Glimmer

of

Hope

The Hope Trilogy

M. L. Newman

1

PUBLISHED BY:
M. L. Newman Publishing

Visit Our Website http:// mlnewmanauthor.com/

First Paperback Edition: November 2013

Editing services provided by LoriAnn Murray

Cover Design provided by Justin Janusaitis

ISBN-13: 978-0615920061

ISBN-10: 0615920063

For my husband, Thanks for your support, unconditional patience and love while on this creative journey.

To my parents, where 'Love turned a house into a home.' I love you both very much; thanks for everything.

For my Nana, 'If there is a will there is a way.' I had the will; thanks for showing me the way.

To Beckie 'My Punkie Pooh', This wouldn't have come to pass without your encouragement and many years of friendship.

For Kristen, You inspired me to write this in 2009; it would still be a thought in my mind if it were not for you. Thank you so much.

To Robert Davis, Thanks for your support as a beta reader and connection to my editor.

In Loving Memory of:

Grandpa & Dad

Table of Contents

Chapter 1
Friday, August 10th

"Wake up, sunshine," Gary whispered.

My eyes lazily opened, focusing on steady hazel gazing back. Leaning down, he brushed his lips against mine.

"You don't want to be late," he continued.

Sitting up slowly, I observed him walk towards our over-the-door mirror and begin tying his favorite hunter green tie. "I'm up." I swung my legs off of the queen sized bed and rubbed the sleep from my eyes. I watched him focus intensely, preparing for work, my attention gliding over his medium physique. Gary kept his black hair cut short and neat, no matter how much I encouraged him to let it grow.

"Don't forget tonight is the banquet dinner," he advised while slipping on his black suit jacket.

"I want to wear the navy dress tonight," I huffed at him, already knowing that he wasn't going to approve.

"Not on your life, Becki. It's too revealing for every occasion outside of this apartment. Besides, one of our important clients may be joining us, and I'll need to focus on him."

Gary always used the same excuses as to why that particular dress couldn't be worn in public. It had become routine. I don't know why I even bothered to bring it up anymore.

"How about the emerald one?"

"Yeah, yeah, I'll wear it but I won't be happy about it," I spat back at him, finally going to the closet and picking out my outfit for work.

"Why are you so snippy? Too much to drink last night?" he asked, frowning.

"No, it's because there is no coffee waiting for me." I glared back for a moment before a chuckle escaped my lips. He wrapped his arms around my waist, planting a gentle kiss on my nose.

"I'll see what I can do about that," Gary said while slipping out of the room.

Collecting my work outfit, I headed in the direction of the bathroom to get cleaned up for the day.

While in the shower, Gary shouted into the door, "Coffee is ready and waiting for you, babe. I have to run in early so I can prepare for tonight. We're leaving at six, so don't be late, okay?"

"I know, see you tonight," I shouted back, trying to finish rinsing shampoo out of my light brown hair. The blonde highlights stood out beautifully after straightening it, and gratefulness overcame me at the thought of my best friend and co-worker, Lily, taking the time to do it. I slipped into my work outfit and grabbed a mug for my favorite liquid breakfast.

Walking back into the bedroom closet, I was drawn to one of my most favorite possessions. Lifting the navy dress from the clothing rack, my fingers slid down the shiny silk with the black lace fringe on the

7

cleavage top. Turning it around, I sighed while gazing at the practically backless dress with black lace covering just below the shoulders down to just below where my behind would start.

"One day I will wear you out," I promised my favorite dress. Grabbing the emerald cocktail dress, I hung it up on the back of the door while pulling out my black sandal heels. I also chose a black choker necklace with gold outlining and an emerald dangling from the middle.

After living in this one bedroom apartment for the last four years, I used to be under the impression that my savings account would be filled up enough to move to a nicer place. If I still lived back home in North Carolina, I'd be able to have my own house, a nice backyard with a built-in pool and a picket white fence. But, no, I decided to move up north to New Rochelle, New York, believing my college diploma and savings account would suffice for me to make enough to have my own house. Even having Gary living with me for the past two and a half years hasn't helped us save up even close to the amount that we needed to move into one.

On my way to work, I made sure to slide the rent check under the landlord's door for our second level apartment. For paying roughly two thousand dollars a month, it still boggled my mind that the apartment was only six hundred square feet. After decorating it fully, it became my home, but the tiny kitchen with dining room attached almost made me walk away. The living room was of decent size especially for two people; however, we couldn't hold parties here. The small bathroom wasn't even close to the bedroom, but oddly enough was close to the only door in and out of the apartment. The only perks to the place was that it was close to my job, had a nice view of the park across the street, and was only a month-to-month lease, so we wouldn't be stuck here when we finally got to move into our dream home.

*****

Arriving back at the apartment at five, Gary gave me a glare at the door. "You better dress quickly because I'm dragging you out of here at six in whatever happens to be on your body." I jumped up and kissed him on the cheek before running into the bathroom to shower quickly and get dressed.

As I was stepping into my heels, a funny idea to provoke Gary came to mind. "So you're saying if I put on the navy dress, you would have to drag me out in it?"

Right on cue, Gary came storming in ready to blow his top but froze when he saw me wearing the emerald one.

"If you were wearing that dress, you wouldn't be leaving this room. I'd tie you to the bed until I got back and then give you a good reason to never want to leave this room with it on," he joked and then smirked wickedly. Gary helped me put on my choker and skimmed his nose from my shoulder up my neck and into my hair.

"We have to go in five minutes. No time for that," I reprimanded while pressing back against his chest and letting my behind press into him.

"You'll pay for this later, you know," Gary replied, spanking me gently. After I put my hair up in a classic

9

twist, he opened the front door for us. As he locked the door after us, my eyes took in his grey suit with white button-up underneath. His light eyes crinkled slightly in the corners as he smiled, noticing my examination of him. Placing his hand on my lower back, we headed out to the business dinner.

Gary parked near the front doors, knowing that after dancing in these heels I wouldn't want to hobble a long distance. We walked into the lobby and followed the sign for the *International Publishing House of Floyd Banquet* with an arrow pointing to the right. Following the arrow, we walked into the banquet room that had striking white walls with gold painted moldings. The carpet was purple with a gold design, and a marble dance floor was the centerpiece of the room. The traditional white linen on the tables and bronze colored chairs with white cushions had my feet already aching to walk in that direction.

There were a few people scattered around the room already, and Gary started his rounds while escorting me by the elbow to the first group.

"Good evening, Gary. Glad to see you brought Becki along tonight," Bill said, acknowledging us.

"I have to bring her along to prove I really do have a job; I'm not just twiddling my thumbs all day long," Gary admitted, laughing with Bill.

Bill picked up my extended hand and shook it very gently. I could feel my smile widen in his presence while the light reflected softly from the salt and pepper color in his mustache. Bill came across like an encouraging father figure more than a production tyrant although that opinion of him was held by other associates.

After mingling with a few people, we finally sat down at the banquet table with Gary seated on my left. I sipped my water knowing that if I started drinking the wine now, I would be a mess by the end of the night.

"Darling, I'd like to introduce you to Mr. Whitman. He is one of the best writers we are lucky enough to publish," Gary stated, politely introducing the gentleman across the table from us. Following the conversation, I looked up into the loveliest blue crystalline eyes I'd ever seen. Enraptured by the color, let alone the yellow surrounding his irises, his eyes put my own baby blues to shame.

"Mr. Whitman, this is my girlfriend Becki Austin." I slowly brought my hand up to shake his while being completely sucked into the vortex of his stare.

"The pleasure is truly all mine. It's very nice to meet you," Mr. Whitman replied with a deep, rugged voice, while bringing my hand up to brush his lips. The gentleness of his lips against my skin sent my stomach into a flutter. His eyes never left mine while he allowed my hand to come back to my side.

"It's nice to meet you, too," I replied, smiling like the idiot that I was. Trying to grasp control, I looked up at Gary and included him in my smile.

"What kind of books do you write?" I inquired politely.

"I write about paranormal mysteries—UFOs and such things," Mr. Whitman replied, smiling down

11

kindly at me. He must be tall because he towered over me like I was a child sitting at the adult table.

"That's very interesting," I responded, keeping my eyes lowered.

Silence befell the room as Bill took his turn to speak at the head table. "I'm very proud to have you all here to celebrate not only our production reaching our goal but surpassing it with flying colors. And due to these positive outcomes, we are going to be expanding our company further. We are also lucky enough to have several of our authors here to join us this evening. I won't make you stand, but just know that we are glad you could join us tonight in celebration." Raising his glass, he finished, "To our authors and our associates joined as one happy family." We all raised our glasses to the toast and sipped.

The food was soon rolled out buffet style for guests to go up and pile their plates. I look up at Gary, and he chuckled already knowing he was on a mission for two. He never hesitated to take care of my physical needs or wants which was one of the reasons we had lasted so long. Our relationship was smooth sailing regardless of our bickering at times.

Sipping my water, my skin tingled as I felt Mr. Whitman return to the table rather than actually seeing him. Glancing up, I noticed all the food he had piled on his plate and chuckled softly.

"Did I miss something?" he asked curiously. Shaking my head, my smirk was obstructed while taking another sip of water.

"Not hungry?" he questioned further, gesturing to my empty placemat.

"Gary is grabbing me a plate," I replied, causing him to chuckle now.

"Lucky him."

Gary returned with a little of everything on my plate: macaroni and cheese, a little salad with a dinner roll and a slice of beef brisket. Picking at the salad with my fork, the easy conversation flowed around the table. Gary respectfully included Mr. Whitman with the ongoing conversation but received minimal responses at best.

Leaning into my ear he whispered, "Keep talking to Mr. Whitman. It'll make him feel more welcome, and maybe he'll come to more of these events. He is a very important client."

With an inaudible sigh, I stuck a fork with a big piece of brisket into my mouth to chew on and nearly choked as I noticed Mr. Whitman observe my nonverbal tantrum.

"Do you like to read?" he asked courteously, excusing my obvious misbehavior.

"I don't have time to read; I work pretty hard all week and volunteer on the weekends sometimes." Smiling up at him, I quickly realized he has no idea what I did for a living. I'm used to Gary's coworkers knowing about our general background.

"I work at an animal shelter. We take care of animals and find homes for them."

"That sounds nice; you have a passion for animals," he commented before sipping his glass of merlot.

"I do, especially for abused and neglected creatures that can't defend themselves from people who should know better." The frustration uncontrollably escaped past my lips. Without a thought, I glanced up into his eyes and glimpsed him trying to control some sort of emotion. He nodded his agreement while his fork grazed his plate.

"How long have you been writing?" I asked, trying to keep the conversation light.

"I've been writing since I was in high school. I didn't take my writing seriously enough for it to be published until about five years ago," he replied kindly. "Where are you from? I can't seem to place your accent," he asked with his head cocked in my direction.

Smiling from the cute gesture I replied, "I was born in North Carolina, but when I graduated from college I wanted to travel. I was offered an internship at the animal shelter here to get some experience, but I ended up doing such a great job that they hired me." To my parents' horror I should have mentioned. They had expected me to spend a year or two at the most in New York before returning home with my tail between my legs.

"How does your family feel about you being so far away?" he asked.

"They hate it. Every time I speak with them they beg me to come home, but I needed to survive on my own. I didn't want to spend my life wondering 'what if,'" I admitted, shrugging my shoulders.

"Are you from New York?" I inquired.

Nodding his head in my direction, I took notice of his dirty blond hair tied into a ponytail before he continued. "I grew up in Ontario, but after high school I decided to travel, too."

"Does your family come to visit you often since you're so close?" I asked curiously.

"No, they spend more time watching over my younger brother, Dane. He is so busy partying that he doesn't realize that he will have to get a job eventually after he graduates. If he graduates," he said, shaking his head in what I assumed was embarrassment.

"I wish I had a sibling. My family wouldn't be so focused on what I'm doing as much," I confessed openly.

"That's not true," Gary chimed in with a knowing look. "I don't feel that I get less attention because Haylie is around," he advised, nudging my shoulder. I couldn't openly argue with Gary right now, but if I could, I would rub it in his face that his little sister was just as obsessed with him as his parents were.

After dessert (which I skipped completely), the music started playing and some couples got up to dance. Gary retreated to the bathroom, and while I was waiting for him to come back, Bill made his way over with a bow.

"It would be my honor to have this dance with you." Standing up, I curtsied back and allowed him to lead me to the dance floor.

"So when are you and Gary going to finally get married? You've been together for how many years?" he inquired, smiling at me sheepishly.

Chuckling at his forwardness, I replied, "I'm waiting for the same answer as you are; he hasn't popped the question yet. Maybe he wants to make sure I'm worth the investment."

Bill laughed and boisterously said, "That cannot be, you are wonderful in every way. I'll see what I can do to speed up the process. Maybe a promotion might send you two down the aisle sooner rather than later." Bill winked at me as he planned out our future. Shaking my head, my laughter eluded my control.

"May I cut in?" Gary asked as he returned, but Bill promptly declined.

"You haven't yet proposed to this attractive young woman. You will certainly not get a dance until then," Bill advised, smirking at me causing my cheeks to heat up.

"Actually, we need to have a discussion if you have a few minutes, Gary."

"Of course," he replied, and I watched the men head in the direction of the bar. Bill could be so forward at times that it was almost disarming. That may have been the reason he was such a good boss to have—associates never had to wonder what he was thinking.

Taking a slow stroll in the direction of the banquet table, I was accosted by a towering Adonis dressed in a black suit ensemble with a navy collared shirt. He took my hand and wrapped it around his neck while pulling me into his embrace.

"You're a good dancer," Mr. Whitman whispered in my ear while clenching my body even closer almost to the point where our hips would touch if I was taller.

"Thanks. Are you having a good time here?" I asked while trying to keep my composure. My fingers came into contact with his restrained ponytail noting that his hair was only shoulder length. He may have been extremely attractive, but I was with Gary, literally with Gary.

"I am now that I'm dancing with you." Was he flirting with me? I tried to give him a small smile, but I could already feel the huge grin on my face. Compliments were a weakness.

"Is this your first event?" I asked out of curiosity.

"No, but I don't like big social events like this. Bill made it clear that I couldn't get out of tonight." The smooth skin along his jaw line stretched with a slight tension.

I nodded to be gracious but my mouth slipped. "I'm glad that you came. Who else would I be dancing with?" I asked, chuckling to lighten up his mood.

"You could be sitting in a quiet corner reading?" I looked up and saw his smirk, but it wasn't reflected in his eyes. What was he trying to imply?

"I'd rather dance than read; exercise is good for the body. I do enough sitting and reading at work," I stated, holding my head up high to show him that I wasn't backing down.

"An hour of reading wouldn't hurt, and then you can exercise your body in any way you see fit," he replied smugly while raising his eyebrow challengingly. Was he really going there? I'd love to smack that smirk right off of his face.

I pulled out of his arms quite abruptly and headed back to the table. While grabbing my purse, I retreated straight to the bathroom without so much as a glance back. What was wrong with him? I couldn't stand smug people like that, especially saying such rude things to a perfect stranger. It was bad enough I have to deal with Tim's bad taste in humor, but at least he had known me for years. Stupid, handsome writer, why did I even let him get under my skin? Shaking my head in distaste, I finished up in the bathroom stall and then washed my hands, realizing my hands were trembling from the urge to whack him over the head. At least for Gary's sake I didn't do it. I don't think he would have taken me home with him if I had. The tinkling coming from my purse alerted me to a call. I couldn't believe I forgot to put it on silent. Whipping it out, I wasn't surprised to see that it was my mother calling. I hit reject on the call and placed it back in my purse. I could only handle so much in one evening. Walking out of the bathroom, I bumped right into Gary.

"I saw you go in so I was waiting. Are you ready to go soon?" he questioned with a smirk tugging at his lips. What was with everyone tonight?

"Why are you smirking at me?" I asked, trying to keep my annoyance to a minimum.

Leaning closer, he whispered, "I'm thinking of the plans I have for us tonight...getting you out of that dress for a start."

"Oh, Gary, I have a headache. Can we save it for another night? I'm not really enjoying myself anymore." I complained, trying to keep my teeth from gritting.

"What happened? You were in good spirits when I left with Bill." Putting his arm around my waist, he held me close.

"I'm just tired and ready to go home. Can we go now?" Gary nodded and kissed my forehead.

"Let me just tell Bill we're leaving." I nodded back at him and walked into the lobby sitting in one of the big overstuffed chairs. My fingers idly tapped to the beat of distant music while staring into the fireplace. There was no reason to take out my frustration on Gary. He hadn't caused it.

"What are you doing out here alone?" asked Mr. Whitman, standing quietly right behind my chair, spooking me. "Sorry, didn't mean to scare you."

"I'm waiting for Gary; we are going home. I have a terrible headache." I bit the words out at him.

Amused, he leaned down and confessed with a hushed tone, "I'm sorry if I offended you. I was just trying to have a laugh and relax. I get a bit stressed at things like this, and I might have overstepped my boundaries," he admitted, his eyes conveying the honesty within them.

I replied, "You did, but I'll let it go. Apology accepted."

Gary returned and grabbed my hand to help me stand before we said our good-byes to Mr. Whitman and climbed in our car to go home.

"You're serious that you don't want to have a little fun tonight? It's been a while," he cajoled, smiling in my direction all hopeful. I really didn't feel like it, but I couldn't turn him down on a night that went so well for him.

"My head doesn't hurt that bad now, after all. We can." His smile widened, and I already regretted saying I would go through with it. I really was not in the mood.

I'm walking into my favorite bar, Lights Out, wearing a tight white button-up shirt tucked into a black mini skirt and black high heels. The place is completely dark except for a spotlight on the dance floor. I notice a few of the normal patrons on the sides, but they are all acting weird. Tim is bartending, but even he isn't his same happy self. Without even knowing it, my feet start guiding me to that spot on the dance floor where I stop automatically. I can feel a dark presence closing in on me; I look up and see a very attractive man. He grabs my hand and proceeds to whip me around the dance floor to music.

I feel my heart pounding as I begin to stress about the quick steps, then the sensuous dance partner leans down to my ear and whispers, "Don't think...feel," as the tempo slows down just a touch. I can feel every muscle in this man's body pressed tightly against mine; I can feel the rhythm of the music guiding my feet to the right places, his heart, too, pounding in his chest.

He leans down close, now dancing cheek to cheek, feeling his breath on my neck that is sending shivers down my spine. I can feel my entire body warming up even though the tempo is slowing down rapidly. As the song starts to descend, he then dips me gently and then slowly brings me up so close that our noses almost touch. He leans in slightly and just as I can barely feel the brush of his lips against mine…

Chapter 2
Saturday, August 11th

I woke up to the irritating scream of the alarm. After turning it off, I sat up slowly trying to remember where I was. Running my fingers against my lips I realized it was just a dream; who was I dreaming of? I knew he was majorly attractive, but I couldn't see anything about him. I looked over my shoulder and spotted Gary still passed out from our 'late night excursions' as I called it. I headed into the closet and grabbed my holey jeans and a stained t-shirt and hopped into the shower. Today was my volunteer bath day at the animal shelter, and I was on drying duty. That didn't change the fact that I'd be soaked just as much as if I was bathing them, too.

As soon as I got to work, I could hear the familiar howling and barking that greeted me every morning. I went into the kennel room to say good morning with a pet on their furry heads and saw a cage already empty. Walking into the bathing area, I saw a dog was already in the process of being washed.

Tyler, another coworker, was bathing him as I greeted him. "Morning, Ty, how is Barney today?"

"He's good, but I have a question, and feel free to say no, it's just that I'm running out of time and people at the moment," he said, pleading with brown eyes.

"Okay, shoot."

"Could you keep Barney over the weekend? I got a call about ten minutes ago that we have a new batch of rescues coming in from a fire, and it's going to be so cramped. Lily is already out grabbing more cages from the storage room, and we may even have to double up at this point," he explained.

Lily was here? She didn't say that she'd be coming in today. Ty finished rinsing Barney as his medium stature and bronze skin lightly shimmered from the inevitable water splashed on him from the bath. Even his buzz cut was glistening with pebbles of water on it.

"I don't mind taking him home; he's a good Saint Bernard."

"Thank goodness. I am bringing home at least two of the puppies, and I can already see them chewing on my furniture," he laughed. "I don't need Barney here to excite them."

Smiling down at Barney, I dried off his head and ears then worked down the body. Without a word, he sat down and let me finish drying off his back and tail. Ha! Maybe I'll be able to stay dry longer than I thought.

*****

"Now, we are not going to have any barking and not too much drool, okay?" I whispered down at Barney while rubbing his head before putting the key into the door. "Gary? Are you home?"

"Hey, sunshine, I'm just watching TV." As he said that, I could hear him getting up. "Maybe we can go another round now that you're..." he started to say, but the words died on his lips.

Smiling up at him, Barney sat down at my feet.

"What's this?" Gary asks in shock.

I knew he wouldn't take well to having a dog in the house, especially a gigantic one, but it was so much easier to just spring it on him than give him a chance to convince me to back out of it.

"Didn't we already say that we wouldn't be having a house full of pets again especially after that cat fiasco?"

Gary would never let me forget for the rest of my life about the three cats that took over our home for the weekend. Let's just say it ended with us needing to buy new curtains, replacing the carpet and lots of Lysol.

"It's only one dog. There was a fire and we had a full house at the shelter. I'm not the only person having to bring one home, so don't start saying to give him away. Besides he is a good boy," I said.

I made a point of smiling down at Barney and rubbing his head whereby he continued to slide down to the floor. "See? He probably won't leave me all day long," I continued.

"He's going to drool on everything. Why can't our home be ours? You always do this—coming up with excuses as to why this animal needs this or that. What about what I need? After a long week of work, maybe I just want to come home to a quiet house. Did you ever think of that? No, you're too busy thinking of others…well, what about me? Do I not matter?" Gary complained and ranted.

"So you're saying that you want me to get a hotel room for the weekend where Barney and I can stay together? It's fine, it's not like I live here, too. Especially after I've worked hard all week long and went to business dinners for you, meeting asinine people," I said, venting out loud. He expected so much cooperation from me when it came to his job, but he refused to budge for mine. "Come on, Barney, I won't turn my back on you. Let's go for a walk."

A few blocks passed by before I realized that we'd travelled right back to the shelter. Closing the door to my office, I put out a food and water bowl for Barney.

Around six, my phone beeped receiving a text from Gary: Where r u?

I texted him back: Paperwork @ office.

He didn't reply which was just fine with me. Barney was softly snoring in the corner on the pet bed I brought in for him. If there was a bed for me here, I would seriously consider staying, too. Shaking my head, I continued reading over the paperwork that came in with the fire rescue.

"So stubborn you are."

For a moment, I feel like I'm flying and then sense that I'm in someone's warm embrace and being carried away. In a daze, I wrap my arms around his neck.

"I love you," he says as he kisses my cheek.

I open my eyes for a moment to look into Gary's eyes; however, my eyes are stunned by the image of Mr. Whitman running his knuckles down the sides of my cheek and then down my neck.

"I wanted to apologize the best way I know how," he continues.

25

He smiles while kneeling on the bed beside me and closing in for a kiss. My lips begin tingling and my heart starts to race.

"Please don't," I mumble against his lips with my eyes closed.

"Why not, sunshine? Are you that mad at me?" he asks.

I opened my eyes to find Gary hovering over me after all. I shook my head and instead cuddled up in a ball in his arms until we both fell asleep.

*****

Sunday, August 12

Waking up early, I decided to go to the beach and work on my tan a bit. I left a note for Gary next to the coffee maker. I also left a voicemail for Lily to let her know my plans and that she could feel free to meet me there. After packing up the car with needed sunscreen, water bottles and umbrella, I put on Barney's leash, and we drove out to Rye Beach. The highway was clear for a morning drive which allowed me time to think.

It dawned on me that last night I had an intimate dream about the author from the banquet. Was I dreaming about him the first night, too? I don't even know the man; why in the world would I want him of all people to kiss me? If I wanted to hear terrible sex jokes or pick-up lines, I would just go hang out with Tim. Arriving and parking in the somewhat empty parking lot, I checked my phone.

Lily had texted a reply: <u>On my way. Tanning time!</u>

I grabbed my beach towels from the trunk, a bowl, an umbrella and a mini cooler with ice packs and cold water bottles in it. Wrapping the leash around my wrist, I carried everything to a good sandy spot right in the sun's view. Planting the umbrella tightly into the ground, I laid out a towel for me to lie on and one for Barney where I put his bowl and filled it with ice water and put the rest back in the cooler. I slathered on sunscreen before lying down on my stomach. The tinkling of my phone showed that my mother was calling again; I hit reject and made a mental note to call her back later.

Feeling a warm, wet tongue on my toe a few minutes later, I cried out in shock before laughing at myself.

"Oh Barney, are you ready to play in the water?" I asked. Grabbing his leash, we ran and played in the waves. The water temperature gave me goose bumps, but the heat of the summer made the swim worth it. I chased after Barney causing him to run up the beach before I turned and ran away. Barney rapidly turned and followed me back into the water.

"You started without me!" hollered Lily before tackling me into the water.

Barney, getting excited to have some playmates, jumped on top of both of us licking and splashing. After galloping around in the water for a bit, Lily impatiently walked her short self to the towels. Following behind her wet trail, Barney and I laid down on the towels again. I added more cold water to his bowl before closing my eyes and lying on my back.

27

"How'd the banquet go?" Lily inquired as only a best friend can, straightforward and to the point.

"It was fine—food, speeches and dancing. The usual humdrum stuff."

"What dress did you wear?" Lily asked with a raise of her brow.

"The emerald one."

My face must have said enough because she didn't push for further details. She knew all about the wonderful navy dress that stayed locked up in the closet. And why wouldn't she? I never would have found it without her assistance. And definitely wouldn't have tried it on without her insistence. Once it was on, it felt like home. No further pushing was needed to purchase it.

Lily advised me of her weekend with her recent nightcap, Brad. "He was sweet, but his kisses were like sloppy fish lips. I tried all night to get his mouth to cooperate, and finally, I gave up and grabbed a towel."

Lily sighed.

"Wow, that is terribly hilarious…I'm sure it didn't stop you from having a nightcap though," I replied with a smirk.

"Well, I couldn't be rude," Lily explained while chuckling to herself.

"I don't want to know what you are laughing at, not at all…do not go there," I said, rolling my eyes.

"You started it!" Lily teased, smirking at me. Sighing, I realized that I walked right into it. So sue me.

Lily had a way of getting attention from the opposite sex; she looked so sophisticated especially with her new bob hairstyle. The look enhanced her Chinese heritage. Who wouldn't be drawn to her independent, attractive and hardworking skills?

After an hour of sun, we packed up our belongings and stuffed them in our cars. It wasn't as difficult as expected having Barney at the beach. He didn't really seem interested in being too far away from me. Even in the parking lot, he didn't stray more than a few feet from Lily and I.

"I'll see you bright and early," Lily said before driving off.

My fingers hit play on my stereo system, and I decided to cruise around the area for a while. I was in no rush to get back to a tension-filled apartment. Cruising down a side street, I noticed a house that had a 'for sale' sign in the lawn. The neighborhood looked quiet and still not too far from work; it would just be a brief car ride away.

Deep down, the urge to go inside was strong, but I couldn't bring Barney inside, and I wouldn't leave him in the car. Too many bad memories for him—I was sure he'd panic. Instead, we crawled past at a single digit speed to get the best look at the house as possible.

It was a yellow two story with a small front yard. Any size would be better than the shoebox Gary and I currently resided in. And I'd love to have a yard where I could walk barefoot in the grass on the summer days. Even Barney seemed to be interested, with his head hanging out of the window. Oh, the possibilities.

I unpacked the car slowly, dreading going up into that tiny apartment after seeing what could be possible for the future. And dreading dealing with the obvious. No matter how much time I took, there was no getting around it. Barney and I trudged up the stairs, tired out after all the heat and playing at the beach. We entered the apartment where I put down the dog bowl and looked up to see Gary in the kitchen.

"What are you making? It smells good," I said hesitantly, not knowing whether Gary might still be sulking.

"I slow cooked corn beef and cabbage. It's just now finished," Gary said.

I already knew the one thing I wanted to talk about was the one thing he didn't want to discuss, but I needed to say something, or I knew I'd regret never bringing it up. I made sure to wash my hands before getting settled down at the table where I crossed my fingers with hope.

"We had a great time at the beach, sun tanning and playing in the water."

Gary looked up and smiled. "I'm glad that you had an enjoyable morning, while I was slaving over a hot stove all day."

He placed the plates down on the table. It appeared he was over his irritation of last night. Sticking my tongue out at him, I pushed on with the conversation.

"On the way home, I saw a beautiful house for sale right by the beach. Would you be interested in looking at it with me?" I asked, smiling hopefully.

"Becki, how many times do we have to have this conversation? We are not going to be living by the beach. Not only can we not afford it, but I don't want to stay here for the rest of my life," he advised, frowning into his food.

"I was only asking if you wanted to look," I repeated, trying not to scowl.

"What would be the point? Our future isn't meant for New York, sunshine," he said dismissively.

We finished eating in silence before I put my plate away. I took a deep breath at the sink, then suddenly, I felt fingers rub up my back and wrap around my arms.

As I leaned gently into his embrace, he said, "I want us to have a beautiful house surrounded by land. We can get a pool put in since you love the water so much. I feel like I've been living here too long already. After graduating college, I never expected that at the age of twenty-six I'd still be living in this city. Please leave the option open at least so you can see what the world has to offer before saying no, okay?"

I shrugged in response and pulled away from him. This decision wasn't just about what he wanted. If we get married, it was about both of us.

"It's not just your future that I'm concerned about. What about mine? I've just started my career, and I love everyone I work with—my boss, the animals. I feel like if I move that I'm starting from scratch with nothing to show for it at the young age of twenty-four except a boyfriend. No offense," I vented.

31

"I don't think I'll be your boyfriend forever, you know? I'm hoping one day you will be Mrs. Rebecca Taylor," Gary commented, kissing my cheek.

"Actually, I have no idea what is planned for me. Maybe I'm supposed to be here, to hit the lotto or save a life. Maybe some rich guy will decide that he wants to be generous enough to my cause and give me millions," I said with a grin.

"Keep dreaming," he said.

Later on that night in bed, my mind was restless. Marriage had never been a high goal for me. I wasn't against it, but I'd always wanted more for myself than just a wedding band. I wanted to have a career, be self-sufficient, have a house on the coast where I could be close to the ocean. A nice home where I could have my parents come to visit me, where I could have a dog or two to play in the backyard. Gary didn't really like pets, but he'd have to suck it up. I wasn't planning on having kids any time soon. Of that much I was certain.

Chapter 3
Tuesday, August 14th

It was a slow day at work, so I took off for lunch at a local deli getting a half loaf of whole wheat with honey ham, turkey, American cheese, lettuce and a little mayo just on the top half, and a bottle of water. I sat in the corner of the room with my favorite playlist playing in my ears and sank my teeth into one of the most delicious subs I'd eaten in a while. Unable to keep from moaning out loud from the tastiness, I just happened to look up and saw Mr. Whitman grinning from ear-to-ear, staring in my direction.

Removing my ear buds, I heard him say, "Obviously, I ordered the wrong sandwich. Mine isn't giving me the pleasure that yours seems to be giving you."

"What did you order?" I asked, trying to get his smirk under control.

"A BLT on Italian sub," he replied. "It is nice to see you again, by the way."

"Mr. Whitman, it is nice to see you, too. Feel free to join my table if you would like to," I offered.

For Gary's sake, I could be polite. Maybe if I was civil, this wouldn't be such an unpleasant experience.

"Thanks," he said as he pulled out a chair. "I'm having a bit of writer's block, so I came to grab a bite and see if anything inspired me. And please, call me Eric," he added.

Taking a smaller bite into my sandwich and trying to keep the delight of my taste buds to myself,

Eric discussed his new book about a psychic who dreamed up her clients before they entered her establishment and how it became a mystery when one of the clients suddenly and suspiciously disappeared.

"That sounds interesting. Maybe I'll read this one," I teased.

"Well, actually," he continued, "I wanted to ask you a question."

His expression was completely serious, but he had a gleam in his eyes.

"I'm almost afraid to ask...what can I help you with?" I questioned.

"I, uh...well, I hate to ask, but would it be okay if you escorted me around your job for a tour? I'm including an animal shelter, and it would be more realistic if I had a clue about what I was writing about."

Completely surprised by the easy request, I agreed. And with that easy acceptance, Eric's smile widened showing his bright white teeth. Was he nervous to ask me? I'm not mean, so why would he feel uncomfortable asking? He might think that I'm busy; of course, I am busy sometimes, but so far this week things have been slow. I couldn't believe that I was blabbing in my head over this guy.

"I'll make you a deal," I stated, stuffing the last of my sandwich into my mouth.

"Uh oh, what's on your mind?" he asked, worry rippling his forehead.

"I'll give you a tour today and any other time you need it to write your book, if you let me read what you

34

are writing about our center. Deal?" I smiled up at him with my hands folded under my chin.

"How about this—you can get a free copy when I'm finished writing," he countered.

"Nope, I want to see it before you publish it. Or you can find someone else's center to tour," I challenged.

I grabbed up my garbage, stood up and threw my trash away and held the lid back so he could throw his in, as well. Without looking at him, I picked up my purse and started walking out of the door.

Eric following closely behind said, "All right, deal."

*****

Holding my head up high as I walked back into work, I brought Eric into my office for a moment as I dropped off my purse and checked to see if there were any new messages. Finding none, I put my cell phone in my pocket and shut the door behind us. We headed into the kennel room, and I showed him the animals in their cages, explaining which animals were recovering from traumatic situations, some that were abandoned and some that were given up because the owner couldn't take care of them anymore.

We strolled into the bathing room where we found Ty washing down a black Labrador puppy. She made the washing process a bit more difficult as she wouldn't stop wiggling.

"Ty, I know you're busy so we won't bother you. Just giving a quick tour," I said, explaining the presence of our guest.

Ty surprised us with laughter. "You would wait for me to struggle with this one to send a tour through." Rolling my eyes, I introduced the men before we continued back to the kennel room.

Eric seemed really interested in the animals. He didn't hesitate to let them sniff or lick him.

"Do you have any pets?" I asked.

"No, I haven't. Why?" he asked, tipping his head to the side like a dog does.

Smiling to myself I replied, "No reason, just curious."

After finishing up the tour, I showed Eric the bathroom and headed back to my office. Sitting behind my desk, I started looking at the last bit of paperwork that found its way here while we were gone.

When I reached out to grab my favorite blue pen to write my signature, it bounced off of my fingers and rolled to the floor on the other side of my desk. Huffing out of frustration, I walked around my desk and bent over trying to pick it up only to have it roll further back under my desk. Getting on my hands and knees on the floor, I stretched out my arm to reach it.

"Well, this is one way to get my attention," a deep, rugged voice suggestively said behind me.

Eric shut the door behind him and leaned back against it, smirking at me while I was still in a rather undignified pose on the floor.

"It's not to get your attention, that's the last thing I want," I snapped crabbily while retrieving my pen and showing him. As I started to get up, he held his hand out to me for assistance, and I took it. "Thank you," I said before his lips hungrily crushed mine.

"No, don't!" I tried to yell out to him, but he quickly took advantage of my open mouth and slid his tongue in, rubbing it against mine. Feeling infuriated by his forwardness, I attempted to bite his tongue, but he pushed me back against the desk where I found myself trapped. The farther my head tipped back to get out of his reach, the closer he got in my inner space. How was I supposed to explain this to Gary? What if my boss saw us? Just as I started to truly panic, Eric pulled back and smiled down at me with that gleam in his eye.

"Don't worry, I won't say a word."

He leaned down to press his lips to mine again; I felt my face tilting up to meet his lips unexpectedly. His strong fingers ran through my hair at the back of my head and held me tighter to him. I moaned softly into his mouth. Wrapping my arms around his neck, I licked his bottom lip until he opened his mouth. Slowly rubbing my tongue against his, I felt my body molding to his surrendering.

"Look who I found roaming the halls!" exclaimed Lily as she walked in with Eric.

Oh, crap! I was daydreaming. Why was I fantasizing about making out with him? I guessed it happened; I'd finally lost my mind. Shaking the thoughts out of my head, I smiled back at both of them.

"So you've met Eric who obviously has no sense of direction," I joked laughing.

37

"Nice to meet you, Eric," Lily said, batting her eyes at him.

"Nice to meet you, too," he replied politely, a bit uncomfortable with her overt flirting.

Lily dropped more paperwork on my desk. "Enjoy the paper cuts. I've already got two," she commented before turning back to Eric.

"Maybe I'll see you again sometime soon?" she asked, eyeing him.

"Yeah, Eric, you should join us for girl's night out," I teased, laughing at his expression.

"I don't like the sound of that. 'Girl's Night.' Do I have to wear a dress or something?" he asked, amused at my sarcasm.

"No," Lily stated firmly, glaring at me. The glare meant 'be-nice-he-may-be-a potential-nightcap.' "We go to *Lights Out* every Thursday night and have a drink and relax. Ever been?"

"No, but I've walked by it before. Maybe you will see me there," he advised, smiling at Lily as she walked out. His eyes then cautiously looked in my direction.

"Thanks for showing me around. I'll have no problem with my book now," Eric said.

He leaned against the door frame almost like in my daydream.

"No problem, is there anything else you need? I have some pamphlets that have phone numbers and information on how things are done that you might find helpful," I asked, rummaging through my desk drawer and coming up with two. I handed them over to him.

"This'll help. Thanks. I better head out, you have work to do," he said, clearly not wanting to overstay his welcome.

"Yeah, if you have any questions feel free to call me here." Picking up my favorite pen, I scribbled my office number down on his pamphlet.

"Thanks, until we meet again...Becki," he said. While taking the pamphlet from my hand, he smoothly brushed his lips against it before walking out.

Wow, just wow.

*****

Wednesday, August 15th

Hearing the tinkling of my phone, I checked the caller ID and saw that it was my mother. Again.

"Good morning, how are you?"

"I'm doing well. How are you doing?" I asked to be polite.

"I'm all right, just missing my daughter," she said sadly.

And here we go—shall I cue the waterworks now or later? Her ability to lay on a guilt trip was ridiculously easy. It came as natural to her as blinking.

"As soon as I'm available for some time off, I'll come down to visit again. How is Dad?" I asked, trying to derail the onslaught of emotions that I was sure were freight training my way.

"He is good. Working hard during the week so he can enjoy his fishing on the weekends. Nothing has changed around here," she lamented.

Shaking my head, I responded, "I'm just walking into work right now, but I'll give you a call later on, okay?"

"Oh, all right. Just make sure you call. I still don't understand how to work that texting nonsense."

"I will, love you."

"Love you more," she said before ending the call.

Surprised by how easy-going that conversation was, I considered actually calling her later that night. Usually, she pleaded with me to get my head on straight and come home. And if I thought they were mad when I moved here, I hadn't seen the explosion headed my way when Gary moved in. I'm pretty sure I heard my mother's heart stop completely before kicking up in double time and screaming at me to get my butt home.

My father, overhearing the conversation, of course sided with her; he didn't want me to have to live with a man just to survive out here in the big, wide world when I could be safely at home with family. I can only imagine how many grey hairs sprouted after that conversation, but seriously, how was I supposed to get married and have kids if I was still living with my parents? I was just glad that I got out while I had the courage to do so.

Heading into the office, Lily came in on my heels, plopping down in an available seat.

"How did it go? Any problems?" she asked.

She was referring to Frenchie, our new rescue pet from an owner who decided that it was okay to leave their poodle outside with no shade, no food or water on hot cement in 102 degree weather. If we had gotten there too late, poor Frenchie wouldn't have made it. Luckily, the owner relinquished the ownership so that we could take care of her.

"It went okay. For a while I was getting nervous because Frenchie's breathing got a little labored, and she wasn't getting as much water in her system as needed. After hooking her up to an IV, her breathing calmed down and her friendly personality started to come out. I stayed late just to keep an eye on her. She slept well, and all the signs were on the up and up."

"That's good to hear," Lily commented.

"Yeah, Barney was none too pleased with my attention elsewhere, but I made sure to give him a few extra pats on the head."

"You've got a clinger," she chuckled.

"That's okay with me. He's a good boy."

"See you for lunch?" Lily asked. She loved girl chat during lunch.

"I should be free, but send me a message anyway," I said with a smile. I could use some fun today.

"Will do!" she exclaimed as she scampered off.

By noon it was obvious that I wasn't going to be able to go out to lunch, and I let Lily know how impossible it would be. She brought back my favorite sandwich—a six-inch Sweet Onion Chicken Teriyaki with lettuce and American cheese and a cold bottle of water. Lily was the best.

As an undergraduate student, I was so sure that I wanted to be the one out in the field helping to bring in the animals and assist the best that I could. However, after interning here and giving it my best shot, my emotions were a little too high for it. My boss decided to use my skills in the administration area, instead. I still helped out in the field when needed, but mostly I stayed in the office or attended court to press charges against the guilty parties.

I liked the balance my career offered; the joy to rescue pets from dangerous homes, most likely get those pets into happy homes and help prosecute the person/s responsible. What could be better than giving an animal a second chance at life?

Chapter 4
Thursday, August 16th

I finished brushing my hair up into a high ponytail and then examined my outfit. My navy blue tube top dress came down just to the knee. Wearing my black pumps and cardigan, I checked my make up one more time. Navy blue eye shadow with a nude lip gloss on my lips shined back at me. Going to my jewelry box, I put in my navy blue stud earrings and checked myself out one more time.

Why was I getting all dolled up? It was only going to be Lily and I. Tim did give me free drinks when I looked cute enough. Yeah, right, I wasn't a fool. Why was I hoping Eric showed up? Forget it; maybe I just needed some positive feedback to get my spirits up before Gary's family came over for dinner tomorrow.

Gary's family was polite but a bit snobbish, and I'd be getting recognized only by one particular person coming. Shaking my head to forget about future drama, I dabbed some perfume behind the ears and on my wrists. I grabbed my purse and headed out to the bar.

Another fabulous perk to this apartment was that it was only about four blocks away from *Lights Out*. I didn't even need to call a cab unless I'd had over my limit which was rare. The bar had two entrances. On the corner entrance, you walked right into the restaurant side where they made the basics—burgers, fries, sandwiches and sometimes pasta depending on the cook that night. The second entrance was on the side near the complete opposite of the restaurant, that's where I usually came in.

Climbing up on the stool carefully so I didn't flash anyone, I caught Tim staring at me in shock.

"Damn, girl, you look amazing. You and Gary finally break up?" Tim asked, winking at me.

Chuckling, I ordered an Amaretto Sour.

"I'm waiting for Lily to get here like usual. Gary's family is coming for dinner tomorrow, and it's going to be stressful. So I'm drinking it up," I commented, smiling at Tim.

"Tell me you're not planning on marrying that goober. You can do a lot better than that."

For some reason, Tim couldn't seem to get over me. He'd slept around with tons of girls, so I'm sure it couldn't be our one time try at it. And I'm surprised even after that terrible calamity in the back of his car that he would even reconsider being with me at all. If I wasn't so embarrassed by the past, I'd probably give him another chance.

His sea green eyes and brown hair that he styled into a Mohawk for some reason put me on the edge of tackling him with kisses. I could never do that to Gary, but the thought crossed my mind with Tim many a drunken night. Those nights were very rare and few and far between, but I was lucky to have Lily to run interference in that capacity, as well.

"Cheer up! No one has asked, so I'm still just a girl...or girlfriend at this point. And don't you go proposing to me, Timothy," I said firmly, giving him a knowing look.

Feigning innocence, he put his hands up. "Who, me? It looks like your girl is distracted tonight. You may be hanging out with me all night," he said.

Looking over my shoulder, I noticed Lily in her denim skirt and red halter top, talking to an attractive looking guy by the pool table. She patted his chest and then walked over to me while shaking her behind as much as she could in his direction.

"Becki, I think I will be having a nightcap tonight," she said, smirking at me.

"Who is he?" I asked, knowing that I could never deter her from her needed nightcap.

"It's Will. He finally broke up with that slut of a girl, what was her name? Julie? Ugh, good riddance to bad rubbish if you ask me."

"At least you've been with him before. You know what to expect for the most part."

I really liked Will. He was such a sweet man, but I couldn't show how excited I was about her possibly getting back together with him for a night. A nightcap was never guaranteed more than just one night, two if he was lucky.

"True, hopefully that girl hasn't screwed up his skills," she laughed before shouting out, "What does a woman have to do to get a beer around here?"

Tim came over rolling his eyes and poured her one and walked away.

"So, what's up with you and Eric?" Lily inquired while sipping her beer.

"We met at the banquet dinner on Friday." Sipping my drink, my eyes flicked in the direction of the door.

"Why didn't you mention him on Sunday?" Lily asked.

"What was I going to say? He's a writer? I'm pretty sure you could have figured that out." I took a bigger drink from my cup as my eyes betrayed me again. The stubborn door stayed closed.

"Uhuh..." Lily raised her eyebrow.

A shiver coursed down my back. Could she see that I was clearly waiting for him to arrive? Was it that obvious that I was nervous and excited to see him again? What was I doing?

"Want to play pool?" Lily asked, letting me off the hook.

Already sensing this was just a floor show she was putting on for Will, I gulped the last bit of my drink and followed her to the tables. *Never look a gift horse in the mouth*, I thought, and if I was lucky, Will could keep her occupied should I bump into Eric tonight.

After two games and two more Amaretto Sours, I walked over to the jukebox to dance a little bit. Scrolling through the songs, I suddenly felt the heated presence of someone next to me. I spotted Eric, big as ever, leaning against the jukebox. With a quick assessment of his black jeans, royal purple long sleeve button-up that showed off the definition of his arm muscles and black sneakers, I attempted to rein in the slow heat that was building under my skin.

"Didn't expect you to be slinking up here," I said quietly.

Eric replied, "Is that what you think I do? Slink around?"

"It's a very accurate word for what you do."

Without a response, he picked out a letter and number and smiled at me while holding out his hand. Against my better judgment, I decided that I would dance at least one song with him. Placing my hand in his, my skin warmed all over as he led us to the dance floor.

As the song started to play, I realized that I'd never heard it before. Eric proceeded to pull me in close, and we began slow dancing. Following his lead, I found myself pressed up even tighter against his chest, but it felt natural. My heart was pounding away in my chest, and I was sure he could feel it since were dancing so close.

Glancing up at Eric and finding him smiling down at me with a sheepish grin caused a flutter in my stomach. He lowered his face closer to mine looking deeply into my eyes. The daydream from the other day slowly crept into my mind, the feel of his lips manipulating mine. It felt like we were the only people in the bar, dancing and sharing a moment of something forbidden.

Another flutter in my stomach made reality hit hard and fast. I was in a public place with a man I'd only just met. Was I really willing to ruin my future with Gary for the unknown? I smiled at Eric apologetically and laid my head against his chest, closing my eyes. We danced like that until the song ended, and then I glanced up into his incredible eyes.

"You look amazing tonight," Eric complimented sincerely.

"Thanks," I said. "Would you mind joining me for a drink?" I asked hesitantly.

Lacing his fingers in between mine, he walked me to the bar encouraging me to walk in front of him. Was he trying to slyly check me out? Did Gary's family make me that miserable that I was relying on a handsome acquaintance to verify that I was still attractive?

"Pathetic," I mumbled to myself.

"What was that?" asked Eric.

"Nothing," I smiled. "I'll have another Amaretto Sour, please, Tim," I requested.

"Getting trashed tonight? You can stay at my place if you want," Tim offered, smiling wickedly.

"No, thanks." Looking over my shoulder, I witnessed Eric staring impassively at Tim, but the tension to his jaw looked wound pretty tight. "Tim, I'd like you to meet Eric. Eric this is Tim, my friend and bartender," I said.

"Nice to meet you, Eric. What can I get you?" Tim asked smoothly.

"A beer, thanks," Eric said, sliding onto the stool next to me.

"So, how do you know my girl?" Tim asks.

Sliding the beer up to Eric, he smiled challengingly.

"We met at a banquet dinner. Gary introduced us, and now we just can't stop bumping into each other," Eric said matter-of-factly.

He smirked at Tim before turning his piercing eyes on me and giving me his full, bright smile.

Shaking my head at the dig, I smiled up at Tim. "Have you seen Lily?"

"She saw you two dancing, and she hurried out the back door with that guy. It was pretty obvious where they were headed," he said, raising his eyebrows at me. My eyes widened knowing the next remark was going to make a spectacle of me. "My car is in the back if you want to remember old times," Tim said.

Tim had leaned closer but spoke loud enough for Eric to overhear. I watched Eric completely freeze with his beer at his lips before he took a huge gulp, refusing to look in our direction.

Horrified at his words and the awkward silence from my side, I got off the stool as quickly as possible before turning around to see Tim's shocked expression as I slammed down a twenty dollar bill.

"Thanks for ruining my evening, you jerk," I said before heading to the door.

"I was just joking," I heard Tim shout to my back.

Without even looking back, I flipped him the bird and walked out into the humid air. In my rush to get out of there, I didn't even say goodbye to Eric. Oh well, he probably didn't want to talk to me anymore anyway.

Walking down the last block before my apartment, I stepped right off the curb and the heel broke on my left pump. Yelling out of frustration, I grabbed my shoes off and hoofed it barefoot into my apartment. I'd never been so happy to be home with

Gary already sleeping. One less explanation I'd have to give about my night.

Chapter 5
Friday, August 17th

I didn't comprehend until the walk home from work that I had been hoping to hear from Eric all day. I received a bunch of texts from Tim apologizing and offering me a whole night of free booze at the bar. Since tonight I had to cook dinner for Gary's parents, I was considering forgiving him just so I could have a place to drown my sorrows later.

However, there was not a word from Eric. I didn't really understand why that bothered me so much. I mean Eric already knew that I was with Gary; we went for a drink and a dance and had a good time like friends do. And I'm sure he didn't think Gary was my first and only boyfriend. Tim is such a jerk; I couldn't believe he would do that to me.

Lily thought it was a riot. She literally had to sit herself down and clutch her stomach, she was laughing so hard. I'm sure if I wasn't trying to look good in front of Eric, I would have let it pass, but I was with Eric. And you'd think that he would call for more information for his book or even to see if I made it home safely. This was getting me nowhere, and obviously that was just fine since he wasn't talking to me anyway.

Dropping all of my work stuff on the bed, I went directly into the kitchen to warm up the oven. After grabbing the marinated chicken breasts from the fridge, I popped them right into the oven. I grabbed a quick, cold shower to cool off and then finished making a salad and mashed sweet potatoes for a side.

"You are going to love the dessert I brought home," Gary said as he came into the kitchen, carrying the distinctive box from my favorite bakery.

He opened the box and brought it closer to me. I gasped at the vision of my favorite dessert.

"Chocolate cream pie! I could kiss you. In fact..." I got up on my tip toes and gave him a peck on the lips.

"I also grabbed some white wine to go with dinner. When will it be ready?" he asked while taking off his jacket.

"Like five more minutes..."

I turned to see him dressed in his white pin stripe shirt and grey vest. "You know I love that vest," I said, winking at him.

"That is why I put it on, so I could be the reason you smile tonight," he flirted before kissing my forehead.

After Gary set the table, I heard the door bell ringing.

"They're here!" he shouted excitedly while hustling to the door.

I never understood why he ran to the door when his family came. Like the one minute wait was too long for them.

"Gary, darling, you look splendid," Josephine cooed before kissing sounds made it over in my direction.

"Hey, Mom, you look fabulous. Hey, Dad," Gary said, followed by a huff after a hug I was sure.

"Hello, Haylie, glad that you came tonight," I replied cheerfully, belying how I really felt. That kid was a spoiled brat.

Gary grabbed the bottle of wine and filled all the glasses on the table.

"I have good news to share tonight. I wanted to wait for my loved ones to all be here before saying this, but I can't wait until dessert to share." Gary smiled at me and admitted, "I got the promotion I've been waiting for. Thanks to my hard work and Becki's encouragement, I'm moving on up."

Elation surged in my chest at the news. He truly had worked hard for the company and no one deserved it more. Like we needed another reason to love Bill.

"Congratulations, son. Your mother and I are just so proud of you. Both of you," Thomas said, including me in his smile.

Looking up at Josephine, she smiled in my direction but her eyes never really saw me. It was like she had x-ray vision and saw right through me. She wished.

"Yeah, I'm getting a bigger office, bigger pay, and two extra weeks paid vacation. Compared to the perks, I'm not deterred by the location or longer hours I'm going to have to put in," Gary explained while chewing his food.

"Maybe now you can afford to do the right thing and marry this gal," said Thomas, nodding in my direction.

"Don't push him to do something that he may not be interested in doing," Josephine admonished, glaring at Thomas.

Gary spoke up and said, "I'm not sure that she'll have me, but maybe with this promotion, I can show her I'm worth the chance."

Thomas smiled back at Gary, but then stopped and stared at me. "My dear, are you all right?"

"Where are you going to be putting in the hours?" I asked, staring up at Gary, terrified of the answer.

"Well, a former associate made a real mess of things, so I have a lot to clean up. I'll be working from six to eight roughly in the beginning, but after things settle down, I should be able to get on a normal schedule of seven to five," he replied before sipping his wine.

Thomas and Josephine nodded in thoughts about the hours, but I kept staring at him. "Gary..." Looking into my eyes, I saw the sadness creeping into his.

He whispered in my direction, "Arizona."

I nodded my head, already realizing my heart knew he wasn't going to be working here. We all finished eating, and I cleared the table without saying a word and started washing the dishes.

After an hour of conversation in which I stayed hidden in the kitchen, Thomas's voice came across. "Well, son, we have a bit of a drive back up to Shelton, but I plan on seeing you tomorrow morning for golf."

"Good night," Josephine said directly to Gary and walked out the door with Haylie following saying, "Bye."

Thomas came over to me and wrapped his arms around my shoulders. "Good night, dear, sleep well," he said quietly before kissing the top of my head.

"Good night, Thomas," I whispered back, trying to win back the control I had before he touched me.

As Gary walked his family down to their car, I headed into the bathroom and stripped out of my clothes. Turning on the shower to cold, I stepped under the shower head and let the water cascade over my head and down my back, washing away my tears. What was I supposed to do? Was I expected to follow Gary to Arizona, be the girlfriend or maybe wife if he ever asks, just to drop everything for his every whim?

I wasn't that kind of girl. I'd worked so hard to graduate from college with my degree and get the internship of a lifetime. I was lucky enough to be hired at the animal shelter which I loved, and what about my coworkers, my friends? My dream of ever having my own house on the beach would never happen if I was in Arizona.

"Babe?" Gary called through the bathroom door. I couldn't even think about facing him right now.

"I just need some time, okay?" I called out to him, trying to keep my voice steady.

"Are you all right?" he asked, concerned as he tried to open the door and realized I'd locked him out.

Trying to hold my sobs in, I called out, "I'm in the shower, be out in a bit."

"Okay..." he replied before walking away.

I wrapped my arms around myself sliding down to the tub and letting the water fall on top of me. My thoughts kept going around and around, but nothing seemed to make sense except that life as I knew it was going to change, and I didn't know where my life was going to go from here.

Getting myself up and washed, I dried off and wrapped my robe around me and went straight into the kitchen. Grabbing a fork, I opened the fridge and grabbed the remains of the pie. Sitting down on the floor with pie in my lap, I dug in.

Gary came to find me. "You're going to get pie all over yourself like this. Come on, I'll help you up and you can eat it in bed," he advised. "I'll even grab you a big glass of milk."

Pulling me up from the floor, he picked up the pie and put it in my hands and smiled warily at me. I walked into the bedroom and sat on top of the covers. Looking down at the pie, I realized how much I wished life was easier. Life could be as easy as picking up a fork and digging in.

"Here's your milk, sunshine."

I nodded appreciatively and took a big gulp before looking up at him.

"Do you want to talk?" he asked gently.

I shook my head, and he crawled on top of the bed with me. With his own fork in hand, he dug in. Odd as it sounds, we didn't say a single word all night—just continually worked to finish off the pie in total silence.

*****

Saturday, August 18th

I didn't have to get up early, but I knew that pie would catch up to me sooner or later. I figured I'd better take preemptive measures before the humidity set in. Pulling on my red tank top, white shorts and sneakers for a run, I made my way out. After running around the city for an hour, I made my way to the park across the street from my apartment. Sitting on the swings, I let my body start to relax from the exercise while letting the wind from the swing blow the hair off my sweaty neck.

Checking my phone, there were a few missed texts from Tim asking if I was ever going to talk to him again and a missed call from Gary.

I texted Tim back: I'll 4give u if u never do it again.

And I texted Gary: What's up?

Gary replies: Idk where u were.

I texted him back: Went 4 a run. At park now.

My phone vibrated with another text from Gary: I c u.

I looked up to see Gary waving from the window. I waved back but kept on swinging. I liked the peacefulness of this playground. There weren't many kids that played on it, but it was kept up well by the community. I felt my phone vibrate and looked down to see a text.

It was from Tim: Promise. I'm sry. I care about u.

59

I smiled back at it and replied: <u>I care about u more. Taking u up on free booze night.</u>

Tim texted back: <u>Done. C u Thursday.</u>

I walked into the apartment, avoiding Gary, and took a quick shower. As I walked out, I noticed Gary dressed up to leave.

"Golfing with Dad," he said, smirking at me. I forgot I had gotten him on the hook for that today.

"Have fun. Tell Thomas I said hello."

Gary walked over and wrapped his arms around me. He kissed my forehead, and I sighed against him. He leaned in closer and kissed me softly at first and then more passionately than required. Taking my breath away, he wrapped his arms even tighter around my waist. Feeling so loved and cherished, I stroked my tongue against his and deepened the kiss right back until we both broke apart needing to breathe.

"I love you," he said as he picked up his golf bag. "See you tonight for a movie date?" he asked hopefully.

I nodded as the knot in my chest tightened, feeling all the emotions from the night before threatening to explode. I walked to the couch and curled up in a tight ball as I heard him leave. What in the world was I going to do?

Chapter 6
Sunday, August 19th

Early in the morning, I heard the tinkling of my phone. I grabbed it and put it to my ear without looking at the caller ID. "Hello?"

"Becki? Are you there?" asked Lily in a hysterical voice.

"Lily? What's wrong? Are you okay?" I asked, alarmed and immediately awake.

"I need you. Someone broke into my apartment. I...I don't know what to do..."

"Lily, call the police right now. Do not touch anything in that apartment. I'm on my way," I said as I threw on a pair of jeans, flip flops and green halter top with ruffle design.

I left a note for Gary on the kitchen table before sprinting out of the apartment to the car. Arriving at Lily's apartment building fifteen minutes later, I noticed two police cars in front. Dashing up the stairs to her third floor apartment, I was stopped by a police officer at the door.

Breathing heavily, I said, "Lily called me to come over. I'm her friend, Becki. Would you mind letting her know that I'm here?"

The police officer gave me a good once over and then said, "Wait right here."

He entered the apartment where I heard a bunch of mumbling. And then I heard a high pitched voice yelling.

"Becki! Oh, Becki!" Lily sobbed, running into me and wrapping her arms around my neck.

"Are you okay? Were you here when the break-in happened?" I asked, trying to calm her down enough to talk to me.

Shaking her head she admitted, "I spent the night with Will. I just got home and found...Becki, look...just look."

She began crying into her hands. Leaning into the apartment, it only took a second to see it was completely trashed. What wasn't spilled or leaking, was broken and shattered all over the floor. Her door was obviously forced as evidenced by the splintered wood pieces on the floor and the broken frame.

"They stole my flat screen TV, they took all my jewelry, and they took away my home..." Lily said, finally letting it sink in that her home had not only been burgled but destroyed.

After hours of Lily talking to the police, the apartment was dusted for prints but none were found. "Let's go to the hardware store. We'll get a new lock, a chain and a deadbolt, okay?" I helpfully suggested.

Lily stared back at me in horror. "No, I...I don't know if I can stay here...after this." Trying to calm her down before she lost it again, I put my finger under her chin to look into her eyes.

"Let's secure everything that you have left and go from there."

Lily nodded and grabbed her purse which was right next to her laptop. "They didn't steal your laptop?" I said incredulously. "That's great!" I exclaimed, but she shook her head.

"I knew that I'd be staying with Will for the weekend, so I brought it with me so I could get some work done in between...you know?"

Nodding, we headed out of the apartment on a mission. The police helped secure the apartment the best possible way before we all left.

Sending Lily down the deadbolt aisle of the hardware store, I chose to look for the clerk to see if he knew of a good home security alarm system. As I got near the end of the aisle, I tried to scoot around a gentleman in the way, but accidentally bumped into him anyway.

"Sorry," I said absentmindedly before realizing that this gentleman was no gentleman at all.

"No, my fault..." Eric apologized. Surprise flitted over his face for a moment when he recognized me before his jaw turned to stone stretching his skin. "Hey, are you okay? You look a bit—"

"I'm fine," I stated, cutting him off and walking away.

Just remembering the last time I saw him made my stomach hurt. I couldn't help putting my guard up, not with so much going on. If he had really cared, he would have called me in the first place.

Finding the clerk I requested, "Do you possibly know of a good home security alarm system? My friend's apartment was broken into last night, and I wanted to get some information if I could."

"That's terrible, I'm sorry that she is going through that," he replied sympathetically while pulling out some pamphlets that he had under the counter. "Here are the best ones, especially around this area, and here is the phone number." He pointed it out by circling it for me.

"Thanks," I said hurriedly, stuffing the pamphlet in my pocket.

Going back down the deadbolt aisle, I found Lily and was astonished to discover her crying in Eric's arms. Really? I couldn't help automatically shaking my head. Taking a deep breath, I walked over to them and overheard Lily say, "I'm so lucky to have Becki. She's been so helpful. I…I don't know what I would do without her."

She looked up into his sympathetic eyes before she felt my presence and then grabbed me up into her arms again. Rubbing my hands up and down her back as she cried, I glanced up to see Eric's eyes concerned and worried but with an edge to his expression.

"Sorry…again. It's been a long morning for both of us," I explained.

"Do you need help with anything? You are both obviously under great distress, and I don't have any plans for the day, I mean, not really. I'm willing to assist with fixing Lily's door and locks," Eric offered and sincerity showed in his eyes.

"No, thanks," I said coldly. "I've got this under control," I stated, patting Lily's back.

Trying not to sound too rude, I threw out a metaphoric life raft to him. Maybe I was just being too guarded to let him in if he still wanted to talk to me.

"If you need any more information or help with your book, I'm still willing to help. Just give me a call, okay?" Stunned, Eric gazed at me with such concentration that I thought maybe I'd spoken to him in Spanish.

"I shouldn't bother you at work," he advised again with that edge in his voice, and I watched as the skin tightened with stress over his jaw again.

I gasped inaudibly as I realized what was putting him on edge…it was me. He didn't want to talk to me anymore. "Oh…okay, never mind. Forget I said anything. Sorry for bothering you," I replied, turning to walk away with Lily.

"I'm going to wash my face in the restroom," Lily advised before trudging up the aisle. I could feel the heat of him right up against my back, but I ignored it. I didn't know why I was even hoping to hear from him. That was one step closer to the loony bin. It didn't matter anyway.

I couldn't believe this is how my life would be— no more Lily to spend time with, to talk to or work with. No bar with Tim as a friendly face to always greet me. Just Gary and a house in a state that I knew nothing about. I'd be all alone while he was working crazy hours, slowly losing my sanity…starting over from scratch again. My family was going to lose their mind when they found out that I was living on the other side of the country. Oh, yeah, and I never did call mother like I planned.

Hyperventilating, my hands started to shake as my nerves were shot with this morning's events finally catching up with me. What if something had happened to Lily? What if something like that were to happen in Arizona? I wouldn't have Lily to call for help—I'd have no one. Having Lily and Tim made living here more than bearable. Moving sounded more and more like a prison sentence.

"Are you all right? Hey, what's wrong?" Eric asked, encircling my body with his arms just as a few tears began to slide down my face. The somewhat familiar smell of him and his body wash assaulted my senses. I almost immediately realized whose arms I was in and jerked back like I'd been burned.

"I'm fine. You don't have to talk to me anymore. Sorry to bother you," I stated giving him my back again. Trying to will some control over my emotions, my feet started heading in the opposite direction of him.

"You don't bother me, you've never bothered me," Eric said as he grabbed my arm to make me face him before I could get too far away. "What's going on? Why are you so upset?"

Shaking my head and wiping at stray tears I replied, "Just having a rough couple of days. I just feel overwhelmed and tired after waking up to this." Sighing from stress and exhaustion I asked, "Why do you think that you bother me at work? Have I made you feel like you were a bother?"

"On Thursday night...after you left..." he started to say. Instantly, I cringed on the inside at being reminded of something I'd rather have forgotten. "The bartender told me how busy you were and that you

66

were only being nice and hanging out with me for Gary's benefit. Said I should let you be so that you could get your work done. I didn't want to stress you out more, so I didn't call."

Understanding all too well what Tim's motivation was, I shot straight from shaking with tears to shaking with fury.

"Tim is going to get his butt kicked very soon," I stated, clenching my fingers tightly. "Don't listen to Tim. He just wants to get back with me, and I'm not interested. He was one of the biggest mistakes I ever made. In fact, let me give you my cell number. Call or text whenever you feel like. That's what friends do," I encouraged fervently.

Smiling, he pulled out his cell phone, entered my number and gave me his number, too. "I do expect you to use that by the way. Don't just add me to your contacts and forget me," Eric teased while poking me in the side.

Grinning at him weakly, I replied, "Thanks, you're being so nice to me. I'll have to take you out to lunch again. What do you think?"

"I think you're losing your mind. You've never taken me out to lunch," he smirked but finished with, "It sounds like a lunch date. Text me when you are ready to plan it."

Lily emerged from the bathroom looking much better, but her puffy eyes showed she'd had another crying jag in there. Eric assisted us in picking out new locks for her apartment. After Lily purchased them, we waved a hand goodbye to Eric, and I drove us back. Lily settled on her couch with a cold glass of water while I got ready for my handiwork. Installing the new lock, the new chain and deadbolt, I felt a lot better about Lily staying here.

I handed her the pamphlet so she could call the security alarm system office to get the people over to install as soon as possible. I also checked my phone to see that Gary had texted me a while back asking: Is everything ok? Do u need me?

I texted Gary back: Lily's shaken but is ok. Don't worry.

Lily decided to call Will to come over and stay with her, and I waited until he arrived before making a move to go back home. I felt better knowing that Will was there, too. Of all the guys she happened to have nightcaps with, he was the only one she could bring home with pride to show her folks. He had a job; he had his own place and a car. Will was articulate and had a warm smile for anyone who spent time with him. I was secretly hoping that they actually became monogamous, but with Lily it was always a toss-up.

Around two o'clock, I finally managed to get home after Will's arrival. Exhaustion taking over my limbs, I climbed on the bed and closed my eyes.

"You napping, babe?" Gary asked just as I was about to nod off.

"Trying to," I mumbled back.

"Sorry, I just wanted to make sure you were okay," he said, coming to sit on the bed next to me.

Gary was obviously trying to open up the subject of moving. With how drained I already felt after my morning, it wasn't going to happen. I laid my head back and closed my eyes. "I'm dog-tired. I just need a few hours before I can be any kind of companion," I explained, just wanting to avoid everything for a while.

Understanding, Gary left me in peace and closed the door behind him.

*****

Tuesday, August 21st

"Instead of watching TV while we eat, can we talk?"

Feeling guilty and panicked at the same time, I nodded my head. "What do you have on your mind?" I had been trying to avoid this for days.

I stuffed a big bite of burger into my mouth. Gawking at my attempt of shoving everything in my mouth at the same time, Gary started to talk slowly. "Well...I wanted to discuss my promotion. It s something that is a bit of a pressing matter, and I wanted us to be set up before it sneaks up on us."

"Why pressing?" I asked before sipping my water.

"If I accept the promotion, we have to leave in roughly three weeks to fly out there and set up a house before I start working. Bill let me know this morning how urgent it is I give him an answer."

Gulping down too much water making my throat hurt, I stared up at him. "Well...are you going to take it?"

"That's what I wanted to talk about," Gary pressed.

69

"There really isn't anything to discuss. I mean, if you take it, then you're moving to Arizona, and if you don't take it, then you're staying here," I stated, slipping in the fact that he would be going without me.

"I want more from you, Becki. I need more," he said, putting his hands down on the table.

"What do you need? What haven't I given?" I asked, completely dumbfounded at his request.

I need you to be there for me, with me. I want you to be my future, my everything," he stated and quickly finished with, "I'm not saying that you aren't my everything now, but I want it to be permanent. I want you to be my legal wife."

Confused, my brows squish together. "Are you proposing to me?"

Gary choked on his soda and smiled a little. "Not at this moment. I'm just declaring to you what I want for our future. I want to have a family with you."

"I want a future with you, too. I mean, I never thought about us breaking up or anything," I explained.

"I'm so glad to hear you say that. We've been together for almost three years. We make each other happy, and I just want to be with you. After we marry, you can have your IUD removed, and we could start a family right away," he continued.

I nodded in agreement to most of his statement. I wasn't interested in having kids right now.

"So, you are joining me in Arizona?" he asked confidently.

I froze mid-chew on a fry, and he saw the horrified look in my eyes.

"Becki?" he asked worriedly. I shook my head and look down at the table. "You're not going to come with me? I thought we just planned our future together?"

"I'm planning to be with you. I love you, but I don't know if I can make that step to leave everything I love behind, leaving my future behind."

"Becki—"

"No, Gary, please, just leave it. I can't go through anymore right now," I said before pushing my dinner away and heading into the bedroom.

Changing into my night gown, I pulled the covers back and slipped under. Plugging my charger into my phone, I decided to text a friend.

I need to c u 2morrow.

Okay, lunch date? Eric texted back.

Yes pls.

Meet u outside ur office? Eric texted back a moment later.

No come in, it'll make me move faster.

R u ok? he asked.

Not really but we can talk about that 2morrow. Good night. I replied, hoping he caught on.

Night. he responded.

While putting my phone down on my end table, I heard the apartment door open and then shut. As the apartment became silent, I realized that Gary had left. There wasn't anything I could do about how I felt or change the situation that we were in. I'd sleep on it— maybe something good would happen in the morning.

Chapter 7
Wednesday, August 22nd

In the late morning, I received a new case that had just taken place. Setting up the paperwork in the right order on my desk, I plunged into the second abuse case this month. This shouldn't take too long to prosecute in court since the evidence was pretty damning.

The owner's name is Kyle Reynolds (age 39). He was caught in the act of physically kicking his cat across the room by his girlfriend, Jenny Morgan (age 38) before it hit the wall and tried to limp away. Jenny then proceeded in calling the authorities.

The report itself didn't include pictures of the girlfriend, but from the description on this report, it seemed that the cat wasn't the only thing getting kicked around. Shaking my head, I pulled up the papers on the cat's physical when she was brought in. I hated how cruel people could be to animals that hadn't done anything wrong. If you didn't like the animal, why didn't you just give it away?

Kyle reportedly said that his brother is the crazy one, they had the wrong person. The girlfriend insisted to our agents that we had the right person.

Shaking my head in disgust, I put the file in my desk.

I heard a knock on the door. "Come in," I said absentmindedly. Glancing up, I watched Eric come in with a smile, looking more like a male model then a writer in his black jeans and blue button-up shirt with black sneakers.

"I'm almost ready, sorry," I apologized, trying to email the last of the notes from our meeting this morning to Lily as she clearly hadn't been paying attention. What kind of friend would I be if I didn't notice her staring off into space?

"Not a problem. How are you doing?" he asked while leaning against the door frame.

"I'll let you know as soon as I figure it out," I remarked as I finally sent everything and picked up my purse. "What do you feel like eating?"

"Chinese? I know a nice place around the corner," he replied.

Seated in a beautiful Chinese restaurant with music and perfect décor, my breath was taken with how spectacular it was. I wouldn't mind coming back here for another meal. Ordering beef and broccoli to share between us, I sipped my water thinking about where to start.

"So how long have you lived here?" I asked for a polite conversation.

"Almost a year. What about you?"

"I've been living here for about four."

Reading the stress over my face, he lightly grazed my cheek with his fingers to calm me. Unfortunately, it did the complete opposite, and I started to feel that burning sensation in my chest.

"Tell me what's going on?" he commanded in a gentle voice, coaxing my inner emotions to the surface.

"I'm sorry, I'm a mess. Gary and I are going through a serious rough patch, and I think it's over," I said and then comprehended I'd said it out loud and to Eric of all people. I hardly knew the man, and I was pouring out my sob story to him. Someone needed to buy me a muzzle.

"Oh," Eric said. "I'm sorry to hear that."

I sighed inaudibly and continued to explain the promotion and moving issue. "Do you think I'm being selfish by not wanting to go with him? I don't want to stop him from going after his dreams, but it seems like my dreams get stepped over again. I didn't leave North Carolina just to have to follow someone else's life."

Eric, taking a minute to think over what I'd said, replied, "You have to make the best decision for you, not the best decision for Gary or for what makes his life easier. Don't live with any guilt or confusion. You have to be clear with him about what you want for your life just as clearly as he has made his intentions to you."

Silence enveloped us while eating the rest of our meal. Eric probably regretted making a lunch date with me; I couldn't believe I just spilled my guts to him about my relationship.

"Do you enjoy my company?" Eric asked, breaking the silence.

"I do," I replied hesitantly. "Do you enjoy mine?" I asked.

"Yeah, you're easy to spend time with. I wish you weren't so stressed out. Your laughter is nice to hear. It's one of the things I missed," Eric stated before taking a bite of his broccoli.

"I miss it, too," I lamented quietly. Taking a small bite of beef, I asked, "Not to be funny, but would you like to come to Girl's Night tomorrow?"

Smirking, he said, "I don't know, maybe. Shall I dress up this time?"

"You look fine. You don't have to dress up. We usually go around eight, but you can come anytime you want."

Nodding, he advised, "I'll be there."

Thursday, August 23rd

By the time I walked into *Lights Out,* I was so overwhelmed that I ordered two Amaretto Sours in a row and was chugging them down. "You might want to slow down. I mean, they are free all night long," Tim advised.

"My life is falling apart all around me. I just want to escape for a while, okay?"

Shocked, Tim didn't say anything else, but I could feel him watching me. Will and Lily were playing pool, but all I wanted to do was drink until I forgot my own name. Gary was avoiding me like the plague, I probably had to go to court to report as a witness for one of the abused pets instead of just letting my report do the talking, and if Gary decided to go to Arizona, not only would it break my heart, but I had no idea how I was going to afford my apartment without severe life changes. Draining my second glass, I twirled my finger in a circle towards Tim.

By the fourth Amaretto Sour, the clock read that it was almost eleven. I think it said eleven, but my vision was a bit blurry. Lily and Will were nowhere to be found, and Tim was making a drink for another customer. I could make it home—it was only a few blocks away, and apparently Eric wasn't coming tonight even though he said that he would. Not that it mattered; I wouldn't have been much company anyway.

I grabbed my purse and put it over my shoulder so I had two free hands just in case I stumbled. Two blocks away from the bar, I realized that I'd stumbled in the wrong direction. Turning around to make my way toward my apartment, I heard someone behind me, and then I felt someone tugging on my purse.

"Give me your bag and I won't hurt you, lady,' shouted a guy in my face trying to rip my purse off of my body.

Seeing that I wasn't responding, he was about to say something else, but we were both surprised how my body reacted. I threw up everything that I'd consumed for the year, so it seemed, and it wouldn't stop. No matter how much I tried to breathe in between heaving, more liquid spewed out, and unfortunately for the guy, it all landed on his shirt and pants. Freaked out, he ran away while screaming something about me being some kind of exorcist bitch.

Leaning against the wall, I couldn't seem to stop throwing up.

"Becki, is that you?" I heard someone asking me.

"Oh....please....help....." I said in between dry heaving. Having all my nightmares coming true tonight, Eric was rubbing my back and trying to soothe me with calming words. Reaching into my purse, I pulled out a tissue and wiped my mouth and then proceeded to sob uncontrollably into it.

Eric, pulling me into his arms, advised, "It's okay. I think you're done being sick. Let's get you home."

"Eric, don't leave me. I...I was attacked," I mumbled in my still-drunken haze.

Feeling his fingers tighten around my arms and pulling my head up to meet his eyes, he asked, "What do you mean, you were attacked?"

"I was walking home...got lost. I'm a waste face," I admitted, shaking my head. "I was trying to walk home in the right direction. This guy came up and tried to mug me."

"What happened? Where is he?" Eric asked while scanning the area around us.

"He scared the puke out of me...he is wearing most of it. He ran off screaming that I was possessed by the devil."

Eric stopped and stared at me. "Seriously? All right, let's get you home. Do you know how to get there from here?"

I nodded and we walked towards my apartment building. The stairs were impossible for my legs to endure, so Eric carried me up and into the apartment before he sat me down at the dining room table.

"Bathroom?" Eric asked, and I pointed in the direction. He went in and grabbed a washcloth, wetting it. Gently wiping the cool washcloth over my face made me close my eyes and groan in appreciation.

"I take it you are enjoying this?" he chuckled.

"I am...I'm enjoying your company again. We have to stop meeting like this," I laughed drunkenly.

"What the hell?" Gary said suddenly, coming out of the bedroom in a robe. Eric looked up and placed the washcloth in my hand to allow me to wipe my mouth.

"Good evening, Gary. She's had a terrible night. She is going to need some serious looking after. Actually, do you have a trash can?" I pointed in the direction and Eric grabbed it and put it in front of me. As soon as I saw it, my head followed suit.

"Drunk? Becki? What are you doing here with her? What is going on?" I heard the testosterone in Gary revving up for a big one.

"I...was attacked...walking home," I whimpered into the can while Eric held my hair out of the way.

"WHAT?!" Gary exclaimed.

Eric explained to Gary what happened as I was busy being useless.

"Eric...please," I said, holding the washcloth before he took it to the bathroom to run under cool water again.

"I'm sorry, Gary. I wasn't trying to be reckless," I said, pulling my head out of the can. "I was feeling stressed out, pressured and overwhelmed. Tim was giving me free drinks tonight so I took advantage, but my loneliness set in and I just..."

Feeling the washcloth on my forehead again made me look up to see Eric watching me intently. Concern still lingered on his face and more guilt started to plague my chest. I didn't want him to be worried anymore. I was home safe now.

Instantly, Gary walked over. "Thanks for taking care of her for me. I truly appreciate everything you've done to help."

Without another word, Eric handed the washcloth to Gary.

"Eric…" I whimpered, trying to say thank you but the words just wouldn't come out of my mouth. Smiling at me as he opened the door to leave, he nodded his head and said, "Night."

Gary replaced the washcloth against my forehead and sighed. "This is my fault. I shouldn't have let you go out by yourself. Lily usually comes to walk with you, doesn't she?"

I nodded just so I wouldn't have to explain anything else. Gary added ice to my water and made sure that I drank it all up to help keep me hydrated.

"You know that tomorrow is going to be hell, right?"

I nodded as my vision became blurry again, but not from my drinking—from remembering the sad smile Eric gave before leaving. How was I ever going to face him again? Regardless of the attack not being my fault, being a drunken idiot was.

Gary helped me into bed and stripped me down before putting a trash can by the bed next to me.

"Get some sleep, sunshine. You need it," he said before cuddling up behind me and kissing my shoulder.

The night is dark and warm, there is a light breeze blowing the leaves on the tall trees. I can feel the wind on my shoulders, and I wrap my arms around myself looking down to see that I'm not wearing any clothes. I can't seem to care enough about that as I walk into the forest, then picking up the pace into a joyful run into the night. Ahead is a big tree branch that has fallen off a tree. I lie down on top of it, looking up at the stars through the spaces in the tree branches.

Peacefully enjoying the sounds of the owls and night music from the crickets, I become conscious that I'm no longer alone. Looking over to the right, I see Eric completely naked laying down on the grass looking up at the stars, too. He looks up to see me and beckons to me to lie down beside him. Standing slowly, I walk over and lay down with my head on his chest. Feeling his lips press against the top of my head, I sigh in contentment.

"Enjoy your life to the fullest. You only get one shot at it," Eric says.

He uses his finger to tilt my head up to meet his lips.

Chapter 8

Friday, August 24th

Feeling the brush of lips against mine, my eyelids lifted lazily to Gary. "I have to go to work early for a meeting, but I will be home early. I love you."

Being too tired to communicate, I nodded my head. Slowly walking into the shower to get cleaned up, my dream filtered back to me. Hung over or not, I had to make a choice soon. Wearing my sleeveless white blouse and tan skirt with white pumps, I grabbed my cell phone to put in my purse and spotted a waiting text.

How r u feeling? I read from Eric.

Like a Mack truck hit me. What about u?

I gulped down my coffee and brushed my hair up into a tight classic bun. I shut up the apartment and began walking to work when I felt my phone vibrate.

Been better. Sry I was l8e. Eric couldn't possibly be blaming himself for my stupid mistakes. This day couldn't get any better.

No, it's my fault. I got drunk by myself and got lost. I am sorry about Gary. He was worried and freaked out. I texted back, hoping like hell today was a quiet day.

Closing the door to my office as quickly as I could to block out the noises, I went into my desk and rifled around for the Advil. Girl's Night was not happening this week, that was for sure. Especially since I was rolling solo like a fool. Oh, my head hurt. My cell phone tinkled from my pocket. Checking the ID, it displayed my mother was calling. I hit reject. I couldn't possibly have a productive conversation in the state I was in now.

Pulling out the paperwork for the court case that was coming up in a few weeks as well as pictures and doctor's notes from the surgery, I heard a light tap on the door.

"Come in," I said without looking up while paper clipping pictures on top of the paperwork.

"Busy?" asked Lily as she closed the door behind her. Finally looking up, I saw the huge grin on her face and knew she was about to tell me some story about last night.

"It's official, Becki, I'm locked in," Lily said, practically jumping up and down in excitement.

"That's great, I'm so happy for you both. I really like Will," I said, putting the file down and sipping water from my water bottle.

"Hey, what's going on? Usually you're over the moon about anything that has to do with commitment. Talk to me." Knowing that I couldn't escape the conversation, I told her every detail just so I didn't have to go back over anything a second time. I didn't think my head could take anymore talking after I finished with all the gory details.

"Becki! Oh, it's my fault. I should have stayed with you," Lily said, sitting down and putting her hands on top of mine.

"No, it's mine for being an idiot. Drinking alone is always a bad sign. Please don't blame yourself; my head hurts too much to even try to make you feel better."

"For lunch I'm taking you out to a greasy burger joint. Grease makes hangovers go away pretty quick. I'll swing by to come get you," Lily said, smiling before placing down a case file.

"What's this?" I asked with a furrowed brow, my stomach rolling at the thought of greasy burgers for lunch.

"Part two of the Reynolds case. Just came in," Lily said before closing the door behind her.

Opening up the file, I put the paperwork in order before going through the details. The first page said:

Curtis Reynolds (age 37), was just released from prison on August 23, 2012 after serving his full sentence of 12 years on a child kidnapping conviction.

What a colorful family. That was a low blow for Kyle to blame his brother like that; luckily for Curtis, it happened the day before he was released which just happened to be yesterday. A tingle of uneasiness tightened my stomach at the thought of a child abductor being released. The world had enough monsters in it.

It looked like one brother was coming out of prison while another may be quite possibly going in. It didn't sound like they got along too well, anyway. The report showing that Curtis was living with Kyle temporarily looked like a bad omen to me.

*****

Strolling home, a bit more confident in my steps as my headache had finally subsided, I checked my phone. I found one missed call from Gary and a text from Eric.

I understand. Did u tell him that we've been hanging out?

No I never told Gary, it never came up. Lily and I r going to Lights Out on Friday to eat and play pool, no drinking, want to join? I texted Eric.

As I started to put my phone in my purse, it started to tinkle at me.

Gary was calling again. "Hey," I greeted him just as I started to walk into the building.

"Where are you?" he asked sounding a bit nervous.

"I'm coming up the stairs now. See you in a minute," I said before hanging up.

As I reached our apartment, the door was open and the glowing from inside was flickering on the door. Stepping in closer, I saw that there were candles all over the apartment with red rose petals leading from the door to the bedroom. Smiling, I shut the door behind me and followed the trail to find our bed covered in pink petals and a note card surrounded by candles on the night stand.

Picking it up, I read, 'Put down everything. Lie down and close your eyes.' I kicked off my pumps and placed my purse on the floor beside me. I laid back on the bed with my eyes closed and my legs crossed at the ankle as I started to hear soft violins. I smelled a blueberry fragrance and then felt the bed sink at the bottom.

The gentleness of his touch as he began to massage my feet made me groan deep in my chest.

"I hope you had an easy day, sunshine, because I'm going to make sure you have a good night, too," he purred before he switched to the other foot.

"My day is skyrocketing into awesomeness at this point," I replied.

Feeling his firm fingers kneading the tension out of my feet, he slowly started to massage my calves and then on up until he shocked me when his massage changed into much more.

"Nothing is going to get between us tonight. Just you and me," Gary whispered in my ear before kissing me ardently.

Chapter 9

Saturday, August 25th

Trying to catch my breath, I glanced to my left and watched Gary chuckling and huffing, too.

"You are going to be the death of me. Maybe I need to get a restraining order against you and your insatiable sexual appetite," he joked while pulling me to cuddle up against his side.

"How did you get your leg to bend like that?" he asked, bewildered.

Laughing at the tone of wonderment in his voice, I replied, "I have to keep life exciting with some secrets."

Kissing me on the forehead, Gary said, "You can surprise me anytime," before picking out his clothes and going to the shower.

Standing up, I noticed a bit of a wobble. Wow, maybe I overdid it this morning. Wrapping my fluffy robe around me, I went to the fridge and filled up a glass of cold water. Gary popped his head into the living room while I was watching TV. "I have to run to the store for a few things. Do you want me to get you anything?"

"No, thanks. Today is going to be a lazy day," I replied. Just after the door closed, I heard the tinkling of my phone. Begrudgingly, I grabbed it from my purse and answered, "Tim?"

"Lily just told me what happened. Can I see you?" he asked, but I could hear the pleading in his tone.

"Sure, Gary just ran to the store. Come over." I hung up the phone and threw on a baggy t-shirt and jeans before returning to the TV. Checking my phone again, I saw that I missed a text from Eric.

Meet u there. I won't be l8e.

Hearing the knock on the door, I opened it just before Tim scooped me up into his arms. Kicking the door shut behind him, he put me down on the couch and joined me.

"That's a welcome if I ever saw one," I said chuckling.

"You know I'm going to have to cut you off now, right? Why didn't you grab a cab home or call Gary to come get you? I would have been willing to walk you home. Why would you put yourself in danger like that?" he blurted out in anger, frustration, and concern all wrapped up in one.

"I guess my limit is three drinks, free or not. I'm so sorry. I didn't mean to put you in a situation where you felt like you needed to watch out for me. I was so upset with what's going on. I just wanted to drown it all out...I wasn't thinking."

Wrapping his arms around my shoulders to hold me close, he asked, "What's going on with you and that Eric guy? Lily said that he brought you home." Feeling exasperated with this conversation already, I just shrugged.

"He's my friend."

"Listen, your friend wants in your pants," he said, being his usual crude self.

"And you don't?" I asked, laughing at his accusation. "I'm providing information for his book and in return he is being a great friend and listening to me complain about life. That's all," I said in complete seriousness.

"I'm noting how protective you are of him, and I'll back off. I just got this feeling about him, like something isn't right." I turned back to watch TV, not even bothering to respond.

If there was anything wrong with Eric, he would tell me, right? I mean, I would notice, wouldn't I? No...no I wouldn't. I'd been so overwhelmed with everything going on that I wouldn't notice my apartment on fire until it scorched my shoes. Feeling my phone vibrate, I looked down to see a text from Eric:

I will be on watch so no more worrying. I'll c u then ;).

Glancing down at the wink Eric texted me, I couldn't help but grin. Tim, looking over my shoulder, said, "Lover boy? Or Friend?"

Before I could respond to his stupid comment, I heard the door open and then slam shut.

"What's going on here?" Gary asked.

Looking up to see his eyes practically on fire, I tried to understand why he was so upset. I looked back at Tim to see that his arm was still around me, and Gary must be thinking the worst case scenario.

"Tim just stopped by to check up on me. Lily just told him about what happened," I said, trying to cool Gary off by going to stand in front of him.

Gary, side-stepping me completely, said, "This is entirely your fault. You got her drunk and she had to fend for herself. How dare you come into my home, putting your hands on her like everything is okay!"

"I didn't get her drunk! She made her own decision of how many drinks she was going to have. I wasn't the reason she was drinking, and I'm not here to see you. This is her apartment, too, and I'll visit her whenever she invites me," Tim said, getting in Gary's face.

"Stop it, both of you! It was my fault for getting drunk; no one else's," I said, trying to get in between them.

"Becki, tell your 'friend' to get the hell out of our house," Gary said, practically spitting the words in Tim's face. Tim looked directly into my eyes trying to gauge what I was going to do.

"Gary, stop it right now! I'm allowed to have friends over if I want to," I said, trying to calm down Tim before he threw a punch and attempting to get Gary to think rationally. "Tim, thank you for coming over. I really enjoyed your company, but I need to speak to Gary alone. I'll call you okay?"

I tried to make him understand I wasn't choosing Gary over him, but with a stiff, "Fine," Tim stalked out of the room and slammed the door behind him.

"How could you do that to me? I would never embarrass you in front of your company, but you're hell bent on doing it to me every time you come home and I'm not alone," I spat at Gary, not even trying to control my anger.

"Don't even think about it. I went to the store to buy you mace so you could still have your freedom of walking to the bar if you still felt like doing so and came home to find you with another guy with his arms wrapped around you and you not pushing him away. Do I mean nothing to you at all?" Gary asked, fury and pain imploding in his eyes.

"I didn't do anything wrong," I implored. "Tim was trying to comfort me while we discussed the night that I'm obviously never going to live down. You told me that you wanted me permanently; you need me and love me. I believed you whole-heartedly and the trust I gave to you...how am I supposed to spend the rest of my life alone? I'm obviously not allowed to have friends who actually give a damn about me. And after last night and this morning, I thought my feelings for you were quite clear," I vented, looking out the window, too angry to even look at him.

"I don't have a problem with all of your friends, Becki, just him. I know Tim wants you back, and I've always known how he feels about you. Do I stop you from going to the bar every Thursday night? So stop trying to make me look like a terrible person," Gary yelled at my back.

"You had the same reaction when you found Eric trying to clean me up that night. You practically threw him out of the house," I said, shaking my head, remembering that horrible look in his eyes.

"I was concerned about you. I wasn't worried about him," Gary admitted, calming down a bit.

"I've been trying to tell myself the same thing, but every time you come home and there is a male around me who isn't Thomas, you freak out first and ask questions later. That's not fair to them or me," I said, wrapping my arms around myself.

"I will try to not 'freak out' anymore, okay?" Gary said, wrapping his arms around me. "And you will not be alone; you'll have me there with you. You'll be able to make new friends in Arizona. Maybe you'll find an even better job, too. Becki, have some faith in me. I'll make this work," he said, rubbing his hands up and down my arms trying to soothe me.

"Gary, be realistic. You're going to be working long hours. In this economy, I am lucky to have the job that I do. And I'm not worried about making new friends—I'm happy with the friends that I have now. I'm happy with the way my life is now."

"I want more for mine, for us..." he said, leaning down and brushing his lips against my shoulders.

"I'm not going to force you to stay here. I want you to have everything your heart desires," I said, walking out of the apartment.

Sitting on a swing in the park, I pumped my legs with my eyes closed enjoying the warm breeze as I contemplated my future. Having Gary in my life for the past three years had been amazing; we got along and I just accepted that we would get married. If I married Gary, I was going to have to follow him wherever his job took him. I didn't like to move around—I'm just not that person. Starting to stress out, I took a deep breath and opened my eyes in total shock that Gary was sitting in the swing next to me.

"I'm sorry I ran out like that but I just needed—"

"Stop. I'm not trying to pressure you into a decision about moving or anything else." Picking up my hand we swung together. "I have a proposition for you to think about."

Smirking at his business-like tone, I nodded for him to go on.

"I'm going to take this job in Arizona, set up a place to live and you can stay here working if you promise to make a decision about whether you want to join me."

"When do I have to make the decision by?" I asked, a little nervous.

"I'm hoping sooner than later, but after I go, how about two months? That will give you time to try to find a job in Arizona, you can come and see what it's like there before judging it so harshly, and you won't have to worry about me pressuring you. I want our future together. I want you," he said, interlacing our fingers together.

I nodded in agreement as my emotions were too much to try to express with words.

Chapter 10
Friday, August 31st

Finished straightening my hair, I walked to the closet to pick out shoes. Since I was only wearing my peach sundress with white polka dots, I slipped on white sandals that showed off my French pedicure. I looked into the mirror one last time to check my outfit when I overheard voices in the next room. Opening the bedroom door, I spotted Lily hugging Gary before Eric started shaking his hand. What in the world was going on? Was I late? The clock read ten minutes to eight...no, I was on time.

Reading the confused look on my face as I came into the room, Lily came over and whispered, "We came to escort you to the bar. Think of us like your bodyguards for the evening," she said while giggling.

Lily, dressed in her black slacks and yellow halter top with matching earrings and her hair pulled up into a classic bun, looked fabulous as usual. Astonished, I looked over and overheard Gary talking to Eric.

"I'm sorry about last Thursday. I was...an ass," he said, shaking his head and laughing.

"Don't worry about it. It was a very intense and strange situation to be in," Eric replied diplomatically with a relieved smile.

As I took a step to walk into the living room, Lily grabbed my arm tighter and whispered, "Listen, Eric seems to be a little off tonight. He was really quiet and weird. Did you two get in a fight?"

Shaking my head, I responded, "No, not that I'm aware of. Work stress, maybe?"

My eyes took in Eric and saw he was wearing a hunter green button-up shirt with grey slacks and charcoal shoes. He looked absolutely breathtaking with his hair pulled back into the usual ponytail.

Shrugging her shoulders, we walked over to the guys.

Eric asked, "Gary, did you want to walk with us to the bar?"

Gary, astonished, asked, "You go to Girl's Night?" before throwing an intense look my direction.

"I invited him to walk us to the bar so he knows where to pick me up tonight," Lily said, grinning and batting her eyes at Eric.

"Oh...no, I think you girls are in safe hands with him. I have a few things I need to do tonight...work related," Gary said.

Watching Eric and Lily walk out the door, I leaned up and kissed Gary lightly on the lips. "I love you," I cooed.

Holding me even tighter to his body, his hazel eyes bore into mine. "I love you, too. How does Lily know him?" he asked.

"You know Lily and her nightcaps. I'd never guess that they knew each other until she mentioned it at work," I replied, trying to hide my nervousness.

"Huh. Small world, I guess," he stated before kissing me again. "Who's bartending tonight?" he asked, letting me go.

"Tim. I need to make sure he is okay. Regardless of your dislike for him, he is my friend," I said, turning away from his scowl.

At the bottom of the stairs my friends were waiting. "I can't believe you two are trying to escort me around. Who am I, the president?" I asked, laughing at them.

Lily joined in laughing and said, "I don't mind spending more time with you, but this idea didn't come from me." We looked over to Eric who wasn't even grinning.

"I just wanted to make sure you made it to the bar safely. I don't know why you'd think this is funny. Something bad could have happened to you," he scolded before stoically heading through the lobby. Lily grabbed my hand and squeezed it, letting me know to tread lightly. Apparently, we were now in hostile territory. The thought alone made me want to laugh harder, but I bit my tongue.

"I'm sorry to offend you, Eric. I was just surprised is all." Not responding, Eric opened the door for us to go through.

"I'm so excited to see Will tonight. Shall we play pool, couple versus couple?" Lily asked, directing the question to me.

Hoping that Eric didn't notice my heated cheeks, I managed to say, "I'm down if Eric is."

"Sure," was all he replied and then went back to his silence.

Arriving at the bar, I let Lily go in ahead of me and then walked to the side of the building. "Have I really upset you? I never meant to…if you want me to apologize, I will."

Taking a deep breath, he replied, "No, I just…I have a lot on my mind."

"Is there anything I can help with? Is it the book?" I asked, trying to help him for once since he listened to me whine about my life. Eric wordlessly shook his head. "Listen, if you're busy, you don't have to stay. I can call a cab home or have Lily and Will walk me home. You don't have to waste your time here with—"

"You're not a waste of my time. I don't spend time with people I don't like," he said sternly.

Without thinking, I wrapped my arms around his waist and pulled him into a hug. "I like spending time with you, too."

Sighing, Eric clutched me close to him and then leaned down, whispering, "Are you going to Arizona?"

Looking up into his bright blue eyes, I realized I couldn't lie to him. I couldn't lie to myself anymore, either. I knew what I wanted regardless of how hard it was going to be. I shook my head in response, laying my head against his chest, and I could feel his heart thumping.

"I'm sorry. I shouldn't have asked you that. It's none of my business."

"I'm being honest with you. I've been wracking my brain to try to see myself moving away, and I can't. I don't want to. Not even if it means that I lose any chance of being with Gary. I need to live my life my way. I only get one shot at this," I said, looking down at my hands.

His finger lifted my chin up to look into his beautiful eyes. "Becki, you have so many options available to you. You don't have to feel obligated to anyone; it's their loss if they can't appreciate you for who you are."

Smiling, I lean into his chest and start to fully relax knowing the pressure is finally off my shoulders before realizing the implications of his words. Glancing up, I witness Eric's burning stare go right through me.

"I—"

"We should get in there; Lily and Will are waiting for us to play," he said, effectively cutting me off and opening the door.

Walking in with Eric, I felt Lily scrutinizing my facial expression. I glimpsed Tim's smile for me slip a bit before giving me his back. "I have to go talk to Tim for a minute. Can you please let Lily know I'll be there soon?" I asked Eric. Nodding, he headed over to the pool tables.

"Tim, I need to talk to you."

"What's up?" he said, not looking at me.

"I need to talk to you in private if you can spare me a moment of your time," I said, pleading with my eyes at him. Coming out from behind the bar, he clasped my hand and brought me to the back room for employees only.

"What's on your mind?"

"I wanted to thank you for being there for me when I needed to talk to you. I wanted to apologize for Gary's cruelty to you, and I wanted to let you know that no matter what, you are special to me." Blinking in shock he picked me up and twirled me in a circle.

"Oh, man, I thought you were going to tell me that you weren't going to talk to me anymore or you were going to stop coming in," he said in my ear, holding me close to him.

"I'd never let that happen. I mean, unless you pissed me off, I'm pretty much not planning on kicking you out of my life," I said reassuringly.

"And I wanted to ask you something," I said, trying to catch my breath. "Can you please try to be nice to Eric? He is going through some personal stuff and you trying to snub him by bringing up our past or being rude is not helping him or me. I need to be there for him because he has been a good friend to me. Can you understand?" I pleaded with my words and eyes to Tim.

"I guess. Just be careful, okay? I really have a bad feeling about the guy." After a big hug, he walked me back to the bar with his arm around my shoulders.

"Hopefully, Eric is good at pool because I am terrible," I said, laughing with Tim.

Unable to hide my smile while I headed over to the pool table, I calmly nodded to Lily and tried to include Eric in my smile but noticed that he was back to his reserved self, obvious by the tension in his jaw again. Before I had the chance to ask him if he was okay, Will racked up the balls while Lily handed out cues. Will, wearing his signature blue and white checked shirt with jeans and sneakers, smiled up at me as a welcome. He was the most attractive African American I'd ever had the pleasure to know. I was so glad that he and Lily were together.

"Did you two have a nice talk?" Lily asked while handing a pool cue to me.

"Eric?" I whispered back and she shook her head. Instantly, my eyes widened, and I realized that Eric must be wondering what Tim and I discussed in the back room. Lily chuckled and handed Eric his pool stick.

"You want to shoot first?" Lily asked, but Eric declined.

I shouldn't have to explain my actions to anyone, especially Eric. He had no right to get upset while I was still with Gary. Regardless, he should have been aware that the relationship was basically going to go nowhere. Did he think I was going to choose him because I was so lost? Did I look that weak like I can't survive without a man in my life? Getting slightly miffed, I grabbed my pool stick and leaned over the side to line up the cue ball to break. Of course, I didn't get a single ball in a pocket, but I did do a good job of separating.

"Good break," Will commented while lining up his shot and sunk the orange solid ball.

After Lily hitting the cue ball several times off of the table and my terrible shots of knocking in almost all of the solid balls, it was surprising Eric and I won at all. Cheering and smiling up at Eric, I saw that he had mellowed out a bit but was still keeping his distance from me. After getting change from Tim for the jukebox, I turned around to see Will and Eric deep in conversation and Lily looking bored. I nodded my head to her in the direction of the dance floor and she slipped away unseen and joined me. Lily picked out the songs and we grabbed hands and danced together, laughing away all of our problems.

As the song ended, we both just happened to look over and see Will and Eric leaning against the wall watching us. I stopped abruptly, unsure if it would be okay to dance with Eric. Will took Lily by the hand and started to swing her around in time with the music. Watching Lily smiling as she enjoyed her time with Will, I sighed and went back to the jukebox looking for something I'd like to hear.

Picking out a newer techno pop song, I leaned against the wall waiting for it to come on. Eric was acting so weird tonight that I didn't really want to go near him. I was trying to have a good time. After the first two notes of our song played, I heard Lily exclaim and then come running, leaving Will in her dust.

"I can't believe you put this on!" she yelled at me and then we did our favorite kind of dancing. Basically, it consisted of us dancing really close with our eyes closed so we didn't end up laughing at each other but not bumping into anyone else. Getting lost in the music with my arms over my head, I felt hands suddenly around my waist pulling me close. Not wanting to ruin the moment, I kept my eyes closed and just went with it.

In my mind, it was Eric's hands wrapped around me, and I was finally starting to relax when I just happened to open my eyes to distinguish Eric talking to Will on the other side of the room by the bar, clearly not paying attention to the dance floor. Looking at Lily, she had made the same mistake that I did. I pulled away and saw that it was a complete stranger.

"Aww, don't stop now, the song isn't over yet," the stranger complained with a bit of a slur, grabbing me by the arms and pulling me back into him and then trying to spin me around.

Panicking, I cried out, "Lily!"

Suddenly, I was falling to the floor and sliding on my side.

Unable to catch my breath, I saw Lily rushing over to me.

"Are you okay?" she asked and started trying to pull me back up to my feet. I was enamored by the scene in front of me; the stranger who was dancing with me was on the floor rolling around with Eric and Tim.

"Becki, answer me," Lily insisted, trying to shake me into speaking.

"Ow!" I yelped as she shook me, and I felt the beginning of a bruise starting to form on my ribs. This is great. Like I needed another incident at the bar. Gary was never going to let me out of the house again.

Suddenly, I heard yelling and turned to see the stranger had Tim in a headlock and was punching him in the head. As quickly as it started, it ended with Eric punching the unsuspecting stranger squarely in the face and knocking him out. Tim yelled at the stranger's friend to get him out of the bar before he called the cops. Throwing his friend over his shoulder, he carried him out of the bar, grumbling.

Lily took her thumbs and started wiping the tears off of my cheeks and confusion swept through my system. I was crying? Why? Lily took my hand to walk me to the bathroom, and I practically fell over with the pain that was setting in from my ribs. No distractions were even possible to fake that I was okay.

Panicking from the pain and the adrenaline, I started to hyperventilate. "Becki, come on. Take slow, deep breaths with me," Lily instructed, trying to get me focused.

I tried, really, I did, to follow her instructions, but just as I started to take a deep breath, my rib protested and I cried out again. I looked down expecting there to be blood or something, but my dress was just wrinkled.

"What's wrong?" Lily asked, trying to understand why I was practically incapacitated.

"She went down pretty hard on her side," I heard Eric say as he pulled my arm over his shoulder and lifted me up and carried me into the ladies room. "I'll wait right outside the door, okay? I'll take you home after Lily checks you out," he said respectfully and headed out the door.

Lily quickly pulled up my dress and shook her head. "That is going to look disgusting in the morning. It's turning purple, and I wouldn't be surprised if you had quite the shiner."

Finally calm enough to speak, I said, "It's going to be a long night. How am I supposed to get home? How am I supposed to explain to Gary that I got knocked down when a bar brawl started because some drunk put his hands on me?" I started to panic again.

"Don't worry about it. You don't have to explain that. Just say that you were walking and tripped over a curb on the walk home. That happens to people all the time, trust me I've seen it," Lily said helpfully.

"What happened?" I asked. "One minute I'm being manhandled, and the next I'm on the floor."

Lily, shaking her head, advised, "Tim saw the look on your face and hopped the bar. He was running so fast that when he collided with the guy, you just went flying. He didn't mean to hurt you; he was trying to protect you. Eric saw you go down but then saw Tim tackling the guy and having a hard time and jumped in to help him."

"I thought I was dancing with Eric." My voice came across sounding defeated in my admission. Not needing to respond, Lily rubbed her hands up and down my arms.

"Let's get you home, okay?"

I nodded and started to walk towards the door slowly. One thing I loved about Lily was that I didn't have to explain every detail to her about my life. Most of the time she just accepted what was and went from there.

Pushing the door open, Tim and Eric were talking next to the door.

"Are you okay?" Tim asked, worriedly.

"I'm bruising as we speak, but I'm fine. Don't fret over me. Thanks for stepping in. I didn't really know what was going on until it was too late." Tim nodded understanding.

"I hope you have a quiet rest of the evening," I said, waving a hand at Tim and started walking to the door.

"Can I bring you home?" I heard Eric ask behind me.

"If you want to," I replied, slowly making my way out the door.

"I can drive you," Eric offered, but I just shook my head and keep trudging home. "Did I do something wrong?" he asked, concerned, but I continued to shake my head.

"Becki, talk to me," Eric said, stepping in front of me.

"What am I supposed to say? I'm sorry I ruined your night by getting hurt?" I made a point of walking around him and continuing down the sidewalk.

"What? Why would you say that? I was having a good time," he said, looking at me like I had two heads.

"Could have surprised me. You barely said two words to me all night long. Listen, I get it. You're going through some stuff and that's fine. It's none of my business. I just wanted to have a good time tonight to make up for last week, and it turned out pretty crappy. Just forget it; you don't have to walk me home," I said, picking my head up and trying to walk at a faster pace away from him. I tried to take deep breaths in between steps, but the pain reemerged with a vengeance.

As I stepped up the curb on the other side of the street, I gasped out loud from the pain and leaned against the building. I couldn't even storm away from an unwanted conversation. Pathetic with a capital 'P.' Trying to keep my tears from brimming over the edge, I tried walking again and felt a shadow behind me. If I was going to get mugged again, then so be it. I didn't have any fight left in me for this crap. Feeling an arm go around my waist and then gently picking me up, I distinguished concern written all over Eric's face.

Laying my head against his chest, I let the tears fall down my cheeks as he admitted, "I want to walk you home. I don't like the idea of you being hurt and trying to get home alone."

"I'm sorry," I whispered, wiping the tears away from my face before he noticed.

"Did you think that guy you were dancing with was me?" Eric asked out of the blue. I shrugged my shoulders, not committing to an answer.

"Did you want to dance with me?" he asked again, and I replied with a nod and a shrug.

Recognizing the equipment around us, he sat me down on a bench at the park. Sitting down next to me, he put his arm around my shoulders. "I'm going to have to move," I said automatically. Seeing the beauty of the park at night broke my heart.

"Why?" Eric asked, looking down at me.

"I could just about afford my apartment alone years ago. I'll have to find somewhere to stay where I can get a roommate. Maybe Lily would be willing to live with me," I said, thinking about my future issues.

"Oh, that's right. You don't have any family around here," Eric commented, remembering our first conversation at the banquet dinner.

"No, they're all back in North Carolina. I could never move back home. It took me so long to finally get out of there."

"Do you not like your family?" he asked, confused by my statement.

"No, I adore them. They just smother me to the point that I think they would try grounding me like I was still a teenager. I enjoy my freedom too much," I said, fiddling with my fingers. "Do you like your family?"

Eric shrugged his shoulders and looked up at the sky.

"Were you mad that I went to talk to Tim?" I asked, the words just sliding off my tongue.

"Why?" he asked, not committing to an answer.

"Ever since I talked to him, you were...I don't know...distant, like you couldn't stand to even look at me," I said playing with my fingers again. "What were you thinking?" I asked.

"I was wondering what you guys were talking about. I wasn't meaning to come off isolated to you. It's none of my business either way."

"Eric, Tim is my friend, only my friend. Remember how Gary treated you last week?" I asked, watching Eric nod.

"Well, times that by thirty and that was the confrontation that happened between Gary and Tim. He was hurt, and I wanted to make sure he was okay. That's all."

A smirk came across his face as he took a breath.

"What did you think I was doing? Hoarding alcohol?" I asked, at first trying to make a joke out of it but then actually feeling a bit resentful at that. He didn't know me that well, but he certainly shouldn't be thinking I'm some sort of alcoholic.

Shaking his head, he pulled me closer into his side. "I was just worried about you."

Resentment making me bold, I spat out, "Worried about what? Do you like me or something?" Eric's jaw tensed up as well as his whole body. I turned to face him full on. "Do you?" I asked again.

Aware of Eric's silence, I took it as a sign that I didn't really want to know the answer.

"Good night," I said, walking home knowing that he wouldn't follow me since it was right across the street. Going straight into the bathroom, I took two Advil with a glass of cold water and then lay down on the couch. Tonight sucked, and I didn't think I wanted to ever go to the bar again.

Chapter 11
Saturday, September 1st

Waking up around ten to the vibration of my phone I noticed a text from Eric.

Lunch? I need to talk to u.

Sitting up on the couch, the pain wasn't as bad as last night, but the ache was a reminder of everything I went through. If Eric had just danced with me then I wouldn't be in pain right now. I didn't care that it wasn't a logical accusation; this is his fault. I texted back:

No, I have nothing to discuss with u.

I walked into the bathroom and looked at my bruise in the mirror. Lily was right; it was an ugly looking thing that slightly resembled a butterfly except for the nasty colors. This was a nice way to start the month of September. I hoped my birthday wasn't this eventful.

Pinning my hair on the top of my head, I took a warm shower and then wrapped myself in a towel before heading to the bedroom. Seeing Gary still asleep in bed made my lips lift in semblance of a smirk down at him. I grabbed my white and blue hippie skirt with white tank top and navy blue flip flops. Pulling my hair into a messy bun, I slung my purse across my body and walked outside to a humid day. I ordered a tall Java Chip from my favorite coffee shop before going window shopping for clothes that I didn't need.

Hearing the tinkling of my phone, I put it to my ear.

"Why?" a rugged voice asked, not leaving a minute for even a civil introduction.

"Why what?" I asked while picking up a cute skirt in my size.

"Why can't you have lunch with me?" Eric asked.

"I think it's best if we just don't. I'm going through some life changing experiences, and you are going through whatever situation you're going through, and it's just seems like it'd be better if we didn't," I replied and put the skirt on back on the rack.

"You're really doing this. You don't want to talk to me anymore?" he asked with strain in his voice.

"I'm not hungry so lunch isn't on the list of things to do today; it's too humid to eat," I said, trying to ease out of ignoring his question, but he persisted.

"Do you not want to talk to me anymore?"

"I need today off, okay? We can talk tomorrow. I'll feel better then."

"How's your ribs?" he asked, automatically thinking that's what I meant.

"My bruise hurts but not too bad. Nothing Advil can't fix."

"Then meet me for a drink tonight? Or maybe a movie would be good; the air conditioning would be perfect," Eric enthused.

"My bruise isn't the only thing hurting right now. I have to go. We'll talk tomorrow," I promised, and before he could respond I ended the call.

Lily texted me later in the afternoon: <u>Join me 4 dinner.</u>

I just wanted to be alone today. I hadn't even spoken to Gary, and I didn't want to. I knew anything I said would lead to the Arizona talk, and I just couldn't have that right now. If I went to dinner with Lily, I knew she was going to want the details of the walk home with Eric. She wouldn't ask me, but I knew she would expect me to divulge anyway. I may not have told her about how close our friendship was, but she wasn't blind or stupid. The one person who made me smile is the one person who seemed to keep making me frustrated. I texted Lily back:

<u>Maybe another day, I just need to rest.</u>

Maybe I should go to Arizona; I wouldn't have to worry about anything because Gary would take care of me. Shaking my head at my selfishness, Gary wasn't a security blanket or a hero to save the damsel from her laziness of not wanting to deal with people. My purse vibrated again, causing my eyes to flick down to notice an awaiting text from Eric. I should just ignore it and say my phone died when I talked to him tomorrow. Or I could put on my big girl panties and deal with it now so I didn't have to worry all night about it.

Reading the text, I felt my eyes start to burn from being open for so long. <u>Sry if I hurt u. I enjoy being w/ u. I just wish u were here, it'd make me feel better. I'm free 2morrow; let me know when u r ready to c me.</u>

Just like that, my frustration with Eric evaporated into confusion. There really was no description for our relationship except for friendship—we talked, we hung out and we danced. I didn't consider that cheating as I did the same thing with Lily. And what was wrong with doing the same with him? Maybe Tim was right—maybe I should be watchful about getting closer to him.

Walking down the street, I spotted an ice cream truck and bought a rocket Popsicle which has the colors red to white to blue on the end. Sucking on my Popsicle so it didn't drip on my clothes, I turned the corner to head towards Victoria's Secret and just happened to come across Eric speaking with another young man. They didn't really look the same in their complexions, but they had the same eyes. Eric's blond hair, tied in the usual ponytail, was so different even in texture to this gentleman's black hair that was thicker but in a 'bed head' style. And the young man's shorter stature made Eric look like a skyscraper.

Thinking about turning around to head in the opposite direction, Eric happened to look my way and cocked his head to the side. Why did he have to be here? Why did I let Gary rip the last two bras off of me so carelessly? Thinking about that actually made me scowl; I loved those bras. I watched Eric's face turn into a frown as he thought my reaction was because of him. Taking a deep breath, I maintained walking and tried to place a small smile on my face, but I was nervous that it came across like a grimace. I couldn't just walk by, especially after he noticed me.

"Hi," I said to Eric, trying to be pleasant.

"Hi," he replied, giving me nothing back.

"Hey, I'm Dane," said the young man, holding out his hand to me with a genuine smile. I smiled at Dane while shaking his hand.

Eric introduced us almost reluctantly. "Dane, this is Becki…my friend. Becki, this is my brother."

Very nice to meet you," I said politely, but feeling a bit awkward, I started to back up a bit. "Well, I hope you both enjoy your time together. I must be on my way."

Dane threw a smile in my direction while waving farewell, but Eric stepped in closer. "Can I speak with you for a minute?"

I sighed at him in frustration but nodded anyway. Why didn't he get it? Was I that much of a pushover?

"I'll meet you inside," Eric said back to Dane, and we both watched him head inside the department store.

"What's up?" I questioned nonchalantly while tossing my Popsicle stick in the nearby trashcan. He'd better talk quickly; I didn't want a long, drawn out conversation that would ruin my shopping mood.

Instantly, I was consumed by the muscles in Eric's arms, and I felt my body actually relax into his embrace. Even my body was betraying me now, how ridiculous. "Eric—"

"No," he said.

"Eric, I—"

"No," he said again firmly. "Please, just be here with me," he whispered almost to himself.

Looking up into his eyes, I could clearly see the trouble written in them. "What's wrong?" I questioned.

He shook his head in response but didn't loosen his hold on me.

113

"How am I supposed to be here for you and with you if you don't trust me enough with the truth?" I started to pull away, but he held on tighter. This was really great—everyone was just staring at us while we made a show of ourselves. What explanation would be plausible to explain this to Gary should he walk up on this scene? Feeling Eric place his head on my shoulder, I stopped squirming completely.

"I can't talk about it right now. Are you sure you can't join me for dinner? I do trust you. It's just hard to talk about."

Finally feeling like he was going to open up to me, I didn't push him any further. "Where?" I acquiesced.

"The Italian restaurant about a mile from your place is great. I can pick you up," he suggested.

"No, how would I explain that to Gary? I'll meet you there. It's the restaurant with the red awning and big script-like sign, right?" Eric nodded and then stood up to his full height.

"Why don't you tell Gary that we are going to hang out together?" he asked. The horrified expression that instantly befell my face made him cock his head to the side.

"He would never understand. Even if I explained it, he would see it as me cheating, or worse he'd invite himself to come along making it into some business meeting."

Eric, shrugging his shoulders, said, "I have some things that I need to take care of before tonight. I hope you enjoy the rest of your day."

Nodding my head, I watched his back disappear into the store before continuing on my way to my destination.

Replacing my two bras with some lace fringed ones in different styles that both clasped in the front, I made my way back to the apartment. Tripping over my own feet as I opened the door, I stumbled into the apartment but caught myself before I hit the wall.

"Ah!" I gasped right away from the pain of my bruise protesting against the movement. Noticing Gary walking towards me, I tried to straighten up and smooth my face over, but I could already see the anger in his facial expression.

Trying to play it cool, Gary leaned against the wall. "What happened?"

"I tripped over my own feet. Nothing new," I advised, turning to close the door behind me and taking a deep breath to calm myself.

"That's not what I meant. Last night?" Flicking a quick glance into his eyes, I saw that he must have known about the bar fight.

"It's not a big deal," I replied dismissively, shrugging my shoulders not committing to anything.

"How heartless can you be?" he spat back at me before charging into my face. "Were you ever going to tell me?"

Aghast at his words, I cocked my head to the side. "What are you talking about?"

"I saw you at the park last night with some guy. He had his arms wrapped around you and you practically dissolved into his side. You didn't even come to bed. Afraid I might smell him on you?!" he yelled.

Knowing what he saw, I understood why he would think I was cheating on him. Walking even closer until I was practically touching Gary, I slowly pulled my shirt off over my head. Backing up, I could see he was about to say something terrible so I cut him off with a stern glare and pointed my finger to my ribs. Once Gary got started in a temper tantrum all bets were off.

Finally getting full view of the bruise in its glory of purple and blue with a yellow tinge, his face turned bright red. "Is that your excuse?" he threw in my face.

"There was a fight at the bar last night with some drunk, and Tim was trying to get him out. I got trapped into it, unfortunately." Looking down at the bruise, the memories came flooding back, and I shook my head to make them go away.

"Who was the guy, Becki?" he asked pointedly, not showing any emotion to what I had just told him.

I blurted out the first name to come to mind and explained, "Tim, he helped me to the park. We talked and he apologized and then the pain set in really bad. I wasn't cheating on you; I was trying to get comfortable with this stupid thing." Pointing down again I continued, "I didn't come to bed because I didn't want to have to explain everything about the fight. I didn't want you to tell me I couldn't go back to the bar. And worse, I didn't want any chance of rolling around on this or you accidentally bumping into it. I was safer on that stupid, uncomfortable couch."

Tinkling erupted from my pocket. Shoving my hand in and pulling it out it read that mother was calling again. I hit reject quickly, but Gary's eyes were alight with fire. "Is that him?"

"No, it was my mother, so stop trying to make this into something that it isn't," I stated back defiantly. What was wrong with him? It's not like I'd changed all of a sudden. I was participating in all the normal activities for the past four years.

"Do you want to be with Tim? Just be honest with me. I'd rather know now than later," he said, his eyes still icily glaring at me, but I could see the hurt in them.

"Gary, I love you. I truly love you. I would never get back with Tim even if he was the last man on the planet." Gary nodded his head, but his eyes never stopped glaring at me.

"I'm leaving this Saturday for Arizona," he said matter-of-factly before going back to the living room to finish watching TV. Well, it seemed that I'm damned if I do and damned if I don't, so I grabbed my shirt and bag and went into the bedroom. Putting my new bras in the drawer, I laid down on the bed and stared at the ceiling.

There was no way Gary was going to let me go out tonight and not scrutinize my actions. Picking up my phone, I saw a text from Lily:

How do you feel?

Fine. Gary thinks that I'm cheating on him w/ Tim.

And with that, my phone started ringing. I picked it up and quietly rehashed the whole argument to Lily. "I can't believe he would think you'd get back together with that loser. I mean he is your friend and all, but I

117

know you haven't forgotten why you two broke up. He isn't the one."

Smiling into the phone, I said, "Yeah, well, apparently my standards suck. I'm going to rest for a bit," I concluded before hanging up.

Remembering Eric again I thought back. Was I cheating on Gary? I wasn't kissing him, I wasn't sleeping with him, and I didn't treat him any differently than I do Tim. Actually, I treated Tim a bit better. Sending a quick text to Eric, I wrote:

I can't make it tonight. Lunch?

I need to c u tonight. It's really important. He was begging. I'd never heard him say anything like that or sound so desperate.

I can't escape tonight. Gary is livid. I left it at that.

Spending the evening watching TV with Gary and receiving the silent treatment was hard. Every time I sighed due to being uncomfortable in the same position, his eyes flickered at me from the corner of his eyes. Finally unable to take it anymore, I got up and grabbed some ice from the freezer, put it in a sandwich bag and placed it against my ribs. Closing my eyes, I moaned softly out of the pleasure of coolness against the ache. I was ready for this to be healed and gone.

"What are you doing in here?" Gary asked, abruptly pulling me out of my peacefulness. Turning around he saw the ice bag against my ribs and then nodded with his eyes tight. Grabbing a water bottle and two more Advil, I sat back down on the couch and felt my phone vibrate in my pocket.

"Who were you talking to earlier?" Gary asked, appearing beside me.

"Lily," I said, exasperated.

"What about?" he persisted.

"My bruise," I replied just as curtly. There was no point in checking my phone now that he seems to be acting like a tyrant.

"No plans for tonight?" Gary asked, leaning in closer, scrutinizing my appearance.

"Recovery," I said and then got up and went to bed. How was I supposed to deal with a man who was so jealous? I could just imagine him telling me to stay in the house and the only friend allowed was Lily, and at this point, I'm sure he was sick of her, too. Huffing out a deep breath, I prayed for sleep to hit me, but it didn't come as quickly as I wanted it to.

Hearing the vibrating phone again, I remembered that I never read the previous message or responded. Checking my texts I saw that they were both from Eric. The first one read:

Did u tell him? and then second text read: R u safe? I smirked at his protectiveness. I quickly texted back:

I'm safe and sound. Going to sleep. C u @ lunch.

And then I turned my phone off not wanting to be disturbed.

*****

I'm at the JFK airport walking up to the security frisk lines with Gary.

"You sure you want to join me, right?" Gary asks with his carry-on duffle bag over his shoulder. I nod at him but inside I can feel that I'm still not 100% sure of my decision. After walking through the metal detectors and being patted down, I collect my purse before walking to the end to grab my shoes and slip them on. As I look back up to see where Gary is, I realize that he is nowhere to be found.

"Gary?" I ask out loud before starting to walk around.

Tapping a security guard I ask, "Have you seen Gary? He was just behind me."

With a shake of his head no, he continues on with his job studiously ignoring me. What am I going to do? Heading in the direction on the boarding area, I check to see if he is there, but I don't see anyone.

"Hi, I'm trying to find my boyfriend. He is supposed to be on this flight with me," I say to the lady at the counter showing her my ticket.

"I'm sorry, Ms. Austin; you've missed your flight. It took off fifteen minutes ago. Would you like to set up another flight out?" Oh no, I've missed my flight. Gary must have gone on without me.

Gasping awake from the nightmare, I clutched onto Gary's hand without thinking. I then cried out in pain as my bruise let me know that it was unhappy.

"What?! What happened!?" he asked, searching the room for an intruder and then looking back at me. Gulping down air, I looked down at my trembling hands on him.

"Nightmare, bruise," I said to calm him but only managed to bring on my tears.

"Are you okay?" he asked, concerned about my pain but still holding back from me.

"Yeah," I said. I took my robe and wrapped it around me before heading to the couch to sleep for the rest of the night.

Chapter 12
Sunday, September 2nd

After my shower, I came out to see Gary picking up his briefcase. "I'll see you tonight," he said, glancing my way and then stopped when he saw my facial expression.

"Do you not want to be with me anymore?" I heard my lips saying. Gary, stunned, looked deeply into my eyes but refused to come closer.

"I do. I just need to get to work. I'm finishing up a project before my last week." With that he closed the door behind him, leaving me with my thoughts. Maybe he should just break up with me. Then I wouldn't feel so guilty about everything.

It was his right to want to go to Arizona and start a life that he so desperately wanted. I don't have to be the girl he wants to spend the rest of his life with. Maybe I'm just not the girl. I remembered Eric's face from the park when I had asked him if he liked me. He never replied, and maybe that was best. Maybe I wasn't as amazing as Gary once thought; maybe Tim just wanted to finish off the job he started years ago. Getting depressed, I turned on the radio to listen to music while I finished getting dressed.

By the time lunch time arrived, I was no longer interested in going but felt bad about blowing Eric off last night, so I continued on my way. The lovely Italian restaurant had candles on every table and flowers all around the walls. The hostess, seating us in the very back corner of the restaurant, lit our candles after we sat down to brighten up the small corner. Feeling an edge to this corner already, I looked up and saw

Eric's face making the same assumption. I laughed out loud at this situation and blew the candles out.

Eric, cocking his head to the side, asked, "Why'd you do that?"

"Too romantic for my taste. This is just a lunch hang out after all," I said, trying to keep my distance from anything that could seem skewed.

"Are you all right? You seem a little flustered," he noted while keeping his head cocked to the side and staring me down, concerned.

Shrugging my shoulders, I sipped my water. The waiter came over and took our order and headed back into the kitchen.

"Becki, tell me. What happened last night?" he said more firmly.

"Gary is breaking up with me. He doesn't want me anymore," I said, calmly trying to be numb. "He thinks I'm cheating on him with Tim."

"I see," he said with his eyebrows pulled tight together. "How do you feel about that?"

"Confused," I admitted, shrugging again.

Looking into his intense eyes, I blurted out, "He doesn't want me...to go to Arizona with him. He is preparing to cut off all ties."

Raising one blond eyebrow, Eric asked, "Wasn't that the plan?"

"We weren't breaking up because I didn't want him...our future was separating us. He hates me and I feel..." I stuttered, unable to finish my sentence.

"Hurt? Upset?" he offered.

123

"Lost."

The waiter brought over our meals, and I stuck a fork into my broccoli before popping it into my mouth.

"Do you want to go to Arizona...with him?" he inquired, but I heard the inflection in his tone. Why did he care? This was not the reason that I came here today.

"I don't want anything." Trying to change the subject, I asked, "So, what did you want to talk about?"

"Nothing really. I just wanted to touch base," he said before eating a fork full of pasta.

Dropping my fork onto my plate, I glared at him. "Really?"

"What?" he asks shocked at my tone.

"I guess I should go," I stated, grabbing my purse.

"No, why?"

"What's the point? One-sided conversation is quite dull," I replied cattily.

"I just don't want to upset you more, but I seem to be doing that anyway." Shaking his head, he took a deep breath and continued, "I finished my shelter scene so I wanted to extend my part of the deal back to you."

Noticing my glare disappear but my eyebrows raise, he continued, "Also, something has come up, and I wanted to explain to you why I might not be around as much."

Oh, hell no, now he was making a break for it, too? It must be my lucky day. Seeing the frustration on my face, Eric advised, "It's not what you think."

Raising his hands in a stay put gesture, he took a sip of his wine and confessed, "When I was twelve years old, I was kidnapped by a lunatic." My nerves that were shot before just had a huge bucket of cold water doused over them. "When I escaped...the police put him in prison."

Taking another breath, he looked up to meet my stunned gaze. "He was released from prison the day you were attacked, which is why I was late."

Not wanting to interrupt his story, I placed my hand on top of his, silently trying to send my calm to him. "My brother came down to visit me to let me know some stuff. That guy moved here, registered on Friday of last week. I don't know why or what he has planned, but I won't be hanging out at the bar anymore."

Comprehending how scared he must have been, the worry came out of my mouth, "Are you okay?"

"I'm not afraid about him finding me," Eric said, reading into my words. "I'm afraid about him seeing us hanging out together. With Gary leaving, you will be alone in your apartment. It's not safe."

Losing my appetite, I nodded. He asked, "Does Gary know that you are here...with me?"

"No, he's not speaking to me." I shrugged again.

Hearing the tinkling of my phone, I picked it up and apologized with my eyes to Eric.

"Where are you?" I heard Gary demand.

"I just went to grab a bite to eat."

"Who are you with?" he asked, seething.

"Why do I have to be with anyone? Why can't I eat alone?" I spat back in a whisper.

"Come home now," he demanded.

"When I'm done with my sandwich, I'll be there."

"NOW!" he yelled into the phone. Flinching at his yell, I hung up the phone.

"What the hell was that about?" Eric asked looking concerned, worried and slightly angry.

"I have to go. I'm sorry," I said, putting my phone back into my purse.

"Why was he yelling? Tell me what's going on," he insisted. I reached in my purse, grabbed some cash and put it on the table for my half of the bill.

"I don't know. Gary needs me home," I explained and started hurrying out of the restaurant.

Arriving at the apartment, I felt the onslaught of butterflies in my stomach.

"Gary?" I asked, shutting the door behind me. Seeing movement from the corner of my eyes, I spotted Gary coming out of the bathroom.

"Why are you never home anymore?" he accused.

"I wanted to get a sandwich from the deli," I said defensively.

126

"You have all these excuses—hanging out with your friends—when are we going to spend time together?" he asked.

"What is wrong with you? I'm always home every night. I only go out like once or twice a week. What's this about?" I asked, throwing my hands up in the air.

"I'm leaving in a week," he stated soberly.

"I know that. We have this conversation every day. What else is there to say?"

Hurt coming across his eyes, he said, "You were never planning on leaving with me. You're already trying to get back together with Tim."

Horrified by his statement, I yelled back, "I have no intention of being with Tim! You are pushing me away. Some proposition…you said you wouldn't put pressure on me but you have. The same conversation of moving, the cruel and undeserved temper tantrums you throw at me. You don't want to be with me. You want to own me," I spat back at him before going to the bedroom and slamming the door behind me.

*****

Friday, September 7th

The whole week went by in a blur, the silence was deafening, but worse was the fact that I didn't do anything all week. No girl's night, no lunches with friends, not a single activity did I engage in all week long. The only slice of happiness was Barney keeping me company. Walking into my apartment after work, I was welcomed by a bunch of cardboard boxes. Upon seeing Gary packing his suitcase full of clothes, I headed into the bedroom.

127

"Hey," I said to be polite.

Nodding in my direction he kept packing.

"Do you need any help?"

"I'm almost done packing," he said, headed to the bathroom. Sitting on the bed, I waited for him to come back. As he packed his toiletries in his suitcase, it finally hit me that he was really leaving.

"Can I ask you something?"

"Shoot," he said, zipping up his suitcase.

"Do you want me to go with you to Arizona? And think about it before you answer. Do you really...want me?"

Feeling his gaze on me, I looked down at my knotted fingers. "Is that what you think? That I don't want you?"

Wrapping his arm around my shoulders, he continued, "I know I've been crazy for the past couple of weeks, but it was just the stress of the job getting to me and having you hanging out with your ex wasn't helping. I thought you wanted out."

"You've been so mad at me. I admit to avoiding you at times, but that was because we were always fighting. I thought you were going to just break up with me."

Sighing, he lifted my chin with his finger to meet his gaze. "I think we're both afraid of the inevitable. I'm leaving...and I know you well enough to know you aren't following. It doesn't change how I feel...how much I love you."

"I love you so much, Gary." I whispered.

"I know. My offer still stands, if you want to move with me or even visit. I'd love to have you."

Glancing into his tear-filled eyes, I tilted my head up and brushed my lips against his. Deepening the kiss, he ran his fingers through my hair. My heart breaking, I whimpered into his mouth. Finally breaking apart, we wiped each other's tears off of our faces and held each other for a while.

"My plane leaves early in the morning, and I have to forward my boxes. I'm going to stay at the airport hotel," he said, grabbing his suitcase and heading out the door. After helping to put the boxes in the car, he kissed me deeply again.

"I want you to have this," he said, handing me an envelope. "Open it after I leave, okay?"

Nodding, I leaned in and kissed him a final time before he slid into his car and drove off.

Walking into my half empty apartment, I sat down on the couch and began opening the envelope to find a check for $3000 written out to me. Unable to control my emotions any longer, I curled up in a ball letting loose of body-jolting sobs.

Chapter 13
Monday, September 10th

Work was a blessing in disguise. It gave me a reason to get out of bed, a reason to get dressed, and a reason to continue working on my future. Taking a scalding shower, I let a few tears escape while washing my hair and body. Using lots of hair spray, I scrunched my hair into a style I'd never tried before. I thought it looked nice. I pulled out my outfit for work—tan slacks, blue short sleeve blouse and my blue flats. Filling up my to-go cup with coffee, I headed out to work.

Getting to work a half an hour early, I settled in to work on a bit of paperwork before helping with rescue cases that came in.

"So you're just not going to answer your phone?" Lily said snottily to me at the door. Glancing up, I saw that she was wearing her royal purple boat neck shirt with grey slacks and grey flats.

"My battery died, and I wasn't in the mood to find the charger," I said, shrugging my shoulders.

"Do you want to talk about anything?" she asked, walking closer to my desk.

"No, I just need time. And stronger coffee if I'm to get through all of this before the next case comes in."

Lily chuckled and said, "Coffee I can fix, and I think I have a spare charger." Hurrying out for her task, I watched her leave. I loved having Lily in my life; she knew how to make me happy so easily.

By lunch time, I was famished and grabbed my purse to walk to the deli with Lily. Sitting in the back corner, I sipped my water and chomped on a simple six-inch meatball grinder with American cheese.

"Do you have any plans tonight?" asked Lily.

"My plans consist of jammies, popcorn and a movie. What about you?" I mumbled with a mouthful of sandwich.

"I'm in the process of moving in with Will. I still feel weird in my apartment, and I spend most of my time with him anyway. It'll be cheaper for both of us."

Delighted, I asked, "How did you manage that one?"

"He protects me from my nightmares that I have sometimes. I just feel so creepy there, I can't do it," Lily advised before munching on her chips. "Have you spoken with Eric?"

Shaking my head, I confessed, "I'm not ready for that conversation just yet, either." Lily took the cue and started gabbing about sales that were going on at our favorite stores this coming weekend.

Back at my desk, my cell phone charged thanks to Lily. Waiting for it to power up, I checked my messages on my computer, but it seemed we were having a quiet day. Looking back at my phone, I noticed three voicemails waiting for me.

Calling my voicemail box, the first message was from Lily saying, "Hey, Becki, it's your one and only gal pal. I miss your face and wish you would pick up so we can go out and buy some shoes. Call me back when you get this." Smirking, I hit delete and moved on to the next message which was from Eric.

131

"Hi, I'm getting worried. You're not answering my texts or picking up your phone. Please let me know that you are okay even if you don't want to talk to me."

Sighing, I hit delete and moved on to the final message from Gary. "Hey. It's me, Gary. I just wanted to let you know that I arrived safe and sound in Arizona. Call me if you want to." Taking a deep breath, I hit delete and then called Gary back.

Getting his voicemail in return, I left a message. "Hey, it's Becki. My battery died, and I can't find my charger. I'm glad that you made it there safely. Call me if you want to. I'm available. Um...okay, bye."

Before I lost all control of my emotions, I called Eric.

"Thank God, are you okay?" he said, dripping with anxiety.

"I'm fine, Eric. What's going on?" I asked, unable to resist a smile to myself at his obvious concern.

"I couldn't get a hold of you, and I thought something had happened. I..."

"Don't worry, there isn't anything wrong. My battery died, and I can't find my charger," I said to get him to understand.

"Oh, okay, good. By the way, I was wondering if you were busy tonight? I would like to have you read my book, if you still want to." Just as I was about to shoot him down, I thought about my plans tonight. I was just going to cry myself asleep again.

Sighing into the phone I said, "Sounds good. Where should I meet you?"

"At the park, that way we can go straight to my place. See you when you get off, okay?"

"Sure," I said before hanging up.

Around four, I got a call from Gary checking up on me. "So, you are okay?"

"As good as it's going to get for a while. What about you?" I replied.

"I'm surviving. I miss coming home to you, though," he said, his voice tinged with sadness.

"I miss you, too. This will get easier, and I hope that we can continue talking. I'm not losing you as a friend," I said to him, and he laughed.

"Of course not! We're in different time zones now so it'll be harder, but I don't plan on leaving you behind. Talk to you soon?"

"Sounds good," I replied, and we hung up in a hopeful awkwardness. The sound of his voice, while comforting, also seemed to leave a slight edginess in its wake. At least I wasn't getting in the way of his work. It would have been awful for him to get to his dream job and screw it up on account of me.

An hour later, I grabbed my purse and walked to the park. I was interested in seeing where Eric lived; I mean, he had been to my place twice. I wasn't much of a critic, but it would be interesting to review what he wrote about my place of work. A block from the park I was stopped by an older gentleman who was a little taller than me and slender with dark brown eyes.

"Excuse me, miss. Do you have the time?"

I checked my cell phone. "It's ten minutes after five."

"Thank you kindly," he said, tipping his head and smiling showing straight teeth but the left front tooth was missing. Smiling, I continued on my way to the park.

Seeing Eric sitting on the bench, I walked over and sat beside him.

"Your critic has arrived," I stated in all seriousness.

"Well, then, I might change my mind on letting you read it," he said, smirking at me. Holding my hand, we stood and he guided me over to his black vehicle. Opening the door for me to slide in, I noticed the grey interior with black console and built in GPS. Buckling our seatbelts, I was surprised to see him take the exit to the highway.

"Where do you live?" I asked, puzzled.

"Rye. It's really quiet there so I can get my writing done," he replied.

"So, whenever I asked you to come to the bar, you had to drive like a half hour? I'm sorry. I wouldn't have asked if I had known that."

Frowning, he glanced my way. "You don't want to hang out with me?"

"I do, but that is crazy to drive all the way to *Lights Out* just to hang out with us," I said, looking out the window.

"I go to enjoy an evening with you."

My stomach fluttered from his words and tone.

Pulling into a nicely paved driveway, I opened my door and gaped at the house before me. A beautiful white-sided house with many windows on every side greeted me. Walking up the brick patio toward the front of the house, I saw white pillars holding up the second level.

"Eric, how many rooms are here? Do you have a roommate?" I asked, astonished at the beautiful sight in front of me.

"Four bedrooms, three bathrooms, game room, a large kitchen, dining room, living room, den and office. There is also a balcony and garden in the back," he said, studying his home and smiled down at me. "I don't need a roommate to afford this."

"May I ask how much it was to purchase?" I requested as he unlocked the front door.

"You don't want to know."

"I'm just curious because I was saving up my money to buy a house on the coast," I said not wanting to force him, but I was dying of curiosity.

"$1,850,000," he said, leading me into the beautiful white kitchen. Wow, Gary was right. I would never be able to afford living on the coast around here.

Looking around the granite counter tops, all stainless steel appliances including dishwasher caught my eye. The walls were a warm cream with crown moldings on the top and the floors were marble. Turning around to face him, I glimpsed what had his attention; I'd never seen so many locks in my life for one door. There were two deadbolts, a chain, and a home security system, where I think I saw him place his finger on a scanner for the door to lock. Looking up, he saw me watching and shrugged.

"Can't ever be too safe. Let me show you around."

The tour around the house was amazing, stunning, breath-taking and depressing all at the same time. There was so much space to do so many things, but he only used one-quarter of the space of the entire house. "And finally this is my office," he said, guiding me with his hand on my lower back.

"This is where the magic happens," I said, fluttering my fingers out like fireworks.

The room was very spacious with tan walls and a white marble fireplace. A cherry wood desk overflowed with papers and notebooks, and an overstuffed dark brown chair with tiny rollers was placed to the right of the fireplace. To set off the lighting was a beautiful candle chandelier hanging down; however, I noted the small lamp on the left side of the desk. The walls surrounding the door were covered in filled bookcases and there was also a love seat kitty-corner to the desk and fireplace.

"Some of the 'magic' happens here, some in the living room or the garden. Would you like to eat now?" he asked, smiling.

"Depends. What are we having?" I asked, raising my eyebrow.

"Already prepared salad and soup from a can," Eric said with a huge grin.

My laugh eluded my grasp before I responded. "Sounds delicious. I'm in."

Walking back towards the kitchen, I viewed the pictures in the hallway. They were all landscapes. "Your house should come with a map," I joked.

"Noted. I'll print one out for you," he said, laughing with me. "Okay, the choices are chicken noodle, minestrone, and tomato soup."

"Tomato, please," I replied.

While Eric started warming up our soups on the stove, I opened the fridge and pulled out a bag of premade salad. The fact that Eric can't even take the time to cut up a salad made me want to whack him with the bag. Shaking my head, I started opening cupboards to find bowls. He had to be surviving on more than this.

"The bowls are—"

"Shh! I'm hunting down dishware," I said, doing my best Elmer Fudd impression. After my fifth attempt rifling around in the cabinets, I found the bowls and salad plates. Setting the bowls next to the stove, I filled our salad plates and then set them on the dining room table.

Walking to the fridge to pull out Ranch and French dressing, I blurted out, "Do you travel a lot?"

"No, I just like to have nature's beauty surround me." Cocking my head to the side, a learned behavior from the master cooking over the stove, I thought back through the rooms he took me through.

"Do you have any photos of your family?"

"Um...I have a few, but they're mostly in photo albums." Oh, yeah, he didn't really seem to admit whether he liked his family or not.

"Oh." I quickly picked up the dressings and hustled into the dining room before I delved any deeper. I couldn't seem to bite my tongue around him, and one day it was going to bite me in the behind.

"Do you like being an only child, other than the unwanted constant attention?" he asked, suddenly behind me as he placed down our soup bowls.

"Yeah," I said noncommittally and then turned to go back into the kitchen.

"Nope, you sit. I'll grab the utensils and water with lemon?" Smiling back at him, I nodded. I shouldn't be surprised that he knew what I liked to drink; he was my lunch companion.

We sat down and ate our salads, waiting for the soup to cool.

"Are you close with your brother?" I inquired to see their relationship.

"Our age difference is pretty wide; we don't have much in common."

"He seems nice. You tower over him, though," I noted.

"Different fathers," he admitted, sipping his water. Biting on my fork, I kept my questions to myself. I wasn't going to push him. "My father passed when I was six years old, the Gulf War," he stated without emotion.

"I'm sorry," was all I could manage to pass through my lips.

"My mother remarried, and Dane came soon after that."

Nodding, I practically stuck my head in the soup bowl, not wanting to continue the conversation.

After a few moments of awkward silence, he asked, "What do you think?" Glancing up at me, his head was cocked to the side with a smirk.

"It's good, thank you. Are you enjoying yours?" I asked, feeling my cheeks warm.

"It's okay," he commented. After the meal, I helped load the dishwasher, and we headed back to his office.

"Here is the scene," he said, handing me a bunch of papers. "Let me know what you think."

Reading the four page scene with its incredible detail left me in awe of this man. I couldn't imagine how he made our bland looking shelter sound so impressive. "Wow. I may actually read the whole book when you're finished," I declared, putting the scene on his desk.

"I'm glad you approve," he remarked with a smirk.

Glancing up at the clock, I saw it read nine o'clock. "It's getting late. Do you mind taking me back?" Eric's smirk faded, but he stood up and walked me to the front door, undoing all the locks.

Enjoying the silence while he locked up the front door, I closed my eyes and enjoyed the luxury of having the peacefulness surround me for the moment. I loved the beach, and I wished I could afford to live in a beautiful house like this. I could tan all summer long living so close to the coast. Feeling the caress of fingers rub up my back, I opened my eyes and headed towards the car with his hand still on my lower back.

Arriving back at the park, it seemed harder than usual to say good night to him. Eric's company felt like more than just comfortable friendship. "Thanks for having me over for dinner. I had a really nice time," I stated politely.

"I'm sorry my cooking skills aren't up to par, but we made it through all right," he replied, chuckling before opening his arms in my direction. I willingly leaned in and closed my eyes, listening to his heartbeat and his easy breathing. Eric placed his chin on top of my head and sighed softly. I wished I could stay like this for hours, just relaxing in his arms.

Knowing that I had to get up early in the morning, I reluctantly unlocked my arms from around him and slowly pulled away but found his face so close to mine, my breath ceased for a long moment. Eric ran his fingers up my back, up my neck and into my hair, and I watched as a slow burn started to take over his eyes.

Laying his forehead against mine, our lips were so close to touching that I could practically taste his breath. Is this really what I wanted? Did I want to be with Eric officially when he still hadn't expressed his feelings for me? I ran my fingers across his cheek and gave him a small smile.

"Thank you for tonight. I really enjoyed spending time with you. Drive home safely," I said before exiting his vehicle.

Climbing the stairs of my building to my apartment, my thoughts were running rampant in my head. I knew that I ruined what could have been a perfect kiss, but I wasn't ready. I didn't want to make any mistakes. I didn't want him to be my rebound guy;

he is my friend. I couldn't take advantage of him or let myself be put in a situation I couldn't get out of later. Eric Whitman, the most amazing author I'd ever met, almost kissed me and I walked away. Maybe I was starting to lose my mind.

Laughing to myself, I pulled out my key and started to turn the lock when I got the instinctive feeling that I wasn't alone. I quickly entered the apartment, shut the door behind me and flicked the lock. I've lived by myself before. Why was I so jittery?

*****

Tuesday, September 11th

In the afternoon, Lily was sitting on the opposite side of my desk laughing at my expense. "I can't believe you. Three days and you are already getting the creeps. What kind of best friend would I be to deny you the company you obviously need?" Lily said, chuckling.

"Thanks for making me feel bad," I replied, good-naturedly. "Actually, I had an idea I wanted to run past you. What do you think about me adopting Barney? I wouldn't have to worry about being alone, Barney likes me anyway, and Gary isn't around to complain about pets."

Lily smiled. "I was wondering how long it would take for you to pick him up. Go for it! It's not like you are unqualified to care for him."

Back in my apartment, Lily and I laughed the night away with comedies and popcorn. Just as my eyes started to get heavy enough to sleep, Lily rolled over to face me. "How are things with you and Tim?"

141

Rolling my eyes, I said, "Normal, why?"

"No reason, really. I just saw him yesterday, and it seemed like something was seriously bothering him. He wouldn't talk about it with me, but I don't know."

"I'll text him and make sure he is okay." Nodding her head, we both fell into a deep slumber.

Chapter 14

Thursday, September 13th

Lily, otherwise occupied by a romantic dinner date with Will, cancelled our Girl's Night plans. And after my last solo adventure at the bar, it'd be wise to keep tucked away. Warming up a can of chicken noodle soup, I ate on the couch watching some reality show about finding love in a pitch black room. I didn't understand why everyone seemed to be so obsessed with finding love on reality TV. It's not like it is real. After washing my dishes, I plugged my phone into the charger which I had discovered was hiding under my bed. I crawled into bed almost immediately falling asleep.

Hearing a loud bang, my eyes flashed open and I sat bolt upright in bed. With my heart racing, I tried to listen very carefully to see if the bang came from inside my apartment or from outside. Then hearing the sound of boots walking in the living room made my breath stop completely. I grabbed my cell phone right away from my end table, silently slipped into my closet and shut the door, closing me inside. Hiding behind my long gowns, I punched in 9-1-1 and heard the sound of feet walking back toward the bathroom.

"This is 9-1-1, what is your emergency?" said a monotone voice.

"My name is Rebecca Austin; my apartment is on 643 Holden St, Apartment 202, in New Rochelle, NY. There is an intruder in my apartment, please send help."

"Are you home alone?" the voice asked.

"Yes," I whispered as I heard the footsteps coming closer towards the bedroom.

"A patrol car is on the way. Stay on the line with me," the voice said again. Holding my breath with my arms wrapped around my legs, I tried to put myself in a Zen-like meditation to keep calm my frantic heartbeat. Suddenly, the bedroom door squeaked open and the sounds of low, heavy breathing got closer to the closet. Just as suddenly, I heard the sounds of a police siren coming closer and closer.

The breathing paused before the loud thud of feet started running out of the room. Staying put in my closet, I kept my eyes closed and held my position, too frightened to move a muscle. What if he hadn't left the apartment?

"Ma'am, are you still there?" the dispatcher asked.

"Yeah," I whispered as quietly as possible.

"The officers are coming into the apartment now," the dispatcher advised.

I heard two sets of feet come into the apartment followed by the voice of a man. "Hello, Ms. Austin? This is the NYPD."

Hearing that, I began to climb out of the closet and ended up opening the door just enough to fall out onto the floor.

"I'm here," I said, trying to make sure they didn't mistake me for the intruder. The officers came back into the bedroom.

"The officers are here," I stated to the monotone dispatcher before it was okay to hang up.

144

"Have you been harmed?" one officer asked. I sat down abruptly on my bed, rubbing my hands across my face, trying to get ahold of myself.

"No, when the sirens got close enough to hear, I heard the intruders' footsteps head out of the door. I never saw if it was a man or a woman. I just hid and called you guys."

After hours of questions with the police, I called the one friend who could get to me as quickly as possible.

"Hello?" said a sleepy voice.

"I need you. Can you come and get me?" I asked, trying to keep the shaking from my voice.

"Becki? It's three in the morning. Where are you?" Tim asked.

"I'm in my apartment. Someone broke in tonight, and I need a place to stay," I responded, still shaken.

"Shit, I'm coming now," he said and hung up. About fifteen minutes later, Tim came into the doorway.

"Becki?" he called out. Running into his arms, I collapsed into tears. With officer assistance, Tim and I shut up my apartment.

Walking into Tim's apartment, he kept his arm wrapped tightly around my waist. I'd been in his apartment before, but usually there were lights on, and right now I was just too tired to look if anything had changed.

"I can sleep on the couch. You go get in my bed and get some rest, okay?" Tim said, obviously concerned. Grabbing his hand, I pulled him to join me in bed, too afraid to be left alone again.

As I slipped under the covers, I looked to see Tim hovering in the corner unsure of what to do. "Tim, I don't want to be left alone. Please stay. Just don't—"

"Don't worry. I'm not even thinking about that right now," he said, cutting me off. Climbing in bed beside me, he let me lay my head on his chest and pass out.

*****

Friday, September 14th

The screeching of my phone alarm going off jolted me from Tim's arms. Pressing the dismiss option, I laid my head back on the pillow and tried to think about what needed to be done. I had to go to my apartment and get dressed, go to work, change my locks when suddenly, my head started hurting with the most intense pain.

"I'll drive you back to your apartment," Tim whispered in a raspy voice. Rolling over, I saw the worry drawn on his face. I nodded and tried to smile back which earned me one in return.

"Come on, you don't want to be late for work," Tim said and helped me out of bed.

Tim, insisting on going into my apartment first, started to look around before letting me enter.

"It's empty," he beckoned. I went in and observed that my apartment was pretty much the same way it looked last night with the police here—a little disarray but nothing missing which mystified the police and thoroughly freaked me out. "Grab a shower, and I'll sit here."

Without another word, he sat down on the couch and turned on the TV.

Back in my bedroom, the horrible memories came flooding back of the terror I felt, the sounds of the footsteps getting closer and the sound of his breath... Squeezing my eyes shut, I pushed those thoughts to the side long enough for me to grab a t-shirt, jeans and flats. Making my way back out of the bedroom, Tim's easy laughter reached my ears. My insides relaxed slightly feeling the comfort of a friend close by.

Rushing into the shower, I didn't even take a minute to reflect on what I had been through; I just needed to keep moving. After drying off, I slipped into my shirt and stepped into my jeans when I heard a knock on the bathroom door.

"Hey, do you mind if I fix your lock and stuff for you?" Tim called through the door.

"Tim, you are being a life saver for me right now," I said and opened the door while running the towel through my damp hair one last time.

"I know I can be an ass sometimes, but I do have a heart," he said, mocking hurt.

Smirking back at him, I leaned in and gave him a kiss on the cheek before going to sit down on the couch to slide my flats on. "So do you want to come back to my place tonight to stay?" he asked, being nonchalant about it.

"I have no idea. I'm bringing Barney, my favorite doggy friend, home with me tonight," I explained.

147

"Don't sweat it. I'll bring you to work and walk you home after." And just like that, some of my worries disappeared.

Once in the door at work, I waved a hand to Tim before heading to the kennels. Hearing the familiar yelp of my dear friend Barney, I saw him in the kennel farther to the left.

"You are spending the day with me," I said, opening his cage and rubbing his head. Filling a bowl with water and some ice cubes, I turned to walk up to my office and proceeded to bump into Tyler.

"Stealing?" he asked with a chuckle, pointing to Barney. I nodded with a tight smile, entered my office, and closed the door.

Three stacks of paperwork finally finished and ready to be sent out to my boss for signatures, I leaned back in my chair. My life had been a rollercoaster for the past couple of weeks. This wasn't the life I thought I was going to have without Gary in it. Listening to the calm breathing of Barney sleeping on his pet bed in the corner, I couldn't help but smile down at him. Not even thinking, I got down on my hands and knees crawling over to him and cuddled up and laid my head on his back and rested my eyes.

"This is a first," I heard an amused voice say from the door. Squinting into the direction where the voice came from, I spotted Lily propped up against the door frame. "Sleeping with dogs?" she said, smirking at me.

"Oh, Lily, you have no idea," I replied in a croaky voice and chuckled along with her.

"You're lucky that today has been slow. You would have had your butt kicked if anyone found you in here like that." She laughed again. "Couldn't sleep?"

"Worse, I spent the night with Tim," I said, and seeing her eyebrows raise practically into her hairline, I quickly added, "Someone broke into my apartment last night while I was in bed. The police said I could go home with Tim to sleep."

"Did they know you were there? Did you scare them off?" Lily asked, helping me up off of the floor.

"I don't know if the person knew I was there or not, but it didn't seem to stop them anyway. I hid in the closet and called the cops." I shuddered at the memory of the night before.

"Well, at least it's Friday. You can just relax all weekend long. Will and I can spend the nights with you if you want?"

"I think Tim is trying to take advantage of the situation, but he's harmless enough. Barney is coming home with me tonight so I can have a cuddle buddy," I said, rubbing his head while he yawned.

Rolling her eyes, Lily asked, "Have you talked to Eric?"

I rolled my eyes back at her and said, "No, I don't have to bring him into my crazy world. I'm not even going to tell Gary."

"Here, I'll help you take these piles to the boss's in basket." Lily offered kindly.

We finished just before Tim came to the office. "Ready?" he asked, holding out his hand. Lily smirked at him, and after I took his hand, she started laughing out loud at us. Ignoring her, I held Barney's leash in the other hand.

*****

"I have a surprise for you," Tim said, pulling me closer to wrap his arm around my shoulder.

"Oh, yeah?" Opening the door to my apartment the smell whacked me in the face.

"Oh, my…" Inhaling deeply, I closed my eyes. This smell was so familiar and comforting, I followed Tim to the oven before he hit the light and I peeked inside to see lasagna waiting for us. "You did this—"

"I did this for us to celebrate. Life is too short to not enjoy the pleasures of food among other things," he said, playfully raising his eyebrows at me.

While Tim set out the dinner with glasses of Sangria for us, I filled up Barney's two-sided bowl with food and water.

"So how long have you two been together?" Tim asked, nodding toward Barney.

With a chuckle, I admitted, "I've had my eye on him for a while now, but I'm considering adoption." I then laughed with Tim.

"He suits you. He seems happy but doesn't seem to terrorize your apartment."

"We have an understanding," I said before laughing again.

By the end of the meal and the third glass of wine we were practically holding onto the table with laughter. Tim was doing impressions of drunk customers and passing along the gossip of who is hooking up with whom—I practically had tears running down my face from the hilarity. The tinkling of my phone made me pull it out of my pocket and see that it was my mother calling. I hit ignore. I'll call her back tomorrow.

Filling up my fourth glass, we headed to the couch to watch a comedy where the laughs only got louder and longer. At one point, I clutched my side and stomped my foot on the floor because breathing was becoming a serious issue. I could have died right there on the couch, and Tim wouldn't have been able to save me. He was too busy rolling on the floor in his own fit of laughter.

When the show finally ended and we are able to take a big breath, my throat was killing me. Laying our heads back on the couch, we watched some reality TV show. Curling up into a ball and laying my head on the arm of the couch, I started to doze off asleep.

*****

Rolling over, my legs tangled up with someone else's. What the heck? I sat up looking around to find that Tim and I were in my bed together. I looked down and saw that I was still fully dressed and sighed. At least he was gentleman enough to not undress me. Sinking back down into bed, I put my hands under my head and pulled my legs free from Tim's and tried to get back to sleep. Suddenly, I felt his arm thrown over me. Trying to push it off because it was too warm, I accidentally woke him up.

"Huh?" he asked.

"I'm hot," I said, trying to make it clear for him to roll over, but instead he cuddled up closer into me.

151

Trying to scoot in the opposite direction away from him, I notice that he wasn't wearing his shirt and his thick arm muscles were right up against me.

"Just take off your clothes; you're too comfortable to not cuddle into," he said, pulling me back into him before settling his head on my shoulder and breathing on my neck. I was such an idiot. I knew he'd try to sleep with me, but I never comprehended how much he cared for me. Kicking off the blankets helped, and I took a deep breath and settled back into a deep sleep.

Chapter 15

The tickling of hair against my collarbone made me sweep my hand across only to find a mass of hair followed by a forehead.

"Tim," I whispered, trying to roll his body off of me to the left side but he wasn't budging.

"Tim…roll over," I whispered again, and this time I thought he was finally starting to move until I felt his hands go right to my waist and then he snuggled his head even more into my chest.

"Tim, wake up," I said, forcefully trying to roll him over with my arms and hips until we both went over and I ended up on top of him.

Huffing out exasperatedly, I tried to move back to my side of the bed but then his hands gripped my waist holding me down on him. No! This was not happening.

"Wake up, Tim!" I said, whacking him on his shoulder. His bright, sea green eyes jolted open before crinkling into a smirk.

"This is the best wakeup call I've ever had," he said, grinding his hips against me.

"Let go. You were sexually assaulting me in your sleep," I said, trying to hold onto my aggravation but then cracking up at the sound of it. "No, really, I have to take Barney for his morning walk," I insisted.

"I'll take care of it," Tim said, leaning up and kissing my cheek before hopping out of bed and throwing his shirt back on.

I crawled out of bed to fill Barney's bowl again with food and water.

"Now, Barney, be a good boy for Tim," I said, petting his head and clasping the leash to his collar. Setting the coffee to perk, I went into the bedroom and grabbed my flared jeans and navy halter top with navy flip flops. "I'm taking a shower, okay, so when you come back just let me know that you're here," I said, sticking my head out of the bathroom door.

Tim came over and held my gaze with his eyes. "I wouldn't do that to you," he said and left after locking the door behind him.

Locking the bathroom door, I took a quick shower and washed my hair. After drying and dressing, I took out my blow dryer to dry my hair and give it some thickness. Shaking it out a bit and then putting it in a high pony tail, I smiled at the results in the mirror. Hearing the unmistakable sound of scratching at the door, I chuckled.

"Tim?" I called out to make sure.

"Yeah, you're okay, baby girl," he said but his voice seemed strained. Unlocking the bathroom door and coming out, I found Barney sniffing my legs and Tim leaning against the wall staring at Eric who was inspecting the door frame.

"Hey, Eric, I didn't know you were coming by," I said, giving Barney a few more pets before walking into the kitchen and pouring a cup of coffee. "You guys want a cup?" I asked, cringing at the thought of both of them just hanging out here all day together.

"No, I have some things that need to be taken care of. Is there anything I can get you?" Tim asked, coming closer to me. I shook my head before looking up into his striking eyes.

"I'm okay. Are you working tonight?"

"Yeah, I had to switch days to cover a vacation."

Leaning in closer to my ear he whispered, "Listen, I won't be getting off of work until late. If you want to come to the bar, you are more than welcome. And if you want to crash at my place, you don't even have to ask."

"Thank you for everything. I wouldn't have been able to cope without you getting me filled with booze and laughter," I said, chuckling to take the seriousness out of his voice. I took a step back and sipped my coffee already sensing that one of us was going to move to touch the other. I could honestly feel the pull of wanting to clutch Tim to my side and not letting him go to work. More selfish thoughts…I needed to get a grip.

"Talk to you later," he said before petting Barney on the way out.

"See you around," Tim said to Eric before taking the stairs down to the lobby.

"Do you mind locking that up?" I asked Eric, taking my coffee to the couch. Hearing the door shut and the click of the lock, I took a deep breath already guessing what was going through Eric's mind about all of this. I was harder than I expected to adjust to being around Eric after spending the last two days with Tim. Slowly, he sat down next to me on the couch but angled himself directly at me.

"How's your week been?" I asked, being polite and sipping my coffee.

"Not as exciting as yours, apparently," Eric replied coldly.

I shrugged my shoulders. "How's your book coming along?"

"Really?" he asked, making me look up into his eyes.

"Am I not supposed to be interested in what you do?" I asked, confused.

"Becki..." he said, trying to reign in his frustration as it would seem to me. "Why didn't you tell me? Why didn't you call me?" Tim must have told Eric what was going on. It made sense now thinking about Tim using my coined 'baby girl' nickname.

"I didn't want to—"

"DO NOT say that you didn't want to bother me. You know or you should know that I would have been here for you. To have to come here and see the damage, to already know how bad it could have been...do you know how that makes me feel?"

The memories from that night rushing back, I started to shiver and almost dropped my mug of coffee all over myself. I put my mug down on the coffee table and took a moment trying to regain my light-hearted composure that Tim encouraged in me.

"Please don't," I begged.

The couch sinking on my right side made me glance up to see Eric opening his arms for me. Laying my head against his chest, I took slow deep breaths inhaling the scent I knew to be him. His hand rubbed up and down my back soothingly.

"Eric, what did Tim tell you?" I asked, not looking up. Feeling his arms tense up around me, I wished I had kept my mouth shut.

"He told me about the intruder, about you calling him and how he's been sleeping with you since," he stated, practically biting his tongue off by the end. His admission didn't surprise me in the least; Tim would have made sure to keep Eric at a distance.

Shaking my head, I chuckled with dark humor. "We didn't, I mean—"

"It's none of my business," Eric said curtly, cutting me off. Using my hands, I grasped his smooth face making him look into my eyes.

"We literally slept. I just couldn't be alone, especially here. This isn't my home anymore..." I said, looking in the direction of my surroundings. "And I didn't want to wake you up and make you come to take care of me. You're going through your own situation right now, and it just seemed selfish to make you go out of your way to come get me. Being here was just making my skin crawl. I needed out," I admitted, looking back into his eyes boring as much honesty as I had into them.

"Have you found a place to move into yet?" Eric asked. Shaking my head, I cocked my head to the side unable to decipher his line of questioning. "What would you think about moving in with me? I have the room, I'm a terrible cook and I write. It would be nice

157

to have you around," he said with excitement in his eyes.

"I...I can't. How would I get to work?" I said, furrowing my brow in confusion.

"I have another car in the garage you can use. You can even bring him with you," he said, thumbing in the direction of Barney.

Barney, curious as ever, came over and climbed awkwardly into our laps. Rubbing his head, I questioned, "How much is rent?"

"Free. You pay me in cooking so I don't starve to death. I'm not hard up for cash, and if you want to have your own place on the coast, you'll need to save up every penny," he advised, smirking at me.

The invitation warmed my chest that he would be willing to take me in. And all the reasons Eric listed were good points, but something in me knew there was more.

"Why? I'm delighted you asked—don't get me wrong—but it's a very big deal to just move into another person's house. I just..." Shaking my head, I couldn't seem to get the right words out.

"Becki, just trust me."

"Eric, trust works both ways. You always demand information from me. I'm only asking," I pleaded with my eyes. Pulling out a crumpled piece of paper from his pocket, he handed it over. As I started to read it my entire face paled. I could actually feel the blood draining from my cheeks.

"This is..."

"Yeah, I found it in between my front door and screen door."

In bold letters it read: I TRIED TO HAVE A GOOD TIME WITH YOUR GIRLFRIEND BUT WAS INTERRUPTED. NOW SHE IS HAVING A GOOD TIME WITH SOMEONE ELSE. GLAD TO SEE YOU ARE STILL GETTING FUCKED OVER EVEN AFTER ALL THESE YEARS.

"I didn't understand this at first when I found it this morning. When it finally hit me, I texted you, but I got no reply; I called you and you didn't answer. I panicked and drove over here to make sure you were safe and saw Tim sliding a key into your door," Eric explained.

Stunned into silence, I accepted his invitation with a nod and went to my bedroom, pulling out my suitcase. Hearing the door open and shut, I stuck my head out to see Eric carrying in some cardboard boxes. Running my hands through my clothes in the closet, I stopped on my favorite dress. Taking it out and holding it against me, I looked at my reflection in the floor length mirror. Some crazy guy is stalking Eric and trying to get to him by attacking me. What if I hadn't called the cops in time? What if I hadn't woken up and he had put his hands on me? My heart started pounding hard and fast as I began to panic with my thoughts.

"That's some dress," Eric commented in amazement, leaning on the door frame. Sighing out a long breath, I folded it up before placing it in a cardboard box that Eric placed on the bed for me.

"Have you ever worn that to an event?" he asked.

159

"I tried, but Gary refused to let me out of the apartment in it." Sighing again, I finished packing the clothes from my closet and drawers.

"Where'd you get the boxes?" I asked out of curiosity and hopelessly tried to get my thoughts on a different path.

"I was never sure how long I would be living somewhere before I had to leave or if something came up. I'd rather be prepared," Eric said softly.

A few hours later, the only things left behind were items that were too big to fit in the car—the couch, TV, dining room table and chairs. On the drive back to Eric's, my cell phone tinkled at me. Checking the ID and seeing that it was Tim, I answered. "Hey, how are you?"

"I'm good, how are you doing?" Tim asked.

"I'm good, where are you? It's pretty loud," I asked, trying to figure out the background noises.

"I'm at a birthday party for my friends' son. Sorry. I just wanted to check up on you before I left and went to work…and to see if you were going to spend the night at my place…" he added coolly.

"Actually, I've been invited to move in with a good friend, and I'm taking up the offer. I need a place I can feel safe in, and even with your fabulous handiwork, I still feel weird out there. I'm sorry."

"Huh, a good friend?" he asked, and I could only imagine what his response was going to be.

"Yeah," I stated, looking out the window.

"So you go from straddling me this morning to moving in with him a few hours later? I'm hurt!" Tim said, rejected and sarcastic.

Immediately, I felt daggers being thrown in my direction from the driver who I'm sure overheard Tim practically yell over the phone. "No, you're not. We're not together, Tim. You are my very good friend who tries to make my life hell with sarcastic remarks," I said, refusing to look to my left.

"I have to keep your life exciting. Well, I'm going to head to work. Text me later?"

"Sounds good," I replied before hanging up. He drove me up the wall, but I must admit he was there when it really counted; he was truly a good friend.

Smiling to myself, I looked up to see Eric glaring at the road and his knuckles white from gripping the steering wheel. "Can I guess that you heard what Tim said over the phone?" I asked in a calm voice.

"Like I said, it's none of my business," he said crisply. I didn't know why, but seeing him angry about something so idiotic made me want to laugh. The next thing I knew I was doubled over in laughter and clutching my ribs to keep it together.

"Wow." And as soon as the word left my lips, more bouts of laughter came pouring out of me. Wiping the tears from my eyes, I laid my head back against the head rest.

Why would Eric react like that if he didn't have any feelings for me more than friendship? Pursing my lips, I tried to think back to the last time I asked Eric if he liked me. He still never said no, but he didn't say yes, either. Moving in with him was a huge step for a 'friend' to take regardless of the stalker issues he and I were having right now.

"When you think of our friendship, what comes to mind?" I asked and forced myself to look out my passenger side window so I didn't see his reaction.

After a few moments of silence, he finally said, "I don't know. I've never really had a friendship like this before. I just like being around you."

"Okay, I have a question, but you really have to give me a full answer. No, I don't know answers, all right?" I asked, trying to corner him into giving any information. Seeing his nod I continued, "Why do you care if I slept with Tim?"

After a moment, he simply replied, "I know you can do better than that." The subject promptly ended as we pulled into his garage.

I opened the back door letting Barney hop out and wheeled out my suitcase. In silence, we followed Eric into the massive house, up the stairs, where he stopped outside the first door on the left.

Pointing at the door he said, "This is my room, so if you need me during the night for anything you can knock." Eric led us to the second door on the right and pushed it open.

Setting down the two boxes he was carrying on the floor, I walked into the second biggest bedroom here. The vaulted ceiling with fan dangling down gave the feel of the room being much bigger. The queen-sized sleigh bed made with cherry wood matched the rest of the décor of the house. The bed set was a beautiful cream and beige design and made the whole bed look even more comfortable. The flat screen TV hung over the dresser and bureau in the same wood color on the opposite side of the bed.

I walked towards the mirrored sliding closet door, but as I pushed it aside, I saw that it was much deeper than I thought it would be.

"There is a light switch on the left for the closet," Eric said from behind me. Switching on the light, I stepped into the closet—this was all my space for clothes. I didn't have enough clothes to even fill half of this closet. The perfect challenge for a female.

'You have your own full bathroom, but it's down the hallway to the left of your room," he stated with no emotion.

In response to the sound of his voice and the slight scowl on his face, I said, "Eric, I don't have to live here. I don't want to make you uncomfortable. I can figure out my living situation somewhere else."

I didn't look him in the eyes for the fear of what I'd see. I could sense from his tone that he thought having me move in must have been a bad idea. He already regretted asking, and I hadn't even spent one night.

"What? Why would you say that?" Eric asked, furrowing his brow. He was way too nice to take back the offer, especially if he believed we were friends. What kind of person would that make me?

"Don't worry about it, okay? I'll just call a cab and go back," I said, grabbing the handle to my suitcase.

Stepping in front of me, he stated, "Please don't go. It's not safe for you there." Lifting his finger under my chin to make me look into his eyes, he said, "Stay with me."

163

I nodded slowly, mesmerized by his soulful eyes and then watched as he cracked a smirk. "I won't survive without your cooking."

He picked up my suitcase, put it on the bed and opened it up. "You start filling up the drawers, and I'll grab the rest of your boxes."

He was an odd man. He obviously wanted me to stay here, but his body language was giving off so many different signals. My hands combed through the suitcase putting the clothes away in the dresser. After emptying out my suitcase, I wheeled it into the closet and slid the door closed. Hearing Barney yawn, I realized that I needed to find the pet bed to put in the corner so he could have a comfortable place to sleep. My fingers made themselves busy rubbing his head and scratching behind his ears while waiting for Eric to bring up the last box that was marked for him.

"You really don't mind Barney being here, do you?" I asked while Barney lay down at my feet.

"No, I like dogs," Eric replied before rubbing Barney's head, too.

Opening the box up for me, Eric started to try to play with Barney. After setting up the pet bed and some squeak toys, I brought his two-sided bowl down to the kitchen and filled it with food and water. Heading back up to my room, I paused at the door— watching Barney lick Eric's laughing face made me grin. At least they got along; I really did think I would end up claiming him as mine. He was quite perfect for me...Barney, of course.

"Hungry?" I asked, and Eric looked up with a smile from ear to ear and nodded. Heading down to the kitchen, I opened the fridge to be welcomed with hardly any food at all. How was I supposed to cook? I opened the cabinets and revealed that they, too, were very sparse.

"Eric!" I yelled and then heard a stampede coming down the stairs. Barney and Eric raced to me only Barney got sidetracked when he saw the full bowl of food.

"What's up?" Eric asked.

"There is no food here. I'm going to have to go grocery shopping. Can we order in tonight, and I can go shopping in the morning?"

"I guess I'll let you slack tonight since this is your first day moving in," he said playfully.

After eating a meat lover's pizza while watching TV, Barney yawned, padding his way to the stairs. Obviously, Barney knew where he was going by now. Pointing my finger at Eric accusingly I teased, "You were supposed to have a map so visitors don't get lost."

Pausing mid-bite, Eric almost choked with laughter. "Be right back," he said, walking out of the room. Sipping my water, I almost spit it across the room when Eric returned, handing me a hand drawn sketch of the rooms in the house.

"Impressed?"

"Very much so. Thanks," I chuckled.

Chapter 16
Saturday, September 15th

The heavy breathing was the first clue that I wasn't alone. The second clue was the shadow hovering near my bedroom door frame. Glancing around the room, I can see that I'm in my new bedroom in Eric's house, but Barney is nowhere to be found.

"You thought that you'd get away, did you?" says the shadow as it slowly starts to creep closer to me. I pull my legs close to my chest and fling my right hand out to the end table to grab my cell phone, but it's not there.

"There is no one around to help you, just you and me," says the sinister voice, closer. As I try to dodge his hand trying to grab my foot, I roll toward the left side of the bed to try to escape out of the door.

The most intense pain came shooting from my head and arm, but I couldn't hear anything. I felt a tongue licking my legs and a tail hitting my feet, but I still couldn't manage to hear any sounds around me. I felt like I was underwater and all the sounds were muffled. Trying to concentrate on my surroundings, the door flashed open and instantly I tried to crawl away under the bed. Seeing hands reaching under the bed, I could finally hear a fuzzy noise of whimpering. As I looked to the side of me, Barney was panting and watching me from outside of the bed.

When I started to crawl out the other side of the bed, I grabbed my cell phone, trying to call the police, when I felt two big hands clasp around my wrists and push me against the wall.

"Hey!" I heard, slightly less muffled, but I refused to look at the intruder. While trying to think of an escape route from his hands, he amazingly let go but only to push me back against the wall with his arm and turned on the lamp on the end table. Temporarily, I was blinded, but then I was relieved to see Eric standing in front of me. Recognition glowing in my eyes. Eric's arm released me only so I could collapse onto his bare chest.

As my breathing calmed, Eric assisted me to lie back in bed. Sitting up beside me, he held my hands in silence. Closing my eyes, I recognized a throbbing on the back of my head. Letting go of one of his hands, I touched the tender spot, wincing slightly.

"Do you remember your dream?" he asked softly.

I nodded slowly but refused to discuss it. "I must have rolled right out of bed."

Confused as to why Eric was here, I asked, "Did I wake you up?"

"I heard a loud thud and came to check it out. I saw you lying on the floor, tried to make sure you were okay, but…" Completely mortified, I looked away at the door. So it was him who had come in. I really was losing my mind.

"Becki, relax. Everybody has nightmares from time to time, and with what you've been through recently, it's to be expected. You are safe here," Eric reassured.

Clearly, he thought I was going to be a nut case for the rest of the stay here. Great. Maybe packing up and leaving in the morning wasn't such a bad idea. I

167

wasn't his responsibility. Eric pulled up my blankets to cover me up, and I rolled over on my side expecting him to leave. Oddly enough, I was pleasantly surprised when I felt him lie down beside me on the bed.

"You don't have to stay," I said over my shoulder.

"I don't mind. Maybe this way you can spend the rest of the night in bed and not on the floor beside it," he said, trying to make me laugh. Sighing, I saw what a fool I must've looked to him. Leaving in the morning sounded better and better.

"Well, if you're going to sleep in here, you might as well get comfortable," I said, pulling the blankets down for him to crawl under.

After a moment, I felt Eric slip under the covers but surprisingly didn't feel him against my back. It wasn't like I was trying to seduce him. He wasn't interested anyway. I scooted over all the way to the edge on the right side of the bed and clutched my pillow between my arms.

"Night," I said over my shoulder as I closed my eyes.

"Night," he replied.

*****

Sunday, September 16th

Waking up from a blissful, dreamless rest of the night, I heard gruff snoring from my left. I looked over my shoulder and saw Eric deep in sleep with his arms up around his head. I couldn't believe I put him through that last night, on my first night here. He heard me hit the floor like a sack of potatoes and came running from his bed to me.

Taking a quick look over my shoulder again, I saw that the covers had slid down a bit exposing his bare chest and abs. I never knew Eric worked out; I mean, he wasn't extremely muscled up and buff, but he was toned and well-defined. I glanced from his glorious chest down to his toned, flat stomach where the mystery continued at his happy trail and the covers started. Did I really just check him out? Wow, and I called Tim a horn dog.

Cautiously sliding out from the covers so I didn't disturb his sleep, I headed into the bathroom and checked out my crazy bed head. Allowing the hot water from the shower to soothe the knots in my neck and back after my tumble the night before, I gently washed my hair before shaving my legs. I pinned up my hair into a messy bun and then wrapped myself in my robe and headed back into my room. Stepping into my closet, I pulled my lime green sundress off the hanger and slipped into it. Then, walking back to the dresser, I opened up my jewelry box and pulled out my costume set of pearl earrings and necklace. I might have felt like crap, but at least I could look good.

The tinkling of my phone made me run to the end table before it woke up Eric.

"Hello?" I whispered.

"Where are you that you have to whisper?" Lily asked, confused. Thinking on my feet, I quickly ran into the closet, turned on the light and slid the door shut behind me.

"I don't want to wake up Eric," I said honestly.

"You slept with him? Are you guys together now?!" Lily exclaimed excitedly.

"I couldn't stay at my apartment anymore. Eric offered me a room in his house. No big deal," I said, shrugging even though I knew she couldn't see the gesture.

"Then why are you whispering? Go to your room," Lily persisted.

"I'm in my room."

Letting that sink in for only a moment, Lily yelled, "You slept with him!" She got excited again.

"Literally, I ended up with nightmares, and he spent the night watching over me. How pathetic, I know."

"Be honest with me, do you want to?" Lily asked directly.

Sidestepping the answer, I admitted the truth. "He isn't interested in me like that. We're just good friends." Even I could hear the slight melancholy in my voice.

"Did you ever figure out what was going on with Tim?" Lily asked, wisely changing the subject.

"No, I forgot, but I will make sure to call him today. Do you think he is in some kind of trouble?"

"I really don't know, but I have to get going. Text me later."

"Sure," I replied, and as I slid open the closet door, Eric was standing in front of me.

I hoped he hadn't heard any of that conversation. I hoped I hadn't woken him up. I smiled up at him trying to hide my discomfort.

"Good morning. Did you sleep well?" I said nonchalantly as I bounced out of the closet as if it were perfectly normal.

"Yeah, did you?" he asked, but I noted the edge in his voice and the minor tensing of his jaw.

Nodding I replied, "I'm sorry if I woke you. Lily was calling to check up on me."

"I woke up on my own," he said but still with that twinge in his jaw.

Awkwardness seeping into the silence, I advised, "I'm going to make a food run. Anything you want particularly?"

"Actually..." he said casually, then I watched as his back retreated to his room. A few minutes later, he returned holding cash. "You'll need this," he said, trying to place it in my unloosening fingers.

"No, I take care of the groceries. That was the deal," I insisted.

"No, the deal was that you would cook meals for us. Don't be ridiculous and take the money," he said sternly.

"See you later then," I said, walking away from him, the bills still in his hand.

I unlocked, unchained and unbolted the front door, but it still wouldn't budge an inch. Hearing the cluck of his tongue against his teeth, I didn't even bother acknowledging him.

171

"Glad to see that my security system works properly," he teased.

I crossed my arms across my chest. "It'd suck if I was trying to escape from a fire. I guess I'll just burn to death," I said sarcastically to the door.

"The alarm system would go off and open the doors right away if that were the case. I paid enough for it." Shrugging my shoulders, I refused to look at him. Feeling Eric's body heat right behind me, he leaned in close and whispered in my ear.

"I'd appreciate it if you would let me pay for the groceries."

If I wasn't mistaken, I could have sworn I felt his lips lightly brush against my earlobe. Nope, my conversation with Lily must have been crossing my mental wires.

"Eric, I have a job. I'm not paying for anything here. The least I can do is—"

"Live here with me. Just having you here is enough," he said, sliding his hands up my back and around my waist. Just as his fingers lightly grazed under my bra, he slid his hand in between my arms and forced me to turn around to face him.

"I've moved you far from your job, your friends and a fun hangout. Let me foot the bill for food," he insisted, leaning in even closer to me before slipping the money into my hands. "Okay?" he asked.

With no further argument coming from me, he scanned his finger on the wall and the door opened slightly.

"Here are the keys to my car. I have a full tank of gas so you can get there and back." Nodding, I took the keys from his hand and set out on my journey.

Almost an hour later, I finally arrived back at Eric's house with a backseat filled with all types of groceries. Meeting me outside, we only made three trips each, but I unpacked all by myself. I thought back to the ordeal he put me through before I left. Next time I refused him, I'd have to be stealthy about it. While I was thinking about it, he was going to have to let me have a finger scan option, too.

Walking back into the kitchen after all the work was done, Eric asked, "What would you like to eat?" I pulled turkey burgers out of the fridge and handed them to him.

With Eric outside using the grill, I whipped out my cell phone and texted Tim to see if he was busy. My phone started tinkling, and I answered right away.

"How are you?"

"I've been better, but that's life right? How are you doing?" Tim asked.

"It's weird for me to not be in my apartment but good, too. I had a nightmare attack last night, and I think Eric now has some gray hair on his head," I said, chuckling into the phone.

"You know, if it doesn't work with you there, you can come and live with me. No tricks—just a place for you to stay," Tim responded.

"I know, and you'll be the first person I call. I promise," I said, trying to mend his hurt feelings. "Tim, is something bothering you? Other than me, of course. I just want to make sure that I'm there for you if you need me."

"I'm just having some girl problems right now, but thanks," Tim stated as a fact.

"All right, well, I'm hungry so I'm going to go eat."

"What are you having?" Tim asked curiously.

"Turkey burger," I replied cheerfully.

"Well, you enjoy that," he said wistfully before hanging up.

In the backyard, Eric was grilling our burgers while Barney was chewing on a squeak toy. I had no idea what my future held, but I hoped it would consist of me finding the man of my dreams to make this scene actually come true for me. Setting down the iced tea on the table for us along with paper plates and condiments, I sat down and crossed my legs.

The nice weather allowed me to relax completely. I should have worked on my tan more this summer but at least I wasn't pale. Watching Eric flip our burgers, I noted that he must have taken a shower and gotten dressed while I was gone. Smirking at remembering his half naked self in my bed, I closed my eyes trying to enjoy the memory. It sucked that I had to be crazy last night, but it was worth him spending the night with me.

Reopening my eyes, I assessed his outfit—cargo shorts, a white short sleeved button-up and sneakers. Why wasn't he a model? I understood his love of writing, and he was really good at it, but he could do so much more with his life. Sliding my hand into a bag of chips, I started to munch while daydreaming of the future.

174

"Don't get too full on those. The burgers are ready," Eric advised, sliding a patty onto my bun and then one onto his.

"Yes, father," I said sarcastically and then ducked as he threw a chip at me.

"Hey!" I complained. Barney, seeing the chip hit the ground, came running over and gobbled it up.

Biting into my burger, my eyes rolled into the back of my head with delight. "Mmmm...this is delicious," I purred. "Thanks for grilling."

"I don't really have people over so I never get to use the grill. It's a beautiful day, and I have a new roommate to celebrate with," he said, smiling at me.

"I know you like the quiet for your writing, but do you get lonely out here?" I asked.

Nodding, he said simply, "When it gets to be too much, I go out to lunch or Girl's Night Out."

"This is going to sound odd, but I'm curious since I basically tell you all about my life and issues. Do you have a girlfriend?" I asked and kept my face serene as though the answer didn't matter.

And it shouldn't matter. We were just friends anyway, and he was helping me out of a mess. Actually, I would have been fine if it wasn't for him; it was his stalker taking it out on me. Having all these thoughts collide in my head, I almost forgot that I was actually waiting for him to answer me. I didn't want to make him uncomfortable so I sipped my iced tea and munched on my chips, paying close attention to my plate.

"Why? Would that bother you?" Eric asked, cocking his head to the side.

"No, I just wanted to know if there were some nights I needed to stay at a Lily's place. I wouldn't want to be in the way," I offered as I took another bite of my burger. Still not getting an answer from him, I glanced up to see him watching me carefully. What was he looking at?

Furrowing my brow I asked, "What?"

"Nothing," he replied, picking up a chip.

"You never answered the question," I pushed again not looking at his face.

"Does it look like I have a girlfriend?" he asked.

"That's not an answer, either," I replied with a wry smile on my face.

Shrugging his shoulders he said, "I don't have anyone permanent at the moment."

His response instantly made me think that he was just having nightcaps from time to time. Who would have thought that Eric was pulling a Lily? I couldn't just give my body away to someone who wouldn't cherish me. Oddly enough, that night Tim and I were messing around in his backseat years ago, we only mauled each other. I hadn't trusted him enough to care for me like I needed at the time and look at us now.

Tim was the only one left from when I first moved here. If he was really willing to commit whole-heartedly to me at this point, I thought I would be open-minded enough to give him a shot, but it sounded like he had someone. Ugh! What was I doing? I couldn't just pick up guys left and right when I felt like it.

"Becki?" Eric asked, waving his hand in front of my face.

"Yeah? Sorry, I spaced out."

"What were you thinking about? You seemed deep in thought and well...I'm intrigued," he said, smirking at me.

"Just thinking about my future, what I plan on doing with my life. I have to figure out where I am going to live," I said.

An instant scowl crossed his face. "You live here," he advised seriously.

"I know, but this is temporary. You are going to eventually get married and have kids one day, and I don't plan on still living here when that happens. I have to find my own place, my place in the world," I explained.

"Becki, you can live here for as long as you want. There is no eviction date. I want you here," Eric said, seriously concerned.

"I'm not saying that. I'm just saying that maybe one day I'll be able to stand up on my own two feet again. The future has endless possibilities for both of us."

After clearing up the plates outside, I started to wash our cups out in the sink. "I'm going to take Barney for a walk. Be back in a bit," Eric called out before leaving through the front door.

I had the house to myself, what should I do? I could do a naked lap around the kitchen and the thought made me chuckle. Feeling adventurous, I headed into the living room to scour the shelves of DVDs. The room had tan walls with a white border and white carpet. There was one long white couch with two overstuffed chairs kitty corner facing it with a big screen TV lined up to face the couch. The wall next to the TV was lined with shelving full of DVDs where I easily found two movies that I absolutely loved to watch.

Unable to make a final decision, I put both back down and sat on the couch to think it through. I didn't want to stick to romantic comedies because that was just awkward, but I couldn't possibly sit through a scary movie. The last thing I needed was a repeat of last night. Hearing the happy yelp of Barney coming into the house, I smiled, as a funny question ran through my mind.

"Eric!" I shouted out and watched as he poked his head in. "How would you feel if you came home and I was running around in my underpants in your kitchen?" I asked with a huge grin on my face.

Surprised at the question, he replied, "Stand in shock and enjoy the show," he said, finally smirking at me.

"Such a guy response," I said, chuckling.

"This is your home, too. So if you feel like being a nudist, go for it," he said, raising a pale eyebrow at me.

"You wish," I said as I climbed the stairs back up to my room.

I put my ear buds in and put my favorite playlist on shuffle. While I was picking out my clothes for the next day, a really good song came on, and I started to rock my hips from side-to-side unable to resist the beat. I set out my tan slacks and white and grey blouse and white sandals. A Latin favorite started to play in my ears and I couldn't resist. As I salsa danced around in my closet, I was suddenly shocked to look up and see Eric gaping at me.

"Hey! Aren't you supposed to knock?" I complained, putting my hands on my hips.

"I did, but got no answer. I didn't see you anywhere and well..."

The intense heat in my cheeks made it obvious that I was blushing furiously at the idea of him watching me dance. "We are going to have to set up some rules about barging into others' rooms. I'll get one of those 'do not disturb' door knob hangers."

"You seem to enjoy your closet; I keep finding you in here," he replied with a grin. My hands pushed him backwards out of my room and into the hallway.

"I'm having Becki time. You go have Eric time," I said playfully, slowly closing the door on him.

"I want to have Becki time, too!" he shouted through the door at me.

Locking the door behind me, no matter how embarrassing that spectacle was, there was no denying that a thrill didn't go through my system.

Chapter 17
Monday, September 17th

Jolting awake from the blare of my alarm, I hit it off. That was the best sleep of my life—no dreams or nightmares, just peaceful blackness. Looking down, my sundress greeted my eyes. I must have needed the sleep. After a fifteen minute shower and a thirty minute hair session, I was dressed and ready for work. Quietly descending the stairs, I headed into the kitchen and started the coffee maker perking.

Mondays were much easier to handle with my favorite liquid breakfast. I was sure Eric would want some breakfast. Pulling out some frozen waffles, I put them in the toaster and chuckled. This probably wasn't what he had in mind for me cooking, but I didn't even think he was awake yet.

Sipping my coffee and putting my laptop bag down at the front door, I remembered that I couldn't get out. Creeping back up the stairs, I knocked lightly on the door and called in to him.

"Eric?" Not hearing any response, I tried knocking a bit harder with the same result. Turning the door knob, I poked my head in and saw that he was cuddled up in his king-sized bed with Barney at the foot of it.

Smirking, I walked over to his side of the bed and lightly rubbed my hand across his shoulder. "Eric, I need you to let me out."

Waking, squinting one eye open at me, he replied, "Let you out?"

I nodded at him to get him to understand. "I have to go to work. You have to let me out of the front door," I whispered again to rouse him gently.

Crawling out of bed in just his grey pajama pants, I led him down the stairs to the door. After scanning his fingerprint, he looked down at me with a small smile.

"I'll have this fixed for you to use by the time you get home. Are you taking Barney with you?" he asked, raising an eyebrow.

"He can stay here for the day unless he'll bother you."

"I'll keep him; he is a very chill dog. Maybe he'll inspire some 'magic' for me to write on," Eric said, picking up my laptop bag and keys to his car, he handed them over to me with a lopsided smile.

"Have a good day at work," he said before he leaned in and kissed my cheek. Trying not to show my surprise or pleasure too much on my face, I smiled sheepishly back at him.

"I will now. By the way, breakfast is in the toaster with already sipped on coffee." With every step in the direction of his vehicle, my smile widened. He had kissed me!

I walked up to unlock my office and noticed a note taped to my door with my name on it. "Lunch meeting today to go over the files before court tomorrow afternoon. –Ty."

Kicking my door shut behind me, I pulled open my file cabinet and retrieved the file holding the witness testimony and photos. I brought the file to my desk and double checked all the information to make sure I wasn't missing any evidence, but everything seemed to be in its place.

Opening up my email, I checked to see if there were any new messages, but there were just newsletters. While sitting down at my computer, I realized that there was one important situation that I needed to handle before it was too late. Whipping out a new adoption form, I began to fill it out. Just as I started to finish up the paperwork, my boss, Judy, walked into my office.

"Just wanted to make sure you have everything ready for the lunch meeting." Holding out the file to her, I watched her thumb through the papers. Her perfectly shaped nails were cut short like her blonde hair. Her short stature changed depending on the shoes she chose; today was a pair of black flats that went with her grey slacks and black blouse. "This is great, thank you," she said, smiling her brown eyes at me.

"What are you filling out?" she asked, tilting her head to the side in an all too familiar gesture.

"I'm interested in adopting Barney. Just finished filling out the paperwork," I said and watched her hand flash out to grab the paper.

"Hmmm…" Nodding her head, she pulled out a pen from my collection on the desk and signed it. "It's official, he's yours."

Blinking back tears of happiness my lips mumbled, "Thank you." With a gentle smile, she patted the top of my hand and left my office.

As I started to walk out of the lunch meeting with Lily feeling accomplished and encouraged that we were going to get the outcome we were looking for, I was stopped by a hand on my shoulder.

"You both have been working so hard on this case and others. Take off the rest of today. Just don't come to court hung over tomorrow," Judy warned, smirking at us.

"Thanks!" we both exclaimed at the same time and then chuckled.

"Want to go shopping?" Lily asked conspiratorially.

"Actually, I want to go to the beach and get my tan in while I can. It's cooled off a bit, but without the breeze it might be our last chance."

Dropping Lily off at Will's apartment, I headed back to Eric's house knowing that I couldn't take too long. I couldn't seem to think of his home as mine yet...maybe with time.

*****

Walking up to the front door, I found Eric waiting for me. "I heard the car pull up so I was curious. Are you playing hooky?"

"My boss let Lily and me out early for good behavior. So we're going to meet up at the beach and work on our tans. How's your day?"

Closing the door behind me, he replied, "Slow. Even Barney walked away from me to take a nap."

"You are kind of boring, you know," I teased before hustling up the stairs.

Just as I placed my hand on the door knob, I was crushed into the door. Trying to wriggle away, he pushed his chest tight to my back. Quickly, his hand grabbed my wrist from the knob and pulled it over my head to make it easier to turn me to face him.

"You're fast...but not fast enough," he said, leaning so closely I could have sworn his lips touched mine until I felt the distinct touch of his fingers on my waist and then slowly creep up until he got to my ribs where he started to intensely tickle me.

With a gasp, I used my other hand and twisted the knob to run away. What I didn't expect was us crashing on to my floor, but that is what happened, Eric lying completely flush on top of me.

"Not exactly how I planned that to work," I commented, trying to control my breathlessness.

"You started it," he accused with a grin as he got up and then helped me up before sitting down on my bed.

Raising my hands, I feigned innocence. "Who? Me?"

Hearing Eric's mirth made me laugh myself. I pulled open my bureau drawer and took out my navy and white polka dot bikini. Hitting the light, I walked into my closet and pulled the door closed behind me and started to change. "Did you want to come with us to the beach? Barney can come, too."

"Um...I don't know about that."

"You said things were slow. Come see the natural beauty at the beach and be inspired," I said through the still-closed closet door, wrapping my navy sarong around my waist and pulling on my white tank top.

As I started to open the door Eric said, "I know, but..."

Seeing the stunned expression on his face, I asked, "But what? Afraid of the sand?" Teasing him was so much fun.

"Maybe I should go after all..." he admitted without further complaint and headed to his room, but I noticed him subtly adjusting his pants.

Well, what do you know? He thought I looked good in this outfit. I slid into my white flip flops before grabbing Barney's leash and heading downstairs to get him ready. I opened the freezer and pulled out some hamburger patties and set them in the sink in water to defrost until we got back.

Putting four water bottles in a cooler with a baggy of ice cubes and some doggy treats, I stood up to see Eric in cargo shorts and a white tank top that emphasized the muscles in his arms. Trying not to gawk, I handed him the cooler which he put on his shoulder.

"I'm glad you're coming," I said, winking at Eric. I wanted to gauge his reaction to my flirtation, but his eyes just tightened a smidge.

"I'm just glad to be invited."

*****

Unbuckling my seatbelt, I opened the back door to let Barney out.

"The party has arrived!" I heard Lily exclaim.

Eric pulled out the cooler from the trunk and followed us while we found our way to our favorite spot on the beach. After setting up the umbrella and

185

lying out the towels under the sun, I pulled out Barney's bowl and filled it with water and a few ice cubes. Eric pulled up a beach chair and reclined under the umbrella with his laptop.

"I need a tan so badly. Thanks for the plan," Lily stated.

Smirking at her, I said, "I'm pale most of the time anyway. It's a struggle." I pulled off my sarong and took off my tank top before I lay back on my towel.

"Don't forget your glasses," Lily said, handing over the sunglasses for me.

I untied my bikini halter top strings so I didn't end up with tan lines. Placing my hands under my head, I closed my eyes to enjoy my rays. Hearing someone choke, I looked over and saw Eric trying to cover up his cough.

"You okay?"

"Yeah," he said, clearing his throat and then looked back at his laptop screen.

Checking on Barney, I could see that he was napping under the umbrella comfortably. My mind started to wonder if Eric was watching me. Glimpsing his face behind my sunglasses, I could see his eyes on his screen but then I saw his eyes furtively glance in my direction. Wow, he really was keeping an eye on me, literally. The thought warmed me up more than the sunshine did.

"Turn over," Lily ordered as she rolled. Turning over slowly onto my front, I stretched out but made sure my girls didn't give anyone a show.

"Are you feeling inspired?" I asked Eric, catching him looking at my lower half. Eric, aware that he was caught in the act, glared at me. Laying my head down on my arms, I hid a grin and closed my eyes again to enjoy the last bit of warmth before fall settled in.

I was startled to feel paws stepping on me.

"Barney!" I said as he climbed over to the side of me and started to lick my face. "Is it playtime?" I asked and watched as his tail began to wag wildly. As I slowly sat up, I tried to tie my bikini top but had a hard time trying to quickly knot it.

"Hey, do you mind helping me?" I asked in Lily's direction but then felt the unmistakable feel of masculine fingers on my back.

"I've got it," Eric said, letting his heated breath escape onto my neck.

"Thanks. Are you going to play with us?" I asked, trying to remain nonchalant, especially in front of Lily.

"Play?" he asked, and I noted his tone was darkening with a whisper.

Was he trying to seduce me? He's the one who said he didn't even like me...well, he never actually *said* it, but he implied it. As he finished the knot at my neck, he let his fingers slowly trail down my back gently. I stood up in front of him, letting my body glide before his eyes while he knelt behind me. I grabbed Barney's leash and headed to the water.

Sticking a toe into the water, I decided to change my mind about going in.

"Barney, it is so cold. I don't think we're going to do that today." Not like Barney could understand me anyway. I threw his tennis ball toward the sandy beach and he went running for it. When he brought it back, I tried to grab it from him but he dodged me.

"Barney!" I said excitedly, and he started sprinting away in the direction I threw the ball.

"Barney!" I yelled out again and he turned to look at me. I ran away and he came barreling back in my direction. When I stopped to try to take the ball from his mouth again, I realized too late that he was running way too fast and he ran right into me, knocking us both over. My Saint Bernard believed he was not only a lap dog but small enough to run through my legs.

"Ow!" I complained but chuckled at him, unable to stop myself. Barney, looking a bit surprised, tilted his head at me and then picked up his dropped tennis ball and ran back to the umbrella where he licked up some cool water and promptly plopped down, tongue lolling out. So much for playing—he took the toy, knocked me down and quit. Picking myself up from the sand, I used my hand to brush the sand off of my legs, arms and butt.

"Finished already?" Eric asked with a raised eyebrow as I came strolling back.

"Apparently," I said, shrugging my shoulders and lying back down on my towel.

Hearing a buzz of a cell phone, I looked up to see Lily looking at her phone. "Oh, great."

"What's up?" I asked, confused at her attitude.

"Will's family is having a dinner tonight, and he just invited me. He's known about it for weeks, and he decided now to tell me to go with him. What am I going to wear?" she lamented and then copped a salty attitude. "I should tell him I can't make it just out of spite."

"Lily, you are in a relationship now. Monogamy. Remember? You have to go. Be the good girlfriend that you're expected to be," I stated.

"Becki, I'm not you. I don't fit in the mold of this stuff," she said, looking a bit down in the mouth.

"You can do anything you set your mind to. Will is already in your head; let him in your heart fully. No safety nets, okay?" I said, trying to coax her from bailing on her future. With a nod of her head, she started to text him back.

*****

Back at Eric's house, I filled up Barney's dish with food and water before washing my hands. Taking the hamburger out of the sink, I placed a frying pan on the stove and turned it on level six to heat up. I opened the cabinet and pulled out the taco seasoning and set it down on the counter. Hunting up some plates and taco shells as well as a box of Spanish rice, I started to boil some water.

"What's for dinner?" Eric asked as he walked into the kitchen.

"I'm making tacos and rice. Is that okay?" I questioned, almost regretting not asking before I started.

"I haven't had tacos in months! I made a good decision moving you in here." Rolling my eyes, I continued to work on browning the meat before dumping the packet of seasoning on it.

189

"Are you interested in learning? I could teach you," I offered, feeling him start to hover near the stove area.

"Maybe one day but not tonight. I'll set the table."

The tinkling of my phone showed my mother calling. Reluctantly, I answered it. "Hello, Mother. How are you?"

"You were supposed to call me back weeks ago, and whenever I call you it goes right to voicemail. Do you not love me anymore?" she complained, quite upset. I really should have let it go to voicemail again.

"Of course I love you. I've just been very busy with work. I have a court case coming up, and I need to be prepared."

"You'd have more time if you moved back home. We can spend more time together. I miss you," she said, going from angered frustration to a whine within minutes.

"Ow!" I called out as some grease from the pan popped at me.

"What happened? Were you shot?" she asked, horrified.

"No, why would you even say that? I'm cooking dinner and the grease burned me."

"You live in a dirty, dangerous city, Rebecca. Why would I not assume the worst? This is your decision, remember?" It was the usual guilt trip scenario.

"I'm going to finish up cooking and then eat dinner. I'll talk to you sometime soon."

"Is that your way of saying that you will not be calling me tomorrow?"

"I have court tomorrow. Mother, please settle down. You should be spending more time with Dad and less time thinking about me. I love you. Good night."

'You're my little girl. I'll always worry about you. As always, I love you more. Good night," she said before hanging up.

Well, at least I can now stop feeling guilty; I spoke with her, so my quota was filled for at least a few days. Maybe I will call home tomorrow just to surprise her and show her that I really do miss them.

After consuming orgasmic tacos and rice, I leaned back in my chair unable to breathe let alone speak. Glancing up at Eric, I saw the same expression on his face. I shouldn't have had that third taco. I was already full with the second, but that guacamole and sour cream with shredded cheese and ketchup was my undoing.

"How much do I have to pay you to do that every night?" Eric asked.

"My cooking here is my rent, remember?"

"Yeah, but...I didn't know you could cook like that," he replied, shaking his head in amazement. I picked up our plates and started to prepare the dishwasher while Eric covered up the leftovers.

"Movie tonight?" I asked, hoping for some activity to wind me down before bed.

"Sure, do you want to choose?" he asked, but I declined. I checked on Barney and rubbed his head

191

before going up to my room and taking a quick shower to get the sand off my body.

Coming back down to the living room in my lavender silk tank top and pajama pants, I sat on the couch and waited for Eric to come down, too. I wondered what he picked for us to watch. Hearing his steps down the stairs, I pulled my legs up onto the couch and waited. Eric waltzed right in with no shirt but a pair of grey pajama pants on with a big blanket over his arm.

"What did you decide?" I asked, looking down at my fingernails trying not to gape at the attractive man in front of me.

"About what?" he asked.

"Movie," I said, refusing to look up at him again.

"It's a surprise." With that, he put the DVD into the player, turned out the lights and sat down next to me.

"Oh, I almost forgot," I said, going into the kitchen and opening up the bottom cabinet. I returned to the living room carrying a few items of junk food.

"What do you like?" I asked with my arms full. Eric smirked and picked out a cherry lollipop.

"Thanks," he said as he unwrapped it and popped it into his mouth. I opened my bag of Twizzlers and started chewing on one. I was so full right now, but I felt like if I didn't put something in my mouth, I was going to say something terribly stupid.

As the movie began, I recognized the music and my smile widened from ear to ear.

"Have you seen this one?" he asked.

"Totally! It's one of my favorite movies," I said, leaning back into the couch getting comfortable. I felt fingers tugging on my toes, and I yelped involuntarily.

"Hey!" I complained, but he smiled in return.

"I'm just trying to get you to stretch out," he said, feigning innocence before continuing to stretch my legs out over his lap.

"Are you comfortable this way?" I asked, feeling a little awkward. He nodded in my direction before pulling out the blanket and laying it over us.

By the time the main characters fell in love with each other, Eric was scooted right up against me, practically with me on his lap. Feeling a bit brave, I leaned my head over onto his shoulder while enjoying his company.

"Here," he suggested and fully pulled me onto his lap wrapping his arm around my waist.

"Can you see?" I asked to be polite but secretly enjoyed every second of being this close to him.

"Don't worry so much," he admonished, kissing my cheek and encouraging me to settle my head back on his shoulder.

I tried to concentrate on the movie, but his hand on my waist was starting to key me up in a totally different direction than I planned for the night. When the main characters went to bed together, I felt my whole body tense up as my breath ceased. For some reason, sex scenes always made me uncomfortable with other people around. I knew we were both adults, but it was such a personal and intimate situation that I always got nervous even in movie theatres.

"You okay?" Eric asked, not looking at me. No, I wasn't okay.

"I'm good."

I instantly felt his hand on my waist start to rub up and down my back lazily. Becki, get a grip...he wasn't interested in you like that. He was just a very nice guy who flirted every once in a while. Looking back at the screen, I almost blanched at the love making that was going on before my eyes.

Taking a deep breath slowly so he didn't notice, I closed my eyes but it didn't stop the noises from the movie creating vivid thoughts of me and Eric together. I open my eyes, and I couldn't stop myself from staring at his lips, thin and soft looking. I bet they tasted like cherries from the lollipop he was sucking. Instantaneously, I tugged the pop from his mouth, and the shock of my action made him open up. I stuffed it into my mouth and chuckled gleefully at his reaction.

"What are you doing?" he asked.

"I wanted a taste."

Savoring the sweet taste of the lollipop still warm from his tongue, I swirled mine around it one last time before bringing it back to his lips. As fun as the idea was, I quickly thought about how he might have felt by that action. We'd never shared any type of food or drink—what if he is a germ-o-phobe? He might not want it back...the idea wasn't welcome.

Not opening his mouth, he gave me an incredulous look. "Sorry, I was just thinking about cherries and that I wanted to taste one. So I grabbed yours," I said, feeling the blush rise in my cheeks.

Raising his blond eyebrow at me, he leaned in closer and nabbed the pop in between his teeth and started sucking onto it hard. Trying to smile at him, I realized that his burning eyes wouldn't leave mine, and my smile was cut off into an involuntary gasp.

"If you wanted a taste, you only had to say so," Eric said before pulling out the pop and then leaning in and gently brushing his lips against mine. Frozen in fear that I was daydreaming again, my body refused to respond. Only when his lips parted mine and I could taste the cherry on them did my mind catch up to what was happening. Wrapping my arms around his neck, I started to kiss him back fervently.

His hand that was lazily rubbing my back before was now clutching me tight to his body as he playfully let our tongues touch, rub and massage each other. I was so going to hate myself tomorrow when I woke up all hot and flustered and this was only a dream. I might as well enjoy this for what it was. Straddling his lap and pulling his mouth even tighter against mine, my guard fell away all too easily.

Just as my breathing started to become a bit more difficult, he slid his hand under my tank top but continued to rub my back while keeping me flush against him. As I ran my fingers through his hair pulling out the ponytail, I could hear and feel him groaning into my mouth. With our chests so close, I could feel our matching heartbeats drumming rapidly like they were having their own conversation. My eyes rolling into the back of my head, I tried to suck on his tongue enjoying the cherry flavor as much as his natural flavor. He tasted absolutely delicious.

Just as our making out became more sensual, I felt Eric's lips pulling back from mine. It felt like there was a fire burning on me, but I knew it was actually within my veins. I leaned in one last time and kissed his lips gently and then settled back across his lap to finish watching the movie. I had no idea what he was thinking, but I was very excited that I could at least say we'd kissed. Lily would describe our kiss as fireworks but that just wasn't enough. It was like an atomic bomb. His radiation was still infusing every fiber of my being.

I tried to focus on the movie, but my thoughts were elsewhere. Did I just fabricate the whole thing? I wasn't that creative, and just as the thought passed through my head, I felt Eric's fingers lightly rubbing up and down my bare back. Sighing, I laid my head back down to his shoulder and tried to calm my pulse. I couldn't believe what just happened...that I let it happen. As the screen turned black and the credits rolled, I realized that I blacked out during the last of the movie.

With the movie ended, I stood up off of his lap letting his hand slide out from under my shirt. Looking over to the corner of the room, I saw Barney lightly snoring.

"I think he has the right idea," I said, chuckling lightly to ease the tension between us but also to give him an easy out. Looking up at the clock, it read nine o'clock. Picking up wrappers, I headed to the kitchen to throw them away.

Coming back into the living room, I observed Eric folding the blanket up with the lollipop stick poking out from between his lips. Unsure of what to say, I just stuck to pleasantries.

"Thanks for picking out such a great movie."

"You're welcome, are you tired?" he asked while pushing his hair back behind his ears. The way his hair just hung so perfectly was amazing. If only he would wear it down more often.

"I have court tomorrow; I need to wind down for the night," I responded. I didn't want there to be weird tension between us. It was obvious that would happen if I just left. I walked straight up to him and wrapped my arms around his waist, hugging him close.

"Sweet dreams," I said, before heading up to my room.

Chapter 18
Tuesday, September 18th

Pulling on my grey pin striped jacket, I stood with the rest of the courtroom while the judge went back into his chambers. Leaning down to smooth out my matching pencil skirt, I took a deep breath that ended with a smile. The judge sided with our case and we could worry less about this person harming anymore animals. I collected all the materials I brought with me and placed them in our box to bring back to the office.

"I've got this. You head back to the office and make sure things are okay," Judy stated with the nod of her head.

It was a short drive back to the office, but as soon as I was through the door, I got a distinct feeling of unease. Going into my office, I put down my jacket before heading into the kennel room.

"Ty?" I asked, getting closer to the bathing room.

"Oh, thank goodness, Becki. Grab some empty crates, please!" he called out to me. Running to the back room, my hands grabbed as many crates as they could hold and I made my way back into the bathing room, spotting Tyler with four dogs running amok in the room.

Getting them all separated in different crates, I finally sat down at my desk. I was pulled out of my stunned silence by the ringing of the phone.

"Hello?"

"Hey, sunshine. How are you?" Gary asked.

"Having an odd day, actually. How are you?" I replied feeling slightly hesitant. It feels like it had been weeks since I last spoke with him.

"Things are finally slowing down enough that I can remember my name," he joked.

"I'll have to mail you a nametag so you don't have to say it then," I chuckled back lightly.

"Maybe. So I have a question," Gary started. "Feel free to say no, but I'd really like to see you. Would you be interested in coming for a weekend? I can pay for your ticket and everything."

"I'll consider it. I'll have to find a sitter before I can make a certain date," I said trying to keep the option open. We weren't even together and he was still trying to get me out there.

"Sitter?" Gary asked.

"Oh, yeah, I adopted Barney," I admitted.

The silence on the other end of the phone led me to believe that Gary still didn't like the idea of pets even in his new location.

"Well, that's interesting," he finally replied. I noticed Tyler poking his head in the door, and I beckoned him to come in.

"Yeah, he's good company. I have to get back to work, but I'll get in touch with you soon," I replied before hanging up. The edginess I felt reappeared just like the last time we spoke. Will this ever not be so strained and awkward?

"So what happened?" I asked Tyler.

Shifting in his seat so his elbows were resting on his knees, he huffed a bit. "I was washing up the poodle, Frenchie, when I heard a noise in the kennel room. I peeked out but didn't see anything or anyone, so I went back to finish the rinse. The next thing I know, three other dogs are running into the bathing room yelping and jumping," he said, exasperatedly.

When I came into the kennel room I hadn't noticed any empty cages or even any open ones. "I didn't see anything wrong in there either," I agreed. "I just had an odd feeling."

"I was lucky that you came in when you did because those three set off Frenchie into a scared frenzy where she peed all down her legs. Needless to say, I had to wash her again."

After a few minutes of quiet, Tyler looked up into my eyes and said, "Here is the million dollar question...where did the other dogs come from? They aren't logged in with us. They look like a bunch of strays, but no one even brought them in," Tyler explained. "I'm going to let Judy know when she gets in," he said, just before slipping out the door.

When the clock struck five, my heels were already swiftly clacking out of the door. It was such an odd day—from being in court to coming back to such a mess. Where had those dogs come from? I figured it was probably someone who didn't want to take the time to go through the animal surrender process.

The closer I stepped toward my car, the more I felt like I was being watched. Turning around, I was suddenly face-to-face with that older gentleman who had asked me the time roughly a week and a half ago. At least I knew I wasn't paranoid.

"Can I help you?" I asked to be polite.

"I was hoping you could. Would you mind delivering this to a mutual friend of ours? I have been quite busy and unable to give it to Eric myself," he responded with a smile while handing me a manila envelope.

"Oh. Um...are you sure you don't want to try to reach him again? What's in it?" I asked, hesitating to take it.

"I would appreciate it if you could. I've been so busy, and I have another appointment I need to get to. It's just some paperwork he requested. Thanks," he said, smirking at me while his tongue flicked in and out of the hole where his left front tooth should've been.

Grumbling to myself, I accepted the envelope and got into the car. I didn't realize I had USPS written on my vehicle or stamped on my butt. My mind wondered what kind of mood Eric would be in when I arrived home; I was able to dodge him this morning completely. Opening the door it was obvious that Eric was watching TV in the living room.

"Hey!" I called out and then heard the sprinting of paws coming my way.

"Hey!" Eric replied but made no move to come over to me.

"What do you want to eat for dinner?" I called out while filling up Barney's food and water bowls.

"Anything will do. I'm not picky," he replied, still not making a move toward the kitchen area.

"I've got some mail for you," I said, placing the envelope down on the kitchen island.

I turned on the faucet, washing my hands before drying them on a dish towel. Feeling the vibration from his feet slink into the kitchen, he picked up the envelope.

"Who's it from?" he asked.

"He said he was a friend of yours. You requested some information?" I said, walking to the stairs.

"Huh," he grunted.

I pulled my jacket off as I got to the top step and then heard "Becki!" being shouted from downstairs. Rushing back down quickly to Eric, I saw his ice cold glare and his jaw wound extremely tight.

"What's wrong?" I asked, confused.

"Did you know about this? Have you read this?" he asked, seething.

"Why would I open your mail?" I asked back, getting pretty annoyed at his insinuation. "What is it?"

Eric turned toward the kitchen island and laid out the papers side by side. Peering over to glimpse the papers, my stomach started to roll with queasiness. They were black and white photographs of Eric when he was a pre-teen, covered in dirt and grime and chained loosely to a wall. There were so many photos of him—some of him crying, some of him eating with his hands, and some of him sleeping. I looked finally to a typed up piece of paper that read:

I haven't seen you in a long time. I miss our long nights together, but hopefully we can rekindle that soon.

202

It was a nice try to get your girlfriend to move in with you, but as you can see, I can still get my hands on her either way. And I plan to do much more than that.

Speechless, Eric's gut wrenching expression was at war with his fury. Stepping in front of him to block his view of the photos, I forced his full attention on me. "Eric, you need to call the police," I said, but he shook his head. He pulled out his cell phone and called one of his contacts.

"Becki, who gave this to you?"

"I don't know him but he knew you. I thought he was a friend of yours." I tried to explain.

"I've got evidence of harassment and proof he is stalking my girlfriend," Eric stated emotionlessly into the phone. Girlfriend? I wouldn't hold him responsible for anything he said right now. The look in his eyes showed me all I needed to know about where his head was.

"I'm going to be here. Swinging by in an hour should be fine," he replied before closing the phone.

I quickly went to the fridge and pulled out a bottle of wine and poured two glasses. Handing one to Eric, I calmly advised, "This isn't going to change anything. We'll just be very careful."

Nodding, he downed his drink but then squinted his eyes as he looked at me, "What did he look like?"

"He's shorter than you, thin with dark brown hair and eyes. He is missing his left front tooth," I replied, but out of all the descriptions the tooth seemed to make him shiver involuntarily.

"What?"

203

"He lost that tooth because of me. I kicked him in the face when he least expected it before I escaped."

*****

I was sitting on my bed about a half hour later when the sound of the doorbell piqued my curiosity. I had wanted to stay by Eric's side to comfort him, but he shut himself up in his office claiming to need to finish up writing before company came. I felt slightly hurt by his actions, but I could only imagine what he was going through. If writing would help him deal with this, then I'd let him escape.

I was almost positive that the person at the door was the mystery contact on Eric's phone. Out of respect and privacy, I knew I should just sit here on my bed and let him explain everything to whoever it was down there. This was his business and none of mine...well, not completely none of mine. Trying to stare at the TV screen, nothing was actually registering in my brain. Oh, hell. I could take a trip for ice cream and maybe overhear something from the kitchen.

While sneaking down the stairs like a bandit, my feet made it all the way down to the kitchen without a sound but I could barely hear a word being spoken. Eric must have him in his office. Sticking one hand in the freezer and pulling out an individually-sized moose tracks ice cream, I dug in when my phone tinkled in my pocket.

"Hey, Gary. What's up?" I asked, licking my spoon and hopping up on a stool by the island.

"I just had an urge to call you when I knew you wouldn't be at work. I was thinking about you all day,

204

actually," he confessed. My chest warmed with the thought that he still cared.

"Awww, well, I've been thinking about you, too. Do you feel settled in your new place?" I asked cheerfully.

"Yeah, but it's lonely here," he said softly, and right away I felt like I was being set up into making a decision to come see him sooner than he offered before.

Hearing voices get louder as Eric's office door creaked open a bit, I tensed up hoping that he didn't think that I was trying to barge in on his company.

"Have you decorated the place yet?" I asked Gary, trying to sidetrack him from making me feel guilty. I took a scoop of ice cream and stuffed it into my mouth.

Feeling the vibration of footsteps coming closer, I closed my eyes and tried to pay attention to Gary's voice.

"I tried to, but it's not feeling like a home. Just another place to store my stuff. I think it needs a woman's touch."

"Oh, well, that's too bad. You should take some pictures with your phone and text me them so I can give you advice on it," I offered, trying to be polite but keep some distance.

From behind me, Eric's voice spoke lowly, "She's on the phone. We can wait in here until she's finished."

Slowly shivering, I heard Gary plead, "Becki, what can I do to get you to come see me this weekend? I'll pay for your flight, and you obviously can stay here with me. You can give me advice in person that way."

"Gary, I don't think it's a good idea for me right now. It's not that I don't want to see you; it's just that I'm having a tough time at work and..." I couldn't finish my sentence. I was no good at lying. Why was he making this so difficult?

"Do you...Are you afraid of being alone with me?" Gary asked gently.

"Of course not, but like I said, I'm just busy right now. When things settle down around here, I'll take a trip out to see you. Okay?" I asked, trying to placate him.

"Okay, sunshine. You're still my favorite girl," he said, and I almost cringed into the phone. I wouldn't be if he knew where I was residing.

"You too, Gary. I have to go, but I'll keep in touch. Night."

"Good night," he whispered.

Pressing the end button, I chucked my cell phone to the other end of the island. Did my mouth really agree to someday flying to Arizona? When a relationship ends there is supposed to be time in order to find a way back to friendship. I think I needed more time.

"Gary called?" Eric asked from right behind me.

"Yeah," I said, not elaborating on the subject.

"Do you have a few minutes? I have someone here that would like to speak with you," he advised to my back. Well, if I was going to have to talk to some stranger tonight, my ice cream was coming along for the ride.

Picking up my little cup and spoon, I chucked another spoonful into my mouth. As I walked into the living room, an older gentleman in his late forties, dressed in a brown suit, with wavy blond hair, dark brown eyes and a pot belly awaited.

Eric introduced me. "Becki, this is Ben Johnson. Ben, this is Becki Austin. Ben is a police detective." I politely shook his hand and then sat on the kitty cornered chair facing the couch.

"Ms. Austin, I just wanted to ask you a few questions if you don't mind," Detective Johnson asked respectfully, but I could see his eyes assessing my body language.

"Becki, please. Ask away," I said before slipping in another spoonful. Maybe if I kept my mouth full of ice cream he wouldn't prod as much. Maybe if I had a pint instead of this tiny little cup it would work.

"Becki, the man who gave this envelope to you, was this the first time you've met him?" My first instinct was to bite my tongue, but this man really needed to be taken off the streets. Shaking my head, I watched Eric's eyes squint at me with a scowl.

"When did you first meet him?" Detective Johnson asked with raised eyebrows. Thinking back, I remembered it was the first day that Eric brought me here.

"It was about two weeks ago. He stopped me when I was walking to the park. He asked me the time and I told him and he thanked me. That was all," I replied before starting to scrape the bottom of the ice cream cup. Crap…my last scoop.

"Did he ask you anything else? Did he talk to you about Eric?" Detective Johnson inquired.

"Just the time, nothing else. He was very polite."

"Needless to say, I need you to be very careful about where you go in the day or night. He is a very dangerous man, Ms. Austin…Becki. He isn't who he seems."

"I didn't realize that he was going to start going after her once he wasn't able to get around me," Eric commented to the detective.

"We have no proof that he was the one who broke into her apartment. You and I may know for a fact that he did, but that will not hold up in court. And even with the notes that he left, there is no proof without a signature or fingerprints."

Eric's frustration getting the better of him said, "What am I supposed to do? Am I supposed to worry every time she goes to work if she will come home safe? Am I supposed to panic every time I hear the door open? Haven't I been through enough?" he shouted, thoroughly aggravated by the end of it.

"Do not misunderstand; we will be keeping a tail on his whereabouts. We can keep some undercover cars outside your home and her place of work, as well. We just don't have the evidence to put him back in prison yet."

With that, Detective Johnson left, but the tension was so thick in Eric's neck, I was waiting for a vein to burst. My eyes were locked on Eric's every move as he locked up the front door before he laid his head against it. Giving him some time to think through the conversation that just happened, I headed into the kitchen and put my spoon and the cardboard cup in the waste basket.

"So, how long have you and Gary been talking?" Eric asked with his head still against the door with his eyes closed.

I shrugged and then realized that he couldn't see my actions so I said, "Once in a while to make sure I'm okay and vice versa."

"Does he know that you are living with me?" he asked, this time turning his head to look in my direction.

"No," I replied again not elaborating.

"Why not?" he asked again, but his voice was strained.

"He doesn't know about the break-in so he wouldn't understand why I'm living with you. I don't want him to feel guilty about leaving me behind, and I shouldn't have to explain what I'm doing in my life to him anymore," I said, almost biting my tongue off in defensive mode.

Striding over until our chests were almost touching, he glared down at me. "Why haven't you *really* told him?"

"I already told you, none of his business," I said, not backing down.

Cocking his head to the side he replied, "Really? So you'd be upset if I gave him a call and let him know that you are spending every night with me?"

Shocked and affronted, my blood started to boil. "It's nobody's business what I do with my nights. Why do you even care?" I retorted.

"I'm your friend, that's why," he replied vehemently.

"Oh, really? That's not what you said to Detective Johnson!" I shouted out at him and then bit my lip as I retreated up the stairs and back to my room. Slamming the door behind me, I gave it a swift kick for good measure. I couldn't believe I just said that to him. I was not going to get in trouble for having conversations with people, or not sharing every detail of my life with others. Maybe that was my dilemma—I told people too much.

Exasperated, I laid back on my bed and kicked off my shoes. The soft tap on the door made me rise up on my elbows.

"Who is it?" I asked just to irritate him.

"The Easter Bunny, and I'm bearing gifts."

"It's not locked...yet," I replied and sunk back down to my bed.

"What did you bring?" I asked, not bothering to look at him.

"Here," he said, handing out my cell phone.

"Oh, thanks. Just what I needed," I said sarcastically.

The next thing I knew, I was being attacked by hands. "What are—" was all I could get out before his hand clamped over my mouth.

"No more of that," he demanded before I realized he was straddling my body. The close proximity of him on me started the heat surging through my veins regardless of why. "You are too feisty for your own good, do you know that? You blow up a completely normal conversation into something that it's not. Take a deep breath, and then I'll take my hand off."

Following his instructions, I took a deep breath, and true to his word he took his hand off of my mouth. Refusing to look at him, I turned my head to my closet—my safe haven—and wished I could just go in there and seal the door behind me.

"Becki," he said, trying to coax me into looking up at him, but I declined to do so.

"Look at me," he said, leaning down closer to my face.

Shaking my head, I could feel my eyes starting to water. Oh, no, the last thing I needed to do was cry and have him think I was weak.

"I don't want us to fight. I don't like it. Please, just look at me," he coaxed again. I shook my head again and traitor tears slowly leaked out of the sides of my eyes. Why was he so frustrating?

"Why must you be so inflexible?" he growled at me.

"Please, just leave me alone," I said, trying to control my emotions. There was some psycho trying to threaten Eric by getting close to me, Gary was still trying to make me go to Arizona, and my 'landlord' just physically attacked me because I wouldn't let him verbally assault me downstairs.

211

Grunting, he climbed off and headed for the door. Instinctively, I curled up into a ball, rocking myself slowly with my eyes closed. I was okay…I was going to be okay. Unable to contain the tears, more of them slipped down my cheek and nose to collect on the comforter.

"I—"

"Just go!" I demanded in a rough voice.

"Are you okay? What the hell?" he questioned, coming closer.

"Please, leave me alone," I begged, wrapping my arms around my waist.

"No, I won't. Not anymore," Eric said, crawling back onto the bed and spooning right behind me. I felt his arms wrap around my waist and help rock me back and forth to soothe me. Finally, after the last tear fell, I could feel Eric's hand gently rubbing up my arm before he started to force me to turn over and face him. I tried to wipe my tear-stained face clean, but it didn't seem to be working.

"Here, I can help with that." He grabbed some Kleenex from the end table.

"Thanks," I said before wiping up the mess of my face. Looking down to see that I was still wearing my clothes that I wore for court this morning, I sat up. Slowly crawling off of my bed, I went to my dresser and pulled out my tank top and shorts pajama set.

"I can go—"

"No, I'm going to use my closet," I said, cutting him off.

"Stay," I commanded before slipping in and getting changed. When I stepped back out of the closet, I put my clothes on a hanger so that I could have my now rumpled suit dry-cleaned.

"Can I get changed, too?" Eric asked softly. I nodded my head and watched his back head toward his bedroom. I crawled up to my pillows and slipped underneath the covers. Turning on the TV to AMC, Eric returned with his grey pants in his hands. He walked right into my closet and slid the door shut behind him.

"What are you doing?" I called out at my closet.

Seeing the door slide back open a minute later, he smiled at me. "You are always in here, so I wanted to give it a try."

"And what's your verdict?" I asked with one raised eyebrow, trying not to laugh.

"It is a nice closet," he replied, chuckling to himself before climbing on the bed and slipping in next to me.

"What are you watching?" he asked.

"Nothing really," I said, laying my head back on the pillow. Why was Eric in bed with me? I must be more pathetic than I thought. A few tears and he's planning on moving into my bedroom.

"You don't have to hang out in here, you know " I said, trying to give him an out and surprised by the returning scowl.

"Are you sick of my company already?" he asked, feigning hurt—at least I think he was.

"No, but I don't want you to hang out with me because you feel bad for me. I've just had a rough week. You don't have to hover," I said, staring at the TV.

"My week hasn't been so great either. There were definite good parts, but overall, it was pretty bad. I'm sorry I jumped you. I couldn't think of another way to get you to stay in one place and talk to me," he replied, also staring at the TV.

Sighing softly, I glanced down to my fingers in my lap. It was true that I did run away from conversation, and I didn't condone getting jumped to finish that conversation, but I guess I understood. I was a handful in so many ways. Changing the subject, mentally I thought back to this week. My favorite part was movie night, but was I going to put him on the spot again? No, I'd learned my lesson.

"What was your favorite part of this week?" I asked, unable to help myself. Okay, so I guess I hadn't learned my lesson. At least I didn't have to worry about crying—there weren't any tears left in me.

"I enjoyed the trip to the beach," he said, and I took a deep, slow breath accepting that he wasn't going to bring it up. "However," he continued, "I think my favorite part would be watching a movie and eating junk food with you."

I nodded stiffly. "Me, too."

I plugged my cell phone into my charger and placed it on the table and set the alarm for work tomorrow. I laid my head back into the fluffy pillows and handed the remote to Eric.

"Watch whatever you want. I'm pretty tired," I said before snuggling up against his side.

With a gleam in his eye, he laid back and wrapped his arm around me so I could lay my head on his chest fully. After one of the weirdest and creepiest days, it was nice to know that I could spend my evening cuddled up to him.

Chapter 19
Tuesday, September 18th

The soft glow of tea candles slowly making a trail from the front door to the kitchen was a lovely surprise. I blow out each one as it stops right in front of the microwave with a note that says: Open Me. Pulling open the door, I take out a small white container that has a note that says: Do Not Open Me. Smirking at the messages, I follow and blow the candles as they continue to the stairs where it has turned into more Post-it notes. The first reads: Do You; the fourth step reads: Still Think; the ninth step reads: That I'm; and the note on the top step reads: Boring?

Following two more candles to his bedroom door, there is a note that reads: Open Me. What in the world has he got planned? The room is astonishingly decorated with thick lavender candles on the dresser, both end tables and bureau. On each side of the lavender candles are white tea candles with a vase of lilacs and baby's breath. The scent alone makes me think back to a dream I had, running free in the forest with nature surrounding me.

As I step closer to the bedside table, I almost jump out of my skin to feel my phone vibrate in my pocket. I whip it out and read a text: 'Place the white container on the bedside table and sit down on the bed while slipping on the black satin sleeping mask.' Without further ado, I follow the instructions to the letter, and I'm rewarded with strong masculine hands sliding up both of my arms from behind. The hands stop on my shoulders where they slowly knead away the tension of the day, and I let my head hang forward enjoying the attentive massage.

With the encouragement from my appreciative groans, his hands slide up my neck working those muscles until they are relaxed, as well. And with expert fingers, he pulls the clip out of my hair and slowly massages my scalp from the back to the crown of my head. After working through to my hairline, I'm slowly laid back on the bed where the fingers continue to rub my temples until I start to worry about falling asleep from the sensual assault. My deep, even breathing must have been the giveaway that I was close to sleep because then the fingers lightly glide down the slender slope of my nose to my lips.

I try to keep calm, but I'm stunned by the dampness left upon my lips. Instinctively, I suck on my bottom lip and taste a warm, gooey caramel flavor. Is that what I brought up? Hearing a light chuckle from my side, I turn my head in that direction, but thanks to the mask I still can't see anything. Those skillful fingers then slowly skim my lips, down my chin all the way down my neck, stopping at my collarbone.

I rub my lips together so the caramel is like lip gloss when I feel soft lips brush mine followed by his tongue. I lick my top while he sucks on my bottom lip and I gasp from the shivers going down my spine. One quick kiss of his lips, I start to wiggle under his hovered body until his hands hold me down firmly. Feeling the gentleness of his tongue licking down my chin, sucking it clean before continuing down my neck I can't help my hips from trying to find his body to rub against.

"Mmmmm…" Hearing his moan against my throat and on down to my collarbone where my secret melting spot is, I feel the tingles shoot through my fingers and toes.

"Eric," I say as it's the only thing my lips are willing to let out.

"Becki?" I heard Eric ask from behind me. Oh, no, I was dreaming.

"Becki?" he asked again, but I felt him rolling over to talk to me.

"Yeah?" I whispered back. With his left arm, he rolled me over to face him.

"You called for me. What's going on? Bad dream?" he asked, pulling me close to his body and rubbing his hand up and down my arm.

How was I supposed to explain this without explaining this? I couldn't lie to him; I wasn't very good at it. I could try, but…

"You can tell me. Trust me, I've had my share of nightmares. Don't worry, I'm right here," he said, running his fingers down my cheek trying to soothe me. I wished it was a nightmare so I could get out of this situation.

"It wasn't a nightmare," I said, laying my head back into the pillow fully.

"Really?" Eric asked, concerned and unconvinced, but as I started to scoot away from him he asked with obvious understanding, "Oh, *really*?" I couldn't see his face in the dark, but I could almost guarantee that he was grinning devilishly at me.

218

"Good night, Eric," I stated firmly as I rolled over giving him my back.

"I don't think that I want you to say my name like that anymore...I liked—"

"Shut it or you sleep in your own bed!" I shouted over my shoulder. I couldn't believe this. He was pulling a Tim on me. I should have never admitted the truth. I wondered what he would think about my dream coming true.

Impetuously, I turned over quickly and climbed on top of him, the shock in his voice evident. "What are you doing?"

"You said that all I had to do was let you know I wanted a taste."

With that simple explanation, I leaned down and pressed my lips against his. I quickly pulled out the elastic from his hair and ran my fingers through it. I loved how his hair felt in between my fingers, so soft. The residual heat in my veins returning from my dream, I started to kiss his neck slowly up toward his earlobe.

"Have you changed your mind?" I whispered seductively in his ear before realizing that he wasn't responding.

Sitting back, I looked down at him, but his face even in the dark showed frozen confusion.

"Eric?" I asked picking up his hands in mine. "Did you change your mind?" I asked, starting to panic that I'd really sexually assaulted him in his own home.

"I...was just surprised," Eric explained but still made no move to touch me back. Feeling mortified by my own actions, I crawled off of him and back to my side of the bed. I'd become Tim. I'd taken advantage of his kindness. What was wrong with me?

"I'm sorry if you—" I began to say, but my sentence was cut off by Eric's lips against mine. The weight of his body pressing me into the bed made me melt all over again.

His right hand cupped the back of my head while his left rested against my waist. All I wanted to do was have my way with him, but this didn't feel right. He must've not really wanted to do this. Tim would've been feeling me up, and Gary would have had me undressed a long time ago. The feel of his tongue slipping into my mouth gave me an idea. I caressed his tongue with mine while I massaged my right hand with his left and slowly raised it to my chest, pressing it firmly against me. Hearing the audible gasp in my mouth, I pulled back to kiss his jaw and see what he did from there.

The trembling fingers on my chest said it all.

"Eric, don't worry about it. Okay?" I said as he slowly rolled over onto his back. "I didn't mean to make you uncomfortable." I pulled the covers back up over both of us before lying on my back and staring at the ceiling.

"Becki?" I heard him whisper.

"Yeah?"

"You're beautiful inside and out." Compliments after scaring the crap out of the man who was still in bed with me, what sense does that make?

"Thanks. You're amazing, too." The sound of a sigh caused me turn my head to face him again. "Are you sure you're okay? I didn't mean to make you uncomfortable," I repeated.

I really hadn't meant to. I'd never had to put myself out there—I'd always been the one pursued. Maybe that made me too confident that I'd expect him to jump at the chance of being with me? Eric didn't mind kissing me sometimes, but something about this just didn't feel okay.

"You didn't. It's hard to talk about."

"Is it me?" I asked, my insecurities leaking out of my mouth.

"No, not at all; but in a way, yes." With a frustrated grunt, he pulled me until I was half lying on him.

"What are you doing?"

"Trying," he said before kissing my lips with fervor. He finally pulled me all the way on his lap, slipping his hands under my tank top and rubbing his hands up and down my back.

Placing my hands tenderly on his shoulders, I kissed him back much gentler than before. He might not have been physically fragile, but I couldn't seem to put enthusiasm back into this. Cupping his face, I leaned back with a small smile and ran my fingers up and down his cheeks. Without thinking, I slid down his body until my head was resting on his chest and started to hum one of my favorite songs softly. The steadiness of his fingers still rubbing my back slowly sunk me into a dreamless sleep.

*****

Thursday, September 20th

"What are you trying to say?" I asked while lounging on the couch in the living room.

Today had been so normal that I thought I had only imagined the craziness of needing unmarked cars to follow me to work and back home. I had to fix myself a glass of wine and put on a musical just to relax after the strange aftermath at work. Thursdays are my active days at work, but no major cases came in; I just helped with adopting some cats to new families.

I received two text messages and three phone calls on the way home from Gary insisting on me going to Arizona this weekend. It was starting to make my head hurt. And to top it all off, Gary complained about me to one of my favorite people; needless to say, I got a phone call minutes later.

"I'm not saying anything, my dear. I'm asking if you wouldn't mind going to see him. He truly is all alone out there and some company might do him some good," Thomas insisted.

"I'm not refusing to go see him; I'm just trying to set the trip for another weekend. I am so busy right now that I think my head might explode from all the pressure of it," I admitted even though Thomas had no idea what had been going on in my life since Gary and I broke up.

"I do have an ulterior motive, darling, and I am sorry for putting you in this position. I want him to come home, and I believe that if he sees you, maybe you could beg him to come back to us...all of us," Thomas said a bit gruffly.

I didn't want to upset Thomas, but how was I supposed to just pack up and go? "Thomas, you know that I care about you and Gary. I didn't force him to leave; he chose his job over being with me. I doubt going out there will bring him home," I replied, trying to keep my emotions in check.

Admitting it out loud was harder than I expected, especially to Thomas. Gary didn't want me enough to stay even when he knew I refused to leave. He made his decision. Thomas was going to have to deal with it.

"Becki, he still loves you. I know he would be willing to come back for you."

I doubt Gary would like to come back for me knowing that I'd moved in with another man. I'm pretty sure Gary would see red and murder us both. Unable to just say no, I placated him. "I'll see what I can do, okay? I'll call Gary and see where it goes from there."

"Thank you, my dear. You know that you are as precious to me as my son is, right?"

Smirking into the phone I replied, "Of course, and I love you, too. Get some rest."

"Good night, Becki," Thomas said before hanging up.

I couldn't believe that Thomas was trying to send a rescue mission out for Gary. Actually, this sounded like something Josephine would have tried…she was smart making Thomas call me. I wouldn't be willing to do a thing for her. Rubbing my hands over my face, I laid my head back against the couch. If I went to Arizona, I was going to have to explain to Gary everything that's been happening. And where would he live? I already let the landlord know that I wasn't going to be living there next month and was able to get rid of my big items from the apartment. I picked up my glass of wine and started chugging it down before picking up the bottle and refilling the glass.

"That bad, huh?" I heard a rugged voice ask from the doorway.

"You have no idea. How's your day going?"

"Not as bad as yours, apparently. Want to talk about it?" he asked, sitting down next to me and stealing a sip from my wine glass. Eric got edgy whenever the subject of Gary came up, but if I wasn't honest with him now, he'd freak out when he found out later.

"I got an invitation for a trip this weekend. I'm debating if I should go."

I thought that was honest enough without details of Gary to tip him off.

"The best way to make that decision would be pros and cons. List them out and choose from there," he advised, handing the glass back to me. I chugged another mouthful and then glanced at Eric's head cocked in my direction. Refilling my glass again, Eric reached out and took the bottle away.

"You are going to hate yourself tomorrow. Slow it down and talk to me," he stated with a raised eyebrow. The truth shall set you free; I hoped that saying was correct.

"I've been invited for the weekend to take a trip, all expenses paid, accommodation taken care of. I won't be able to bring Barney with me," I started taking slow sips of my glass.

"That sounds terrific! You don't have to worry about Barney or anything. I'll miss having you here, but it'll be nice knowing that you're not stuck here dealing with my issues that have seemed to spill into your life," Eric said smiling, genuinely happy for me.

"You're not sick of me being here, are you?" I asked, stupidly thinking of last night's awkward situation. We still had yet to speak about it, and I certainly didn't need to bring it up right now.

"Don't be ridiculous! I love having you here. One of the best decisions I've made in a long time, actually," he said, throwing his arm around my shoulders and pulling me into his side. "Those sound like the pros; so, what are the cons of this invitation?"

Looking down in my glass, I took my last chug for courage.

"The trip is to Arizona..." I said and instantly felt the tension run through his arm. I couldn't make myself look up at him. I didn't want to see whatever it was that he was expressing.

"Gary," he stated emotionlessly.

I simply nodded and placed my glass down on the floor again. When I sat back, I noticed that he took his arm back to his side of the couch. "He's been begging me to go, but I don't want to. I was sure I could put it off until he just gave up, but his father called me. His family is worried about him and they want me to persuade him to move back to New York," I said in a rush to explain everything so that he didn't think I was trying to revive our relationship.

"Are you going?" he asked with an even tone. Shrugging my shoulders, I placed my hand on top of

225

his in an attempt to keep him calm. "When were you going to tell me that you were leaving?" Eric asked with irritation easily laced into his words.

"I wasn't planning on telling you because I wasn't planning on going. Don't talk to me like that," I said a bit defensively.

"Anything else you want to tell me?"

"Why do you do that? You were fine a minute ago," I responded with my blood boiling already.

I knew he would be absurd, and yet I was stupid enough to admit the truth. I stood up to walk away, but then suddenly I was pulled back to the couch.

"No," he stated, glaring in my direction.

"What?" I replied almost biting off the tip of my tongue.

"No more running away from our conversations."

"When you can have a conversation without staring daggers at me, then I will stay. Until that happens…" I warned.

"How did you expect me to take this 'invitation' for the weekend?" he asked, making the quote marks in the air with his fingers.

"I knew you'd take it badly. That is a real reason as to why I wasn't considering going," I admitted, looking down to my hands in my lap.

"Do you plan on getting back with him?"

"You're serious? After last night, you're seriously asking me that?" I asked, completely dumbfounded followed by the burn.

Not a romantic fire, but a slow burning in my chest caused by a crushing blow. No wonder he didn't want to be with me last night. He thinks I'm some sort of whore. I've only had one intimate bedfellow and a few minor excursions, nothing anywhere near Lily and her nightcaps, but wow. I couldn't believe he just said that straight to my face.

His eyes widened, signifying that he realized what he asked was wounding. He placed his hand on mine in a gesture of apology.

"I'm sorry. I didn't mean for it to come out like that. Last night was—"

"I don't sleep around," I stated, seething, while pulling my hands back from his.

"I wasn't trying to imply that you did. I have to explain some things to you."

The ringing of his cell phone interrupted his attempt to mollify the unintended degrading remark. Thank God for small miracles. While he reached into his pocket to grab his phone, I moved out of his reach and headed up to my room.

Taking a scalding shower and dressing up in my faded denim jeans with black halter top and black heeled sandals, I was ready for tonight. I texted Lily:

We're still on tonight, right?

Letting my hair down for the evening, I used my black hair band to keep it out of my eyes. With one quick glance in the mirror, I could see that my outfit was absolutely mouthwatering. I wouldn't need anything to keep me warm tonight except my drink.

My phone vibrated with a text back from Lily: <u>C u there!</u>

I dabbed perfume behind my ears, wrists, and in my cleavage. Normally, I don't use too much make up, but tonight I applied heavy black eyeliner and vanilla tasting lip gloss with glitter in it. I was so getting free drinks tonight.

Almost stumbling down the stairs in my heels, I caught myself before the last step and chuckled. Yeah, it'd be great if I couldn't even manage to walk into the bar. Heading into the kitchen, I sat on the stool and grabbed a banana from the fruit bowl. Checking the time on my cell phone, I saw it read a quarter after seven. I wondered where Eric kept the yellow pages so I could call a cab. I walked through the living room, but I saw nothing helpful. Maybe there was one in Eric's office? The door to his office was closed which usually meant that he was busy. I knocked on the door softly.

"Come in," he said.

"Do you have the yellow pages in here?" I asked while scanning the room from the door.

"Um…"

Glancing at his face, it looked like his jaw had come unhinged. Must be my outfit—good, the drinks will be free tonight. Waving my hand to get his attention, I asked again, "Do you?"

"Do I what?"

"Yellow pages?" I asked, sighing and crossing my arms over my chest.

"Yeah…" he leaned down into one of his drawers in his desk. "What do you need it for?" he asked while pulling it out.

"I need a taxi service."

"I don't mind driving you. All you have to do is ask," he said, shocked that I wouldn't.

"No, thanks. I don't know what shape or mood I'll be in later tonight so it's better if I just get a cab."

As I walked over to the desk to pick up the book, he put his hand over it. "You're going to *Lights Out*?"

I nodded, reaching out to grab it again.

"I'll take you," he insisted. "What time should we leave? The normal time?"

Frustrated, I nodded and walked away. At least I'd be in good company with Tim and Lily. Life was already laughing in my face; I think it's my turn to laugh. I took a trip to my bathroom and brushed the banana out of my teeth and used my mouthwash.

"Becki?!" I heard Eric calling from downstairs.

"Coming!" I shouted back and glanced one more time in the mirror.

Tonight's motto: Knock them out or knock them back.

229

Chapter 20
Thursday, September 20th

The half hour drive to the bar was the longest and most awkward silence I'd dealt with in a long time. Eric attempted some sort of conversation, but I wasn't interested in anything he tried to say. Walking into *Lights Out*, I was welcomed with hoots and whistles; but the most obnoxious comment came from my beloved Tim.

"Wow, baby girl. You want to hop up on the bar? You can do some coyote ugly dancing!" he said with a wink.

"In your dreams, dude. I want to have fun tonight."

"Uh oh, that sounds like trouble," Tim said, frowning already.

"Hey, I have a ride home, don't worry. I'd like to do shots tonight, tequila my poison," I said with a grin.

"Becki?" I heard Lily ask, sitting next to me.

"Hey! I'm so glad you are here. It's shots night."

"What's wrong? You don't do shots unless it's bad," Lily asked, obviously concerned.

"Can't a girl just want to have fun?" I asked, taking one of my shots and throwing it back. The burn felt so good that I upped the ante to double shots.

"I've got my eye on you," Tim said, frowning even more.

"Tim, chill out. If you're nice to me, I'll dance with you," I bargained, throwing back a double shot. Lily, taking her shot, looked over her shoulder watching Will play pool with his friends.

"How did the family dinner go?" I asked, remembering her complaint from the beach.

"It was okay. No drama, really good food. How are things with Eric?" she asked before accepting another shot.

"Not so good right now. I don't really want to talk about it; I just want to have fun," I admitted before getting singles for the jukebox. Picking out my favorite song, Lily and I began to dance the night away.

Between the techno fist pumping, mock country line dancing, and sexy grinding sessions with several hot guys, my feet were killing me. Hopping back on my stool, I took another double shot and asked Tim, "Do you mind keeping these for me?" holding out my heels to him.

Smirking, he put his hand on mine. "I haven't seen you dance like that in ages. When do I get my turn?" he chuckled. The alcohol making me bold, I leaned in close letting my cleavage show a bit more than needed.

"Whenever you want it," I purred.

While finishing my determined last double shot, I looked up to see Tim wasn't behind the bar. I looked down at my phone and saw a text from Eric:

On my way.

Why in the world was he coming to get me so early? I checked the time on my phone, and I was shocked to see it was almost one in the morning.

"May I have this dance?" I heard Tim request from behind me. Laughing, I climbed down and let him wrap his arms around my waist.

Closing my eyes, I laid my head against his chest and let him lead the way. "You know that you look fabulous tonight. Was it for my benefit?" he asked.

"You give me free drinks when I look attractive," I admitted, smirking at him.

"Baby girl, you always look attractive. Even if you were in sweats and a t-shirt, you'd have me on my knees begging you for another chance." His admission warmed my chest. It felt like forever since we'd spent time together.

"I haven't been feeling the love lately. I'm just being whiny. Post break up emotions, I guess," I confessed with a sigh.

"You can call me day or night, you know that. I'll send you all the love you need. You could spend the night with me tonight. I have plenty to share," he said, raising his eyebrows at me suggestively.

With a chuckle, I shook my head. "You're dating someone."

"No one special. I'd easily choose you any day."

"I know that is supposed to make me feel better, Tim, but it doesn't. What if I really wanted to be with you? If some other girl turned your head, would you just leave me like that?" I asked, stepping back from him.

"I just want to be with you, Becki. We were so good together; and no, I'm not referring to just the intimacy. We had lots of fun times, like the trip to Boston or the lake house with the bonfire. Give me a second chance. I'll prove it to you," Tim said, rubbing his hands up my arms pulling me closer.

"Your ride is here," Lily whispered from behind me.

"Did he honk?" I asked sarcastically, turning to look at her.

"Nope," she said seriously, sending her eyes in any direction but toward the door.

"Fabulous," I muttered, and as I started to head in that direction, Tim pulled me back into his arms.

"Becki..." he started, but I placed my finger to his lips.

"I'm emotionally screwed up right now. I care for you way too much for you to be my rebound guy. I respect and love you too much for that. If it's meant to be, it will happen; but for now, I just need 'me' time," I explained and gave him a quick hug before slipping from his arms.

"He doesn't look too happy," Lily warned from my side. I just shrugged because there was no need to explain the craziness that was my friendship with Eric.

"I lost track of time. Sorry for not calling you to come get me earlier," I said apologetically to Eric whose jaw looked like stone.

"Not a problem," he said coolly. As I started to follow Eric to the door, I heard, "Baby girl!" from Tim.

I turned around, confused. "What?" Tim ran over, handing me my shoes. Oh, wonderful. I didn't think I was that drunk, but I almost walked out barefoot.

Smirking at me, Tim said, "See? I care. Hey, Eric," he threw in at the end.

A nod from Eric was all the response Tim got; I must have really pissed him off by being out so late. Oh, well, I could have called a cab. I slipped on my heeled sandals with Tim's help so I didn't fall over.

Smiling sheepishly, I waved at Tim as Eric led us back to the car. "How much did you drink tonight?" he asked as soon as we were buckled up in the car.

"I lost count. Double shots of tequila," I slurred, laying my head against the cold glass. "Did you get anymore writing done tonight?" I randomly asked.

"A bit, but I was distracted."

"Barney?" I asked.

"No, he was fine." He better not be implying that he was thinking about me. There was no reason for him to think about me other than our friendship, unless that's what he was questioning.

"Do you like me?" I asked, smirking at him.

"Of course, I do. I wouldn't have had you move in if I didn't," he answered, confused.

Hah! "Eric! Do you find me attractive? Am I eye candy to you?" The words came out of my mouth but it was the alcohol asking the questions now.

"Becki, we should have this discussion when you're sober," he responded, starting to white knuckle the steering wheel.

"Nope, I don't want to wait. Tell me," I said gruffly in the tone he used with me and chuckled at the end of it.

"You're beautiful," he admitted and then shut his lips tight.

"So, that means yes?" I persisted.

"Becki, why are you asking?"

"You make me feel weird," I stated and then chuckled again.

"I think that's the alcohol talking," he stated and shook his head.

'No, really, most of the time you treat me normal like a friend. Then you kissed me while we were watching that movie. And when I tried to kiss you back last night, you treated me like a leper. I'd understand if you didn't think I was attractive but...then the way you reacted when you saw my outfit tonight made me think differently again. Wow, I'm so rambling," I babbled before pulling the lever to make my seat lay all the way back.

"What a ride!" I exclaimed and laughed again as I moved the seat back up and then lay it down again.

Hearing him sigh, I looked over to see frustration on his face. "I'm not hurting your car, you know?' I said a bit defensively.

"You're fine. Don't worry about it." Pulling the seat back up to the normal position, I leaned over and lay my head against Eric's shoulder.

The stiffness of his shoulder and arm made me raise my eyebrow. "Do you want me to move out?" I asked.

"Why would you think that? Haven't I expressed several times that I love having you live with me?" he asked, frustration slipping from his lips.

"You're angry with me. You don't like me anymore," I moaned, feeling the burn of rejection in my chest.

"I'm not angry, you're just drunk," he said almost rudely, pulling into the driveway before putting it in park. I looked down so he couldn't see the sad expression on my face as the feeling of rejection spread from my chest down to my stomach.

"I understand," I said, fumbling with my seatbelt. My face was captured by his big hands and held firmly.

"No, you don't."

Looking up into his lovely blue eyes, I took a deep, slow breath. Using one of his hands to unbuckle both my seatbelt and his, he leaned closer to me and pressed his lips gently to mine. Afraid to enjoy it, I stayed frozen in place hoping not to cause him to panic or worse, let myself hope for more.

The sparks in my chest started to light a fire instantly warming me up again as his lips brushed once, twice, thrice against mine. Opening our eyes at the same time, we smiled at each other.

"Eric, I want to be honest with you, but you scare me sometimes," I said honestly.

Running his hands up and down my arms he responded, "I don't want to scare you. I'm sorry about earlier."

I should have just told him that I wanted to be with him; the worst he could say is that he wasn't interested. "Eric, I want..." Feeling him lean in closer, I panicked.

"What?" he asked.

"Um...I want you...and I to be closer," I admitted, chickening out. I didn't think there was enough liquid courage in me.

Smirking, he leaned in even closer to me thinking that I meant it literally. Chuckling at him, I wrapped my arms around his neck and hugged him tightly.

"I enjoy being close to you," he confided warmly. Laying my head on his shoulder, I slowly inhaled the scent of him.

"You smell good," I said, slipping the truth again.

"You smell wonderful. I like this perfume," he said, clutching me even tighter. Without thinking, I kissed his neck and then sighed back into the hug.

"Did you just—" he said, sounding surprised. I chuckled and nodded against him.

"May I make a request?" I asked formally and then laughed.

"Sure," he advised, laughing along with me.

Feeling a bit braver, I responded, "Touch me." Not wanting to see his expression, I just held on tightly to him to sense any distress.

"Where?" he asked, sounding confused again. That wasn't the response I was expecting. Turning my head to face him as he turned his, we brushed lips accidentally. Making the most of the opportunity, I leaned in and encouraged more.

"Everywhere," I mumbled against his lips, noting the pause in response.

"Everywhere?" he asked, pulling back slightly.

I nodded and trailed my fingers from his shoulders down his arms to his hands, rubbing my cheek briefly against his hand with my eyes closed.

"I want you...to touch me," I admitted, still chickening out at the end, but saying anything was better than not.

The darkness surrounding the outside of the car making me feel a bit more seductive, I placed his hand on my neck, letting his fingers stroke my collarbone. Releasing his hand, I placed mine at his neck and gently rubbed my fingers up and down, stroking his collarbone, as well. The steady beat of his heart reassured me that I was on the right track with him even though I could feel mine pounding away, too.

"Becki..." I glanced up to see his eyes unsure and wary. I was sure he'd done this before. Why was this like pulling teeth? If all we're going to end up doing is getting me excited and him sleeping it off, I was going to need to get myself a Battery Operated Boyfriend. The thought alone caused a chuckle to pass through my mouth.

"Are you laughing at me?" he asked, seemingly shocked and hurt. I shook my head not wanting to explain where my thoughts were headed.

"Let's go to bed, okay?" I asked, and then froze and laughed out loud. "I meant to *sleep*, not to..." I paused and saw his stricken expression, and I laughed even harder.

"I'm really not laughing at you, I promise. I just keep putting my foot in my mouth," I said and then leaned in to peck his lips before opening my door and climbing out.

*****

Changed into my pajamas with my face washed clean, I walked into my bedroom and saw Eric under the covers with Barney sleeping at the foot of the bed. Was I ever going to sleep alone again? I wondered how many women Eric had slept with? I couldn't imagine him not having a bunch of female fans of his book vowing to marry him; I mean, he's good looking, successful, motivated—what's not to like? Slipping under the covers beside him, I faced him.

"Eric?" I asked even though I should have minded my own business.

"You have a lot of questions tonight. Don't you want to leave a little mystery between us?" he asked trying to deter me.

"How many women have you slept with?" I asked bluntly, unable to curb my question subtly.

"Why would you want to know that? It's personal," he stated, sounding irritated.

239

Oops, oh well. I laid back on my pillow and closed my eyes willing my mouth to shut itself before anything else came out.

"Do you enjoy sleeping with me?" I spat out again. He was going to muzzle me. Hell, I wanted to muzzle me.

"Are you going to talk all night long?" he asked, less irritated but not seeming happy either.

"Fine," I muttered, rolling away from him and grabbing my cell phone.

I texted Lily: What r u doing?

She replied back within minutes: Finished my nightcap w/ Will but he's tired and I'm wired. Shouldn't u be dozing?

I chuckled softly and texted back: I annoyed Eric. So it's ur turn. I wish I could have a nightcap...it's been a long time.

Almost immediately I got a text back: Hook up w/ Eric!

He's not interested.

Lily, not missing a beat, texted: Shall I buy u a B.O.B.?

I chuckled again before texting: No.

"Who are you talking to at this time of night?" Eric whispered close behind me.

"Lily," I stated, not elaborating.

"Why are you so keyed up?" he asked.

"You don't want to know. Just go to sleep, Lily will settle me down in a bit," I replied with a sigh.

"I wouldn't ask if I didn't want to know," he insisted.

Lily texted me back: <u>I will have one on ur desk bright and early 2morrow 4 u to enjoy yourself with. It's even waterproof.</u> I started to chuckle again and Eric grabbed my phone before I could hit reply and read it.

"What's a B.O.B.?" he asked, confused.

"Hey!" I exclaimed and grabbed my phone back. "None of your business, it's personal," I said, throwing it back in his face.

"Wait a minute…are you talking about a sex toy?" he asked astonished. Cringing into my pillow, I couldn't help but laugh. "You are!" he shouted at me even though I was lying right next to him.

Cracking up even harder, I texted Lily: <u>Eric read our texts.</u>

"You're joking with her, right? You wouldn't seriously consider…doing that," he said with his head cocked to the side.

"It's personal," I repeated, and I was practically seizing on the bed with hilarity. "Don't worry; I wouldn't do it with you here in bed with me." I practically blacked out with the intense giggles escaping past my lips.

"Why not?" he asked, shocking the hell out of me into a stunned silence.

"You're kidding, right?" I asked, facing him and trying to pick up my jaw from the floor.

"We're friends. I would understand—"

"Friends don't sleep together let alone have sexual excursions while in the bed with them," I said, shaking my head at him.

"I am intruding in your bed. If you feel the need to do...anything...I have no right to stop you from 'enjoying yourself'," he said, quoting the text he read, and I could hear the smirk in his voice. What in the world? He didn't mind sex as long as he wasn't involved in it?

"Go to sleep, Eric," I stated and checked my phone to see a waiting text: That sux, r u sure u don't want it?

I texted her back: I'm positive.

Chapter 21
Friday, September 21st

The sound of the doorbell waking me up after a night of excessive drinking was the meanest joke in the world. Eric spooning me was a clear sign that he hadn't heard it. Slowly peeling myself out of his arms, I grabbed my robe and slippers and gently closed the bedroom door behind me. Luckily, I opened the front door before the ringing started again.

"How can I help you?" I asked, pulling the door open.

"Ms. Austin, I'm sorry for coming so early, but I need to speak with Eric right away," Detective Johnson explained. With a wave of my hand, I had him sit down in the living room.

"I'll go wake him up."

Just as I started to open the bedroom door, the most intense surge of nausea overcame me, and I ran for my bathroom. After five minutes of dreadful dry heaving, I brought my head up from the toilet. I needed a new way to get rid of stress—no more drinking as an escape. Brushing my teeth twice and washing my face with cold water, I headed back into my bedroom.

"Wake up, sleepyhead," I said, rubbing my hand up and down his arm.

A grumble was the only response I got. Smirking at him, I shook his shoulder a bit to get him to come around.

"It is way too early," he complained before rolling over onto his stomach. I climbed on the bed and straddled his back and playfully beat my fists on it.

"I need you to wake up. You have company downstairs. It's important." Finally, Eric opened his eyes and rolled over knocking me to the side.

"Who's here?" he asked with a raised eyebrow.

"Detective Johnson is in the living room," I said as I crawled out of bed again.

"You're serious?" he asked again, sitting up all the way.

"Go see for yourself," I replied before pulling out my outfit for work from the closet.

I put on my black slacks with a hunter green blouse and black flats after my shower. I put my hair up in a classic twist hairdo and finished up with green earrings. Checking myself out in the mirror, I was surprised to see that I didn't look as pale as usual. At least I didn't have a headache after last night. I'll have to have something greasy to settle my stomach, though.

Humming one of my favorite songs as I headed down the stairs to the kitchen, I grabbed an apple in one hand and my laptop in the other before opening the front door.

"Becki!" I heard Eric shout from the living room. Shutting the door and placing my laptop back down, I trudged into the other room.

"Yes?" I asked politely.

"I need to ask a favor of you," Eric asked with a pleading voice but with eyes that were strained with some uncertain emotion.

"What's that?"

"Accept Gary's invitation for the weekend," he said, grimacing a bit.

"Why?" I asked. Walking over to Eric and sitting down next to him, I placed my hand on his.

"Ms. Austin, the man who passed that envelope to you cannot in any way contact Eric. There is a permanent restraining order forbidding it. However..." Detective Johnson cleared his throat before continuing, "there is no protection order set up for you. Other than the few of us that are keeping an eye out for you as you go about your business, there isn't anything stopping him from coming after you."

I felt the trembling of fingers and tried to grip Eric's hand to calm him until I realized that it was my hands that were shaking. He was coming after me to get at Eric again.

As I glanced in Eric's direction, he shook his head with agitation and said, "You going to Arizona would be safer for you. He wouldn't expect you to be leaving me, and there isn't any way for him to get to me without alerting the police." I couldn't believe that I was being sent away for my own protection.

"I have to call Gary," I stated distantly, not really letting it register why I had to leave.

"Barney will be fine here with me. I'll even have a welcome home dinner set for you on Sunday night," Eric said, but his eyes were telling me something else. He clearly didn't want me to go; he wanted me to stay with him. And I'd never wanted to stay with him more.

"I can have you escorted to the airport this evening," Detective Johnson suggested, but I held up my hand.

"Can't I just get a ride with my friend?"

Shaking his head, he insisted, "It's not a good idea to let him know who your friends are. We don't want to put them at risk, too."

"Eric?" I heard the pleading in my voice even though I was using my best effort to control the fear that was seeping into my bones.

"Everything is going to be fine, okay? I wouldn't let anything happen to you. It's just a safety precaution that you get out of town for a couple of days. He can't leave the state without the authorities taking notice of it," he advised to reassure me.

Detective Johnson handed me his business card. "Call me to let me know the times of your flights. Don't worry; we are on top of everything. I'll see myself out." With a nod, he walked out leaving me gutted.

"Calm down. You're shaking, Becki," Eric said, rubbing his hand up and down my arm. Noticing that his gesture wasn't helping, he pulled me on to his lap where he held me close. "Do you think I'd ever let anything bad happen to you?" he asked.

Unable to speak, I shook my head.

"Do you honestly think that I'd encourage you go to Arizona if I didn't think it was the best option?" he asked, holding me tighter to his body.

I shook my head again but then looked up to see the tension in his jaw. "I don't want to go. I want to stay with you," I mumbled.

"I want you to stay with me, too, but you already knew that," he said, trying to make me smile, but I was too tense for any type of humor.

"Come on, you don't want to late," he said, pushing me up onto my feet but holding my hand walking me to the front door. "Besides, you get to come home to see me before you leave tonight, and I'll be here waiting for you when you get back. I'll get a bottle of wine and we can celebrate, all right?" he insisted, and I nodded in return. Apparently, choosing to quit alcohol consumption right now wasn't the best plan.

Picking up my purse, I placed it on my shoulder not really paying attention to anything that was going on around me.

"Becki."

Running his fingers down my cheek gently, he pulled me up into his arms while bringing his head down to brush his lips against mine. He must have been as afraid as I was except he had some sort of protection. I didn't have any protection other than him, his arms, his voice, and his lips.

Placing me back down, he smirked at me and asked, "You didn't see that coming, now did you?" I shook my head and tried to give him a small smile before going out the door to my job.

*****

"I can't believe what I'm hearing! I'll book it right now," Gary exclaimed through the phone at me.

247

"I need time to pack and stuff, but if there is one around eight tonight, that'd be best," I stated formally over the phone.

"There's a flight at eight fifteen from JFK, and you'd land here by midnight. Are you sure you want to come tonight and not tomorrow morning?"

"Tonight would be better, but I don't want to keep you up if that's too late," I replied.

"No! I don't mind coming to get you. Don't worry about it. I can't believe you are coming. All that begging caved you in, huh?" he asked jokingly.

"Between you and your father, I don't know which of you is worse," I responded.

"You love us both. All right, I just booked your flight for you. I'm emailing you the itinerary now."

"Thanks, Gary, I appreciate this," I said, trying to sound grateful.

"No, thank you. Call me when you get to JFK."

"Will do. See you later," I said before hanging up.

Retrieving the itinerary from my email, I printed it out and placed it into my purse. I was going to Arizona to escape a convicted felon from attacking me on behalf of Eric. No matter how many times I tried to explain the reasons why I had to go, the explanation as to why it would be better for me to be away right now, I wanted nothing more than to be back in Eric's arms. Wouldn't a normal person do their best to get away from the situation?

I picked up the phone and called Mr. Johnson and Eric so they knew the times of the flights and which airport I was departing from. Looking down at my paperwork, I saw that there was another court case coming up on Tuesday afternoon. I knew that on Monday, we would be having a meeting to prepare, so I didn't have to worry about going through the files just yet. I was always on top of things when it came to my paperwork.

Checking my work email, there was nothing new except for the newsletter. Looking down at my phone, I picked it up and called someone I never thought I'd voluntarily call.

"Hello?" asked a gruff voice.

"Dad?" I asked, shocked that Mother wasn't the one to answer.

"Oh, my sugarplum, what's going on? I haven't spoken to you in too long," he said in the easy-going way that I loved.

"I miss you," I said, unable to explain what was going on in my life.

"When are you coming to visit us? You know that your mother and I would love to have you come to see us. You can even bring that man along if you must," he added, trying to coax me.

"I promise as soon as things at work settle down, I will be on my way to see you. I love you," I said, trying to express my feelings to him the best way I could from so far away.

"I love you, too, sugarplum. You enjoy the rest of your day, okay?"

"Bye," I said before hanging up the phone. I may not have spoken to Mother, but at least I'd proven I wasn't such a terrible daughter.

On the ride back home, I couldn't stop my mind from wondering what my life would have been like if I had gone to Arizona with Gary in the first place. I wouldn't have Barney which would've been so sad because he was such a good part of my life. I wouldn't have had my friends or my job, but I would have had Gary. He would have been working, and I would've been safely tucked away at home—cooking dinner for him when he finally arrived home, spending my evenings cuddled up on a couch with him.

I was almost positive that he would've married me as soon as it was financially possible for us. Gary would've been my world, and I would have been his. I would have gotten off of my birth control, and we would have had beautiful children—at least two. I'm sure he would have expected me to be a housewife and stay home with the kids. Shaking my head, I chuckled aloud at the thought. Gary would have made the perfect husband if only he could've gotten his jealousy under control. I was the type of person who was going to make friends no matter where I went, and I was sure none of the male gender would have been accepted.

I pulled the car into the driveway and grabbed my purse and laptop bag. I honestly didn't think my fantasy would have run that smoothly in real life. The one person who I would've hated to have to leave behind as a friend was the one person I depended on nowadays just for shelter and protection. I opened the front door before kicking it shut behind me. Living with Eric could be tense, awkward, fun and exciting, but if it came down to Eric or Gary, I knew who I would choose.

"I packed some of your clothes, but you might want to double check. I might have overlooked something that you want to have," Eric said, holding his hand out to me as I came in the door. Lacing our fingers together, we headed up the stairs and into my room. Checking the suitcase, I saw he had packed everything for me except for my undergarments, hair products and razor. Adding those last few items into the case, I zipped it up and placed it on the floor beside the bed.

"I called you a cab to take you to the airport. That way you don't have to worry about parking," Eric said softly from my side.

"Thanks, I appreciate that."

"Are you hungry? Do you want anything to eat before your ride gets here?" he asked. Shaking my head, I sat down on the bed and Eric followed suit.

"I'd like for you to call me when you touch down in Arizona," he requested gently.

"It'll be really late when I finally get there. I'll text you, so you know that I made it safely." Eric nodded and played with my fingers in between his.

"Are you going to sleep in here while I'm gone?" I asked out of numb curiosity.

"Probably. My bed feels so big and cold. I'm used to being in here," Eric admitted, shrugging his shoulders. Grudgingly, I walked into my closet and shut the door behind me. I slipped on a pair of flare jeans and a lavender fitted t-shirt with sneakers before reemerging.

"How do I look?"

251

"Comfortable," he said, beckoning me with his hand to join him back on the bed. Snuggling up against his side, I tried to keep my thoughts blank.

The honk of a horn reluctantly made us head downstairs. Opening the door, Eric grabbed the suitcase and rolled it to the cab. After sliding it into the backseat, he turned to face me.

"Are you going to miss me?" I asked. His hands quickly rubbed my cheeks up and down.

"I'm going to be hopeless without you. Barney might just run away," he said jokingly but finished with asking, "Will you?"

"I started missing you this morning. It's only getting worse now that I have to do it a second time," I admitted, trying to hold onto my numbness.

"It's only a day and a half, then you will be home and we can celebrate," he said as he pulled my face up to meet his lips.

Closing my eyes, I wrapped my arms around his neck and pulled him tight to me. I didn't want our kiss to end because that meant I'll have to leave. The fire burning in my chest slowly spread through my arms and legs. Slowly, as he started to pull away to break the kiss, I stood up on my tip toes to feel his lips as long as I could. With a satisfied smile on his face, he slowly helped me sit down in the cab.

"Eric?" I asked before he shut the door.

"Yeah?"

"Can I have your hair tie?"

He reached up and pulled out the elastic band letting his hair tumble all around his shoulders. 'Wow'

252

was the only word going on through my head on repeat. Handing it to me without question, I took it and placed it on my wrist. "A personal reminder of what is waiting for me to return," I said softly.

"I'll be here waiting," he replied just as softly with a genuine smile on his face before shutting the door. With a wave, the cab took off toward the unknown.

*****

I sat down in one of the most uncomfortable chairs in the boarding area. My purse sat on my lap with a water bottle in my hand; it was the only way to keep my hands from fidgeting. I only had twenty minutes to wait. I could see the plane outside the big glass window. Every second felt like an hour watching one set of passengers get off, the crew from the prior flight come off and the new crew get on.

I pull out my phone and texted Eric: <u>Waiting for the flight crew to finish cleaning the plane.</u>

A second later I received a text back: <u>I've never travelled by plane before. Just road trips. Did u eat?</u>

<u>No.</u>

<u>U have a long flight Becki. Please eat.</u> Even on the run from a stalker, he had the wherewithal to worry about my diet. I texted back:

<u>I have snacks to munch on.</u>

All I wanted to do was tell him how much I wanted to go home to him, but that would've only made it harder on both of us. Wow, I didn't even feel attached to the house; I mean, it was gorgeous, but it wouldn't have been the same without him in it. Thinking about Eric started to make my pulse race and breath quicken. He brought out things inside that I never knew existed—emotions that had been dormant for so long.

Promise me that u'll make better decisions while I'm not there.

I'm the one who cooked. How did his presence make a difference in my eating habits? Reading between the lines, my lips lifted up in semblance of a smirk.

I promise no drinking, no craziness. I'll save that for when I get back to NY.

Oh thanks.

No problem. Time to board, text u when I land :).

As my section was called by the attendant, I stood in line. Looking out the glass at the big white airplane, I wondered if Eric would be interested in going on a vacation with me. He should experience some of the places that he liked to hang around his house. I gave my boarding pass to the attendant and headed down the small corridor that led to the plane's open door.

I appreciated Gary's attention to detail much more once I sat down in my window seat. While applying some lip balm, I felt my phone vibrate on my lap.

I'll be waiting :). Eric texted back. Smiling, I turned my phone off and closed my eyes.

Chapter 22
Saturday, September 22nd

The flight from New York to Phoenix wasn't terrible, but the puddle jumper from Phoenix to Tucson had my heart pounding with fear. Remembering that Piper plane wreck that killed one of my favorite R&B artists, Aaliyah, at the young age of twenty-two made me want to bribe a cab to drive me instead. I'm sure that would've given Gary a heart attack, not to mention that I would have been breaking my promise to Eric only a few hours after making it.

Arriving at the Tucson International Airport would have been intimidating if I hadn't departed from JFK. Glancing around my surroundings, I noticed a PGA Tour shop on my left side while following signs for the women's restroom. The ladies room symbol right next to the escalator down toward the baggage claim was lucky. After using the facilities, I washed my hands and face with cool water. It may not have given me energy, but it made me feel refreshed in a clean kind of way.

Taking the escalator down to the baggage claim, some of the passengers from my flight were huddled towards the left side of the area waiting for the carousel to start.

I texted Gary while waiting for my suitcase: <u>At the baggage claim, shouldn't be too much longer now.</u>

Taking advantage of my privacy, I dialed Eric.

"Hello?" his sleepy voice answered.

"I'm in Tucson," I replied softly.

"How was the flight?"

"The first was okay, but that puddle jumper almost made me take a flight back home," I admitted.

"I think I would've gone insane if I woke up next to you," he chuckled.

Spotting my suitcase on the carousel, I struggled to tug it off. "Ugh!" I grunted.

"What was that?" he asked, sounding alarmed.

"That was me hauling my suitcase," I responded, huffing a little.

"I'll have to get you to exercise more."

"Do I get a personal trainer?" I asked jokingly.

"You already have one. You just weren't aware of it." Smiling, I thought back to the last time I saw his body. Oh, yeah, he can help me work out any time.

"All right, well, get some sleep. I'll text you sometime tomorrow."

Yawning, he replied, "I'll try."

"Do me a favor?" I asked quickly. "Dream of me."

After a short pause, I heard his rugged voice admit, "I believe I was before you called, but I'll do my best to bring it back. Night, Becki."

"Good Night."

I rolled my suitcase behind me as I walked towards the sliding glass doors. Just as I reached the doors, Gary waltzed in. It looked like he had let his short black hair grow out a bit more. The longer hair enhanced his hazel eyes and his strong facial bone

256

structure. Had he always looked this attractive, or did I forget with time?

"Becki!" he acknowledged as he scooped me up into a hug.

Smiling through my unease of readjusting to him, I politely said, "Hey, Gary. Thanks for coming to get me so late."

"Don't mention it. Here, this is for you," he said, handing me a small bouquet of red and pink roses.

"Thanks." Bringing the flowers to my nose, I inhaled keeping close attention to them.

Gary pulled my suitcase while escorting me to his car. "I'm so glad that you made it. I thought you'd never come," he confessed softly as he leaned in close to my personal space.

"My court case was moved to Tuesday so I was able to get away," I commented as I slipped into my seat. Flowers? I hoped he wasn't trying to woo me into getting back together with him. The thought alone caused that edge to reappear causing anxiety in my stomach.

"Are you hungry? There are more options here than back in my neighborhood," he inquired after putting my suitcase in the trunk and sliding into his seat. Shaking my head, I laced my fingers in my lap while looking out the window.

While Gary drove us down the East Benson Highway, we pulled off on an exit that I would have easily missed had I been driving. Even in the dark I could see some of the landscape around me being shown off from the moonlight. The mostly flat land covered in sand with cactuses and rocks was only broken up by mountains in the distance. Gary chuckled at me when I yelped because a tumbleweed just happened to roll across the road in front of the car. I couldn't help it; I thought it was an animal of some kind.

"How's New York?"

"The same as you left it," I said, unable to stop the words from sounding like a double-edged sword. "Noisy, fast-paced and exciting," I added.

"Oh."

"Are you used to living out here yet?" I asked politely.

"It's going to take a bit more time, but it's a nice change. Although it does get lonely sometimes."

"I'm sure you'll make friends in no time," I replied instantly.

"Well, it seems you already have," Gary said.

My pulse instantly started racing. Was he referring to Eric? Of course not. He didn't know what's been going on. I couldn't help the extra layer of guilt that seemed to pile up on my skin. I stared straight ahead out of the windshield, afraid to look in his direction.

"What? You're not going to tell me about Barney?"

I chuckled aloud allowing the relief to pour out of me. "He is the biggest lap dog I've ever seen."

Gary shook his head in silence. His opinion obviously hadn't changed. Not that I expected it to. I'm surprised he even brought him up. I smiled to myself leaning against the window, thinking of my beloved Saint Bernard. Adopting him was one of the best decisions I'd made in years.

As Gary backed his car up into the driveway of a villa style house, I was pleasantly surprised at how cute it looked. The clay color of the two-story house was complimented by the white shutters and door. The stone path leading from the driveway to the front door was enhanced with the tiny versions of bushes lined up against the front side of the house.

"This is lovely," I heard my voice say without consciously meaning to. Hearing the pop of the trunk, he rolled out my suitcase.

"Thanks, it's much more spacious than the apartment. I was lucky that it came with some furniture."

He slid his key into the front door and let me step into the house first. I wasn't sure what I was expecting the inside to look like, but I was shocked to see how spacious it really was. The stairs on the right hand side led up to the second floor, but my feet kept walking straight ahead toward a huge family room. A kitchen was kitty cornered on the opposite side of the garage and connected to the dining room.

"What do you think?" he asked from behind me, but my face said it all. It was miraculously stunning. Even that description didn't do the house justice.

"Are you tired?" Gary asked while placing his arm around my shoulders leading me back to the stairs. He kindly carried my suitcase up the stairs and ushered me to the first room on the right. This was obviously the master bedroom because it was monstrously big with a king-sized canopy bed, the furniture all black and linen white.

"How many bedrooms do you have here?" I probed out of curiosity.

"It has four bedrooms and three bathrooms; there is one right here in the master," he said, pointing to the door on the left.

I couldn't sleep in the same bed with him—that was just too strange. He chose his future regardless of whether I would be along for the ride. Closing the space between us, he put his hands on my shoulders pulling me into an embrace.

"Are you ready for bed? I can help you unpack in the morning. This bed is so comfortable, you will pass right out," Gary enthused while rubbing his hand up and down my back.

"Would you mind if I sleep..." Unsure how to finish my sentence without offending him, I just nodded my head in the direction of the hallway.

"Really?" he asked with raised eyebrows. "We used to sleep together all the time."

"I know that. I would just feel more relaxed in my own space," I said, hiding my eyes from any type of look he may be sending my way. Taking a step back from me, I could feel his eyes looking me up and down to assess why I might not want to share a bed with him. "And a hot shower wouldn't hurt," I added.

"Okay..." he said politely, but I could hear the strain in his voice

Down the hall, he opened the door to a smaller room. "This is the next size down, the bed is only a twin size because it came with the house, but I was told the mattress is soft." Looking around the room, I noticed a medium-sized closet and two windows overlooking the front yard with the bed pushed against the window.

"Do you want to join me downstairs to catch up after your shower?" he inquired.

"I'm really tired. I've been up since seven my time, and with all the travelling and packing…" My voice trailed off and the echo of the silence was deafening. I wasn't sure what else there was to say. "Can we catch up in the morning?"

"Yeah, okay…" Gary said even though it was clear he wanted to talk tonight. "The bathroom is the next door on the right. If you need me, just come get me," he advised before hesitantly retreating to his own room.

I kicked off my sneakers and tried to stretch out my toes. I was so tired, but there was no way I could get in this clean bed after my long day and flight here. Unzipping my case, I pulled out my pajama top, but when I looked for my bottoms, I spotted Eric's grey pants instead. I didn't remember packing those in here. Did he? Smirking, I grabbed the rest of my toiletries and headed into the bathroom where a scalding shower made me feel like a woman again. Slipping into his pants, I had to cuff the bottoms, but they made my butt look cute. Was this his way of trying to stake a claim on me?

As I walked back towards my designated room, I couldn't stop myself from looking at Gary's bedroom door. I couldn't force myself to take a step in that direction. There were too many warning signals going off in my mind. The last thing I wanted was to confuse him into thinking that we were getting back together.

It was strange being where my future could have led, sleeping in a house where my past was only a few doors away. All while wearing the pants of what? A future? Who knows?

I climbed into my twin-sized bed, and I thought back to the conversation Eric and I had earlier. He said he was dreaming of me prior to me waking him up. With that simple knowledge, I drifted off to the land of nod.

*****

The smell of coffee lured me out of bed into the blinding sunshine streaming into the kitchen. "I knew this would get you up," Gary chuckled while pulling toast out of the toaster.

"It's my weakness," I confessed, chuckling along with him before stretching out my arms over my head.

"How'd you sleep?" he asked while setting down two plates and two big mugs filled up to the brim.

"Really great, actually. You?" I asked, walking up to the dining room table.

"It was okay. What are you wearing?" he asked, confusion wrinkling his forehead.

"Pajamas," I stated while sitting down and lifting the cup to my lips.

"You used to wear a matching set to bed; this doesn't look like you at all," he commented making further observations.

"I used to do a lot of things," I replied softly while taking another big gulp. While Gary looked about to start a conversation that it was way too early in the morning to have, I jumped in first. "What are our plans for the day?"

"Um...I was planning on showing you around town and then maybe a movie?" he suggested, unsure of my mood.

"Sounds good to me," I said, chugging the last bit of coffee down. Leaving the toast behind, I hopped off to shower again.

Washing my hair and then styling it with lots of hair spray, I wore it down with the scrunch look again. I didn't know why, but it made my cheekbones and eyes pop in a good way. I dressed in my skinny jeans, navy flats and my white boat neck shirt with navy stripes. Placing my nightwear under the covers in my bed, I walked out into the living room where Gary was watching TV. His expression said it all—not that I wanted to hear it from him of all people, but it was nice to see.

"Wow."

Unable to keep the smile from forming on my lips anyway, I picked up my purse and placed it over my shoulder. "I'm ready when you are."

*****

The shopping options in Vail where Gary lived were much more limited than New Rochelle, but a half hour trip back to Tucson gave us all the opportunities we needed for entertainment. Luckily for Gary, we just window shopped at a few places that caught my eye, and I assisted him with the few purchases for the house. There were a few things I wanted to purchase for Eric, but I wouldn't have been able to explain that to Gary or been able to fit anything else into my suitcase. After a small lunch at a deli, we walked the few blocks over to the cinema.

"How about a romantic comedy?" he offered, remembering my preference for love and laughter. That genre would be sending all the wrong signals to him. Deftly trying to avoid that, I suggested something else.

"How about action? I'm in an action kind of mood today."

"Since when?" he asked with a dumbstruck expression. "I begged you for years to see at least one and you never would." Shrugging my shoulders, I stepped up to the next empty box office window.

"Two tickets for that Sylvester Stallone movie," I requested while pulling cash out of my wallet.

"What do you think you're doing?"

"You paid for my flight. The least I can do is pick up movie tickets," I said, sliding the money under the window to the attendant.

Grumbling, Gary walked off to the concession stand while I was waiting for my change. I didn't know what the big deal was; I did have a job, and I was my own woman now. I followed his trail, and just as he finished ordering for himself, he turned to me.

"Do you want Twizzlers or do you not like them anymore?" he asked a tad sourly.

"I love them, thanks," I said, turning my head away from him so he didn't see my smile. He was acting like such a child right now. It's not like I was being unreasonable.

"Do you want to share a soda, or shall I buy you a separate one?" he asked, his tone still sour.

"I don't mind swapping spit with you," I replied before chuckling at him. Shaking his head, he continued to order popcorn and paid the cashier.

As I led the way to the auditorium, I felt the unease of being watched again. Looking behind me, I didn't see anyone or anything out of place. How could I?

"What are you looking at?" Gary asked, automatically placing his hand around my waist.

"Nothing, I just thought I saw something." Finding a seat at the very top of the auditorium in the right hand corner, I ripped open my bag of Twizzlers and started munching on them.

"I still can't believe we are actually going to watch this," he said excitedly but still concerned as to why I had a change of heart.

"A little action every once in a while is good for the soul," I said, leaning towards the cup holder to sip our soda.

Halfway through the movie, I got the distinct feeling as though I was being watched again. Leaning forward in the darkness, my eyes scanned around below but nothing seemed to be abnormal. Maybe I was just creeping myself out. Relaxing back into my seat, I felt Gary's arm lightly touching my neck and shoulders. A quick glance to the side showed that he was resting it more on the seat than actually touching me. I didn't need to make this something that it

265

wasn't. I didn't want to lead him on, but I felt like I had been kind of rude to him all day. Sighing, I scarfed down a handful of popcorn.

After the movie ended, Gary asked, "Are you tired? We can call it an early night if you want."

"I wouldn't mind that." With his hand on my lower back, he led me back to the car where I buckled myself into my seatbelt.

"What did you think of the movie?" I asked to be polite.

"I enjoyed it; the guns and fighting scenes were amazing. What about you?"

"It was good. Thanks for letting me choose." Other than the creeps that chilled my body, the movie was filled with humor and lifted my spirits.

Once we arrived back at Gary's house, we sat down on the living room couch and Gary channel surfed for anything good on the TV. Kicking my shoes off, I curled up with my legs under me.

"Becki, I wanted to talk to you about something." Glancing to the side, Gary was angling his body in my direction.

"Sure, what's on your mind?" I asked, trying to stay calm.

"My hope for when you came to visit was that we could work out some kinks from our relationship. However, it seems to me like you aren't interested in trying to work anything out," he stated, boring his hazel eyes straight into mine, evaluating my reaction.

"I wasn't aware that we had anything to work out? You didn't explain anything to me over the phone," I replied, trying to dodge the conversation by pleading ignorance. I knew deep down that this conversation would come up, but it didn't make it any easier. Scooting closer to my side, he placed his hand on top of mine. Unable to stop my body from going completely rigid, I tried to take slow, deep breaths.

"Becki, I'm in love with you. Nothing in the world can change that—not time or space. I have spent the past few weeks here practically miserable. All I think about is you, all I dream about is you, and I want to know what I can do to make this work," Gary spoke sincerely while squeezing my hand. I couldn't tell him that I was seeing someone else because it simply wasn't true. Eric hadn't established that we were a couple, and with everything going on, it wasn't ranked high on the list of things to do.

There was no reason for Gary to be trying to rekindle our relationship. He should be living his life and moving on. "Gary, you made the best decision for your life when you decided to move here. I will always love you and nothing can change that. You just need to choose the best options for your life as you can."

"You were the best thing to ever happen to me, sunshine. I can make you happy here, let me show you." And before I could make a rebuttal, he crawled over me, kissing me passionately. I tried to push him back, but Gary was misreading my attempts to remove him. Pulling my body closer to his with one hand, he used the other to start to feel me up.

"No!" I shouted against his mouth, and slowly but surely, he pulled back slightly.

"Becki, what's wrong?" he asked, noticing the fear I felt inside creeping out in my facial expression.

"I'm...I can't be the girl."

"What do you mean? You've always been the one; I've known it since our first kiss."

Shaking my head to ward off anymore advances, I responded slowly, "I'm not that girl anymore. I'm not blaming you for picking your job over me; I'm not blaming you for moving away, but I've had a lot to deal with since you left. I didn't have a choice except to take care of myself."

"I didn't mean for it to seem that I was choosing this job over you, but don't you see that you did the same thing? You refused to leave New York for every reason you could come up with, not one of the reasons to come was for me. I don't hold you responsible for that, but I'm not letting you go without a fight. I love you, and I want you," Gary said, leaning in close to me again.

"I'm not available for the taking," I admitted, looking down at my hands.

"Wh...What are you trying to tell me? You've moved on to someone else already?" he asked, but I could hear the anger in his voice.

"No, I'm single, but I'm out of commission. I can't be with anyone right now...I don't want to be. I just need to have some Becki time. Okay?" I asked, looking up into his eyes. Watching him take his own deep breath, he nodded.

"I'll be waiting for you when you are ready."

"Gary, you need to live your life. Please don't waste your time waiting for me. In all honesty, I could never move out here no matter how pretty it is. It's just not meant for me." My hands kept fidgeting with the unpleasant conversation. "I'm pretty tired," I admitted softly as I slowly leaned forward and picked up my shoes.

"Yeah...okay...get your rest," he said in a stunned slowness. I wanted to comfort him, but he would only take it the wrong way. I shouldn't have come; I should have stayed in New York.

Shutting my bedroom door, I plopped down on the bed. Gary was right; I chose my career over him just as much as he picked his over me. I never even asked him to stay for me, and he practically begged for me to move here for him. I was so busy being stressed out and overwhelmed that I didn't see the fact that I was running away from him instead of begging him to stay.

Gary clearly told me how much he loved me, wanted a future with me, and my insecurities hindered my view of him doing something for me. Laying my head back into the pillow, I tried to keep my crying to a minimum. I'd hurt him so much without even knowing I was doing so. Hearing the buzz in my purse, I pulled out my phone and read a text from Eric:

Haven't heard from u. R u ok? Let me know.

I'm fine. Hope all is well with u and Barney.

Changing into my pajamas, I pulled the blanket up to my neck. Receiving another text, I reluctantly checked it:

U'll be home 2morrow. Barney and I r impatiently waiting.

Unable to really hold a conversation with him, I texted back: C u then. I'm tired. Good night.

My mind relentlessly regurgitated all my past mistakes while dating Gary. Why would he still want to be with me? I clearly let other people rank over him repeatedly without even noticing.

As I rolled over to my side, I heard a soft knock on the door. "Come in," I said, wiping my face dry of any tears that might still be visible. Gary slowly came in and shut the door behind him. I sat up and pulled my legs up pretzel style, waving my hand for him to sit.

"Did I do something to make you unhappy with me?" he asked, and the ache in my chest burned right down to the pit of my stomach.

"No, I'm just a terrible person. Gary, you are so wonderful, any girl would love to have you in their life."

"Any girl but the one I want," he lamented, looking deep into my eyes.

"I'm sorry," I apologized, no longer able to control my feelings; I leaned my head against the wall and let my tears fall in shame. "I'm sorry that I failed to be the one you needed. I can't give you what you need, Gary. It's not that I don't want to."

"Becki, you have no idea how amazing you truly are."

Shaking my head, I finished my confession. "Gary, I never asked you to stay for me. I wanted you to choose me over your job because you loved me. My issues never even let me offer it up to you; I just let you leave and caused you more pain because of it. Please don't waste your time trying to be with me or anyone else like me. I wish the best for you, but that isn't me," I said, practically hiccupping while crying.

Gary wrapped his arms around my shoulders and let me cry out everything. I cried about our relationship, my issues, his issues, my family issues and work issues. By the time I finished, I thought Gary had fallen asleep beside me.

"You have so many negative thoughts of yourself, sometimes I want to strangle you," he said, chiding me. "Go to sleep, sunshine. I'll stay with you until you drift off. Tomorrow is a brand new day," Gary said before leaning in and kissing my cheek gently. I laid my head back on the pillow and closed my eyes.

Chapter 23
Sunday, September 23rd

The rays of sunlight slipping between the blinds heated up the room temperature. Wanting more sleep, I tried to duck my head under the pillow but something was obstructing my plan. I opened one eye slightly and spotted the reason; Gary's head and arm were on it. I should have felt frustrated or annoyed, but I couldn't bring myself to feel anything. Last night didn't go as planned for either of us so why kick up a fuss about nothing? The slow rise and fall of his chest led me to believe that I hadn't disturbed him. Assessing the conversation we had, I realized no matter how much of myself I gave to Gary physically, I never emotionally let him in.

I accepted our easy relationship with comfort, ups and down just being from our moods, but the passion he held for me always gave me the confidence to go on with my life. Gary was my rock, and I took him for granted without a second thought. Feeling the uncomfortable jab in my side, I found my cell phone that I never put away. Opening it, I read a text from Eric:

Night.

I didn't know what I was expecting to read, but I was underwhelmed to see that.

I slowly tried to climb out of bed without nudging Gary. I picked up a set of travelling clothes from the suitcase and headed to the bathroom. Turning on the shower, I let the water warm up before hopping on in. One quick glance at the mirror's reflection made me want to throw something at it. My eyes were all puffy and bloodshot and my hair was sticking up in every direction. After getting all cleaned up, dressed up and pinning my hair into a messy bun, I walked back into my room.

"You're up early," he accused with a raspy voice.

Chuckling, I nudged his arm. "You took over the entire bed." Gary sat up and took in my clothes.

"What time is it?" he asked, wiping his eyes.

"It's only ten."

"All right, I'm going to grab a shower and then let's get breakfast," he said, crawling out of bed, stumbling toward the door. "How does that sound?" he asked, hesitating at the door. I smiled broadly back at him and nodded.

While packing up my suitcase with all my toiletries and clothes, I thought about my relationship with Eric. We'd kissed and talked a little, but for some reason I kept trying to force him to sleep with me. How was I supposed to expect him to open up to me physically when I couldn't even have a conversation with him without running away? I'd never thought of myself as a runner, but maybe that's because I don't run; I hide and wait for whatever happens to just happen.

Thinking about all the conversations that we've had, the only person divulging information was him. He didn't know anything about me, not really. He knew only of my life in New York while he has disclosed two of the most horrendous incidents of his own. Why would I expect him to want to have a relationship with a live-in stranger?

While making my bed up nicely, I went into my contacts on my phone and hit call. "Good morning, how'd you sleep?" Eric greeted.

"Eh, okay I guess. What about you?" I asked.

"I was having a hard time sleeping all night so I got up and went into my office and attempted finishing my book," Eric stated.

There were so many thoughts going through my head and so many emotions wanting to break out of my chest, I couldn't seem to put words together.

"Is everything all right?" he asked after my silence lasted too long.

"I'm ready to be back in New York," I admitted, not wanting to come off as needy.

"I'm ready for you to be here. Don't forget that tonight we are celebrating."

"Are you going to cook?" I asked, chuckling.

"My lips are sealed. What time does your flight touch down?" Eric asked.

"Around six, but I should be home for half past seven at the latest depending on how the traffic is."

"Sunshine, are you ready?" Gary called out while shutting his bedroom door.

"Be there in a minute," I called back to him with my hand covering the phone.

"Well, I'll let you go," Eric said quickly.

"I'm just grabbing some breakfast before my long flight back. You know, following your instructions to

274

'make better decisions,'" I joked, imitating his rugged voice.

"I don't sound like that," he said before adding, "Do I?"

Unable to hold my laughter in, I put my hand over my mouth. "Sometimes. Enjoy the rest of your day."

"Thanks. See you later," he replied before hanging up.

Rolling my suitcase into the living room, I found Gary patting down his pockets.

"Looking for something?" I asked, cocking my head to the side.

"My keys...last night I put them..." Smirking, I picked them up from the new dish we purchased yesterday. "Here you go," I said, handing them to him.

"Thanks, I guess I will have to get used to that."

*****

Gary and I shared a plate of pancakes with sausage at a lovely diner. It seemed so warm and comforting, like I'd been here before. Maybe it reminded me of my hometown where there was a diner just like this. The cakes were so fluffy I felt like I could eat them with just my tongue alone, and the service was pleasant without seeming fake. I'd love to eat at my diner again.

"Told you that you'd like it here," he commented with a smile before popping some sausage into his mouth. I couldn't even take the dazed look off of my face from the delicious meal. I was going to need to start exercising. I could feel the pounds adding up as I swallowed.

"Thank you so much, Gary, for having me come visit. Your home is so beautiful."

"You only have to let me know, and you can come back. If I can persuade you to stay, that would be better," he admitted, smirking at me.

Shaking my head, I wiped my mouth clean before saying, "I have a court case to get back home to. You should visit your folks, though. I happen to know that you are missed by them a great deal."

Gary sipped his coffee before he said, "I know, but it hasn't been that long. I will eventually make my way back to see them, but I'm still getting settled here. I guess I sort of understand what your family puts you through."

Hearing those words, my face broke out in the biggest grin my cheeks could take.

"Finally." I sipped my coffee while Gary went up to the register to pay.

The thoughts of staying here with him forced themselves upon me. The beautiful home he had which I would love to decorate myself. The extra bedrooms allowed options on how many children we could have. And a backyard where they could play safely in their quiet neighborhood without worries of being in a city. The life I passed up.

"Come along, sunshine. You have a flight to catch," Gary advised while checking his watch, taking my hand and assisting me to the vehicle.

Chapter 24
Sunday, September 23rd

On the cab ride home, the traffic was so horrendous that I figured my whole paycheck would be going to the cab driver. Checking the time on my phone it read out that it was almost seven. I texted Eric:

Stuck in traffic. Might not make it until around 8.

At least the flight wasn't so bad this time. I felt that Gary and I left on such a good note that I didn't have to worry about further confusion of our relationship. Gary was a great boyfriend, and I had faith that he was an even more amazing friend.

The vibration of my phone alerted me to a text:

Running l8e so that works out. Tired?

A little but should be on my second wind by the time I arrive.

Glancing up, I saw traffic was due to a three car accident. Stupid rubberneckers were keeping my free lane blocked up.

Looking back down into my lap, I noticed a new text:

Good to know.

Smiling to myself, I thought over my plan for tonight. The main reason Gary and I ended up coming unglued in our relationship was because I wasn't willing to let him in. Well...that and Eric. I vowed to be more concerned about the needs of my other half and reassuring him of my feelings so that there was no question of my loyalty. I knew that I didn't want to put myself out there because I didn't handle rejection well, but I could at least admit the obvious. Sinking into the corner of the backseat and door, I laid my head on the window and rested my eyes.

The vibration of the vehicle slowing down to a quiet purr made me blink my eyes open. Finally back to reality, I reached into my purse. "How much?" I asked the driver.

"It has already been taken care of, miss," the driver stated, waiting for me to get out. That explained why the driver had been standing at the airport with a sign for me. I pushed open my door and pulled my suitcase out behind me onto the driveway.

"Have a good evening," I said with a wave and trudged up the walkway to the front door.

As I opened the screen door, I looked up into the most beautiful blue eyes I'd ever seen in my life. The tingling in my chest from his presence exploded to every orifice of my body. My cheeks started to hurt from smiling so widely at seeing him, but I couldn't help it. The pure pleasure of being in his proximity was so intoxicating.

"Close your eyes," he said softly, and I followed right on cue. Leaving my case just inside the door, his hands guided me slowly making sure I didn't hit any walls on the way.

"All right, open them," he said, ushering me forward.

The first thing to catch my eye was the mass of balloons surrounding the table with messages saying: 'Welcome Home!' and 'We Missed You!' The next was the beautifully laid out table with flowers that accented the china. Eric pulled out the chair for me, and I sat down and took in the atmosphere in the dining room. Watching him sit directly across from me, I saw that he left his hair down tonight. Butterflies making their presence known in my stomach, I tried not to be too obvious while examining his attire which just happened to be a black long sleeve button-up and jeans. Thank goodness I decided to dress up a bit and wear my ruffled blouse on the way home, or I would have stuck out like a sore thumb tonight.

Eric reached to the middle of the table where a small silver bell was sitting next to his wine glass. Ringing it, I was astonished to see Lily waltz in with chicken parmesan and pasta. She surprised me again when she dished up four places, but I couldn't hide the huge grin on my face when Will followed behind her with a big bottle of wine and filled our glasses up with a stylish flourish. Just as Will sat down to my left, I caught Lily hitting play on the iHome stereo system where classical music started softly playing as background music. Eric hovered over the table and lit two thick candles as Lily dimmed the lights low before sitting down on my right.

Speechless, I looked up at Lily with the biggest smile on my face. Looking to my left, I smiled at Will, and saving the best for last, I smiled hugely at Eric.

"Surprise," he said softly.

"Thank you…so much. I can't believe you all did this for me," I said, the words catching a bit in my throat, glancing at Lily and Will including them in my appreciation.

"Let's dig in! I know for a fact this is going to be the best meal any of you have ever tasted," Lily stated with a smug smile upon her lips. Picking up my fork, I proceeded to 'dig in' to my delectable meal. I should have suspected something. I knew that Eric couldn't cook, but I had no idea that he would recruit my friends into this evening.

With everything that was going on right now, I couldn't believe he would put this together for me. It warmed my heart to know that he was willing to put aside the stress of the real world just to celebrate my arrival back.

"I'm glad that you made it back safely from your mini vacation," Will said.

Mini vacation, huh? "Me, too. You don't appreciate what you have around you until it's gone," I replied, smiling in his direction.

"So what was lacking out there? Other than me of course," Lily persisted while forking some chicken into her mouth.

Unsure of what to say to that, I managed to squeak out, "The town is really nice, but it just isn't for me. I prefer the night life," I said, sipping my water.

"So what did I miss while I was gone?" I asked generally, but I shouldn't have been surprised that Lily jumped in.

"I went purse shopping without you, so we have to make up for that next weekend." I nodded slowly, continuing my meal.

"Yes, please take her. I don't think I can handle another shopping trip," Will moaned, smirking at Lily's pout. Smiling at my friends, I glanced up in Eric's direction and caught him staring at me. I'd missed just being able to be in his company. The thought alone made me smile.

Smiling in my direction, he raised his wine glass. "To Becki." My friends, following suit, lifted their glasses to me. Feeling my face blushing furiously, I raised my glass and took a small sip.

The men cleared the table after we finished eating, and Lily put on her dance playlist. There wasn't enough room to dance in the dining room, but Lily insisted we lift the table and move it to the side. We carefully moved the table so we didn't knock over the candles and turned the music up louder. Pretending to be the guy, I took Lily's hands pulling her close to me and then twirling her out before pulling her back in again. To finish off my wonderful dancing skills, I dipped her back but almost dropped her when we heard a set of hands clapping from the doorway.

Laughing, I pulled her back up prior to pointing my finger in Eric's direction and playfully beckoning him. Watching him gracefully approach, I stifled back my sigh; he was way too attractive for his own good. Grabbing my hips he pulled me tight against his body before swinging me around in time with the music. I didn't anticipate Eric to be a good dancer to fast music, but he surprised me in more ways than one.

A slow song coming on next, I placed my hands on his shoulders and let him lead. His lips lifted into a smile and my stomach fluttered with his easy acceptance of my touch.

Behind me, Will sang along to the music. He was most likely directing it at Lily. Eric took one hand off of my waist and slowly ran his knuckles down my cheek. "I've been waiting for this moment all weekend long."

"So have I," I responded breathlessly.

Leaning forward until our foreheads touched, he sighed relaxing with me in his arms. I so badly want to brush my lips against his, but we had company, and Lily didn't exactly know how off kilter our relationship was. Feeling his hand slowly trail back down to my waist cinching me again, I desperately wanted to be alone with him. As I quickly glanced in my friend's direction, I could see Will serenading Lily romantically. They were wrapped up in their own little bubble. I'm sure they wouldn't notice.

Tilting my chin up slightly, awareness lit up Eric's eyes before he conceded and our lips touched briefly. I swore in that moment birds flew out of the flowers on the table and the candles roared up to the ceiling. As Eric slowly pulled back, the smoldering of his baby blues alerted me that he also felt the intensity of our kiss. Laying my head against his chest, I felt him rest his chin on top of my head while finishing up the dance. I was so happy just to be back in his arms, my peaceful place.

When I reopened my eyes, Lily's face appeared shocked with widened eyes. Figures. She would pay attention to me while her boyfriend was being affectionate with her. Rolling my eyes, I walked over to the table to drink more water.

"It's after ten o'clock, and we have to get up early in the morning. We're going to head back to Roc City," Will said with his arm tenderly draped on Lily's shoulder.

"Thank you both for coming. I wouldn't have been able to pull this together without your assistance," Eric said, warmly shaking Will's hand.

"Thank you so much for doing this for me," I gushed. "I think I'm still in shock," I admitted, chuckling.

Lily, giving me a tight hug, whispered, "You're not the only one who's shocked here, girlie. We have some catching up to do."

I nodded, my smile eluding my control and proceeded to walk them out. I closed the door after them making sure they got into their car safely and locked the deadbolts, chain, regular lock and scanned my finger for the security system.

Spinning around, I was abruptly pushed back against the door.

"Finally," Eric said breathlessly before crushing my lips with his. My heart pounded so loudly it felt like it was going to jump out of my chest and start its own drum line. His lips trailed down to my neck where I was lost to the most pleasurable feeling in the world. Leaning my head back against the door, all I could do was try to breathe, but his kisses finding my weak spot just above my collarbone made my knees tremble.

"Eric," I practically moaned before his lips stopped.

"I've wanted to make you say my name like that all evening," he admitted, grinning at me. Playfully pushing on his chest to make him step back, I slipped back into the dining room. I needed to stick to my plan regardless of how much I wanted to get him in bed. I started to blow out the candles and collect the flowers before I suddenly felt his hands on my waist.

"What are you doing?" he asked seductively. I wished there was a switch I could flip to turn him on and off.

"Cleaning up so we don't have to wake up to a mess tomorrow," I replied, but his hands tugged me quickly back against him and away from the table.

"I'll take care of it later. Right now I just want to be close to you," he admitted, rubbing his nose up my neck to my jaw and then back down.

I really didn't want to make the same mistake twice, but how was I supposed to resist? "Come upstairs with me," he persuaded as he started ushering me in the direction of the staircase. As we got close to my suitcase, I grabbed the handle to take it up only to have Eric take it from my grasp and haul it up for me. Once in my bedroom, I went to my dresser and pulled out my night clothes.

"I need to take a shower. I'll see you in a few minutes, okay?" I said, unable to look up at him.

"I'll be here," he said, going into my closet.

I pinned my hair up so it didn't get wet and set the shower to cool. I needed to have my wits about me when I went back in my room; I needed to express myself to him before having any physical interactions. It was as much for his benefit as it was mine. Drying off and putting on my matching silk pajama set, I strolled back into my room.

"Did you enjoy the surprise I left you in your suitcase?" he asked.

"They kept me warm in my tiny twin-sized bed." I replied, chuckling at the memory.

With a raise of his eyebrow as a response from him, I crawled into bed saying, "It was a comfortable little bed, but I sure missed this one."

"Oh, did you?"

"Yep, this bed is not only big and comfortable, but I get to sleep with a famous author every night. What girl would turn that down?" I said, nudging his shoulder with mine. With a serious expression on his face, he leaned in close to me.

"There are a lot of things I want to discuss with you, questions I want to ask and answers I need to give you that are rather important." I nodded and waited for him to start.

As he kissed my forehead and I felt him inhale against my skin, I brought my head up ready for his questions, but his lips pressing against mine slowed down my thought process. "All of that can wait until tomorrow, though," he continued. "Now that you are home safe," he finished before kissing me again.

No! I needed to figure out how to get him talking. I couldn't get side-tracked.

"Eric…" I said against his lips. "Please talk to me." He cocked his head to the side with a confused look.

"Is there something wrong?"

I took a deep breath. "I wouldn't say that there is something wrong exactly, but I did want to talk to you about everything."

"You want to talk to me about everything...that sounds like it could take quite a while," he said, rubbing his hand gently against my cheek.

The gesture made me feel so cherished and content that I couldn't help but relax a bit against him. "Not too long, actually. I just wanted to get some things off of my chest," I said and watched as Eric assessed my mood before he agreed. No admitting feelings, just facts to get my point across.

"When I was in North Carolina, my parents were always taking care of me. Even when I went to college almost three hours away, they found a way to swing by my dorm constantly or make up reasons for me to come home every weekend. Needless to say, I moved away to New York for some real space." Eric laid back against the headboard and pulled me close against him rubbing his hand up and down my back.

"I guess that is when I emotionally shut down after I moved here. I met Tim at the bar, he was interested in me, and it seemed safe enough being with him because I didn't actually have to do anything. I don't have commitment issues; I just found it easier to not express myself," I confessed and glanced up at Eric. Understanding the seriousness of this conversation, he nodded for me to continue.

"I met Gary soon after breaking it off with Tim. Gary had everything that I wanted from life—the motivation to strive for a better career, the family that lovingly supported him from afar without guilt trips, and the emotional bond that I needed. I've been so emotionally closed off out of fear of being hurt—maybe out of fear of turning into my parents and being a clingy person, I really don't know why—but when Gary left me behind..." Taking a deep breath, I tried to finish my sentence. "When he left, I felt sucker punched."

"Becki, why are you telling me this?" he asked emotionlessly, but I couldn't tell if he was worrying that I was getting back with Gary or that I was going to hurt him, too.

"When I was in Arizona, I had a revelation. Gary, as I predicted, did try to rekindle our relationship which I refused. However, it hit me like a ton of bricks after our conversation that night, we didn't break up because he left me for a job in another state. We broke up because of me, because I was afraid of being able to trust in him. Afraid of letting him in."

"That makes sense. If you were running away from the clingy love from your family, it would set off all types of alarms in your head when Gary was starting to give you the same signs," he said, continuing to rub my back and relaxing a bit more.

"I made a decision that I'm going to stick to. I'm not going to make the same mistake again. I don't want to run and hide anymore, so I'm going to be more honest and forthcoming from now on about myself and things going on in my life," I stated, looking deep into his eyes to make sure that he comprehended everything.

"I'm happy for you that you have had a learning experience that opened your eyes. You know you can always tell me anything," he said, leaning in to brush his lips against mine, but I pulled back before he reached me.

"I think it would be best if we were more familiar with each other."

287

Furrowing his brow he asked, "What are you saying exactly?"

I knew I was going to regret having this conversation, but I'd already said most of it; there was only one last bit left. "I've made the mistake in the past of getting physically involved to easily hide from anything more that I needed to give. I want to give the person that I'm in a relationship with all of me, not just physically." Afraid to look up at him, I focused on his bare chest watching his breathing that was before deep and slow, quicken with stress.

Against my better judgment, my eyes flickered up to his face and saw the frozen panic I hoped wouldn't be there. Sighing, my mouth continued, "I'm not asking anything of you, Eric. I'm just being honest with about what I can and can't deal with. I care about you, and the last thing I'd ever want to do is hurt you. I'm just..."

"Becki...you are the only real friend I've ever had. Please believe me when I say that. I would have never invited you to move in with me if I had felt differently. I do get what you are saying, mostly," he said, clearly missing my point.

I'd laugh if it wasn't so depressing to hear. Eric thought that I was just a friend. There was no way in hell that I was going to be able to finish what I was saying now. I rolled over on to my back and stared at the ceiling trying to think through what I should say, but the 'friend bomb' had been set on repeat. I had the strongest urge to lash out at him, but I knew better than to do that. He considered me a friend, his only friend at that. He deserved better than a tantrum, especially after all he had done for me.

Eric tilted his head in my direction. I smiled for his benefit. "I'm pretty sleepy; my second wind has come and gone."

Feeling the bed sink, I figured he was trying to kiss me good night but I just couldn't go through with it. I rolled over with my back to him and whispered, "Good night."

I shut my eyes in hopes that I could keep him from seeing my heart break apart into pieces. I really had set my hopes high for more with him without even realizing it.

"Night," he replied, bewilderment in his tone.

He clicked the lamp off on his bedside table, and just as I started to silently let my tears slip out, his hands wrapped around my waist pulling me back against his chest to spoon. This was my nightmare come true. I couldn't possibly think of a worse position right now. Concentrating on my breathing, I made sure he wouldn't notice the tension in my back. Swiping away the few tears from my cheek, my mouth opened to take a long, steady breath.

This was payback for all the mistakes I'd made in the past. Karma was making a full circle.

Chapter 25
Monday, September 24th

Assisting Ty in the bathing room, I was drying off a tiny kitten when I noticed how tiny her teeth were when she yawned. She was white with grey stripes on her back and an all grey tail. She was unique to her siblings being the only one with a grey tail. Her relaxed personality made me think of Barney. I recalled our nice morning walk around the block that ended with me rubbing his belly at the front door before leaving for work. Placing the kitten back in her cage with her siblings, I shut and locked it.

"Are you thinking about adopting another pet?" Ty asked from my side.

Shaking my head, I responded, "Just enjoying the happy parts of this job."

"You have a case tomorrow, right?"

"Yeah, I have to go over it one more time just to make sure I have everything ready, but I'm pretty sure we will come out ahead," I advised while placing the bathing towel down on the counter.

Wandering back into my office, I was abruptly taken aback to see Detective Johnson waiting for me at the door.

"Ms. Austin, I'm sorry to intrude on your time at work, but there seems to be a conflict of interest here," he informed, while I shut the door closed behind us.

"What would that conflict be?" I asked, settling down behind my desk.

"I spoke with your boss earlier this morning; you are currently working on a case against Kyle Reynolds?" Pulling out the file from my desk, I was shocked that I forgot all about that particular case.

Nodding in his direction while the details slowly reassembled themselves in my head he replied, "The conflict of interest in the case is Eric."

Confused, I began to ask how, but the details came flooding back quicker than I realized.

"I...I didn't know that," I said, stunned and mortified all wrapped up in one.

"I wouldn't have come across it if the court case pending with Kyle didn't include his brother. Curtis will not have to testify as there is proof of his being in custody at the time of the abuse; however, it would be prudent if this case was handed over to another associate. I've already cleared it with your supervisor."

I tried to unscramble my thoughts, but I couldn't get over the fact that Curtis was the one who not only did this to Eric, but this case was sitting on my desk the whole time. I just never put two and two together.

"Ms. Austin...do you understand what I'm telling you? You're being taken off of this case," Detective Johnson tried to reiterate.

Nodding, he stood up, but instead of leaving like I expected, he leaned in closely and commented, "Becki, I can see how concerned you are for him but trust me that he is well protected."

Giving him a small smile as my only response, he walked out closing the door behind him. I clasped the file together with a rubber band and headed to Judy's office.

"Come in," she said after my knock.

"I have the case file for tomorrow."

"Thank you. I have another case for you to take over," Judy said, handing me a thick folder.

"Okay," I said, turning to leave the office, but she stopped me.

"Becki, you are okay, aren't you?" I could only imagine what she thought having a detective come and pull me from a case.

"Yeah, I'm fine," I replied before shutting her door.

*****

The cool breeze in the air finally got my attention. I didn't exactly know how long I'd been sitting on the beach, and I barely remembered the drive here let alone making the decision to actually come here. Between watching the waves reflect the sunset and my unending thoughts, I didn't even hear my phone tinkling over and over. As I stood up and wiped the sand off of my behind, I headed back to the car not even bothering to call anyone back. I was pretty sure I knew who was calling, and I'd be seeing him soon enough as it was.

Driving up the driveway, Detective Johnson's car was pulled up in front. You have got to be kidding me, I wasn't that late. A quick glance at my watch showed that it was eight o'clock. Opening the front door, I heard paws running in my direction.

"Hey, Barney! I've been thinking about you today," I responded while rubbing his head affectionately.

Kicking the front door shut and locking it up, I headed into the kitchen to fill up Barney's bowl with fresh water. A shuffling of feet alerted me to approaching company. I placed his bowl down for him to drink before heading to the fridge to pull out premade salad for dinner.

"Ms. Austin—" I heard Detective Johnson start, but he was interrupted by Eric.

"Where have you been? I've been calling you for the last two hours."

"I had some things to work through. I'm sorry I'm late," I apologized. "Are you hungry?" I asked while pulling out a bowl.

"No," he stated curtly, walking closer to me but I kept my back to him filling up my bowl.

"Becki, what's going on?" he asked concerned about my too cool response.

I pulled out French dressing and put some on my salad without answering him. "I'm surprised to see you twice in one day, Detective Johnson." Opening up the utensils drawer, I collected my fork and proceeded to eat leaning against the counter.

"Becki..." Eric said, trying to look into my eyes, but I shook my head.

"I just needed to be alone. So, what's new?" I asked, glancing at Detective Johnson, trying to put the spotlight back on our guest.

293

"Curtis has disappeared. We haven't seen him since early this morning. When I called Eric to alert him, he let me know that you were also unaccounted for." Nodding, I kept eating my salad waiting for him to finish. "I'm glad that you were able to come home safely. We are still looking for him, though," he stated and turned to give his full attention to Eric.

"I'll call you when we find any new information," he said seriously while Eric walked him out.

I proceeded to clean my bowl and grab a water bottle from the fridge before ascending the staircase. Safely tucked away in my room, I changed into my pajamas prior to hearing my phone vibrate on the end table. Opening up my inbox, I saw that it was from Eric:

R u mad at me? Starting to feel overwhelmed emotionally, I answered honestly like I promised myself I would.

No. I texted back and then laid my head back on the bed.

Y won't u talk to me? he texted me back a minute later.

Stressed out. No sooner did the text send did I hear the tap on my door.

"Come in," I said, even though that was the last thing I needed right now. I just needed space, but he wouldn't understand unless I explained which I repudiated to do. Slipping in and shutting the door behind him, he slipped under the covers with me.

"I've been thinking about you all day today," he said gently as I placed my phone back on the end table.

"Oh, yeah?" I asked while settling back down into my pillow.

"After we talked last night, I learned a great deal about you. I wanted to let you know that I appreciate you disclosing your past to me."

I was glad that he was happy about it because I was particularly regretting it.

"I…I'm sure it's obvious to you that I don't have any friends, other than you, of course." There was that stupid word again. Maybe I should've just whacked him over the head.

He continued, "When I was young, my father was the one person I could tell my secrets to. I couldn't help but look up to him." Glancing up in Eric's direction I saw that he was lying back on his pillow also staring at the ceiling. "After…he was gone, I also shut down. My mother and I have had a strained relationship since. When she remarried and had Dane, I wasn't much of a son. I was never home; I never participated with family functions…as far as I was concerned, I didn't have a family."

Not wanting to interrupt his story, I rolled over to face him and gently grasped his hand. "It was my mother's birthday. I was supposed to be home getting dressed up for dinner, but instead I was walking around in town. I didn't notice the streetlights come on or where I was headed. Suddenly, I was waking up in a dark room, chained to a brick wall, and I was cold." Noticing him wince slightly, he went on, "You don't want to hear the details of what he put me through. I honestly don't know how I managed to survive at all.

"One day he had unchained me from the wall expecting me to be too weak physically to be any

295

challenge to him. All I could think about was my father, how he would have wanted me to fight for my freedom. For me to be a soldier like him. So when he wasn't paying close enough attention, I was able to kick him in the face as hard as I could. I don't remember the exact layout of the place, but I ran up the stairs and out the first door I could find leading outside. I didn't stop running until a police officer grabbed my arm."

I could feel my eyebrows furrow between concern and confusion. The look didn't go unnoticed as Eric glanced down at me and pulled me to snuggle against his side. "Detective Johnson was the one who noticed me. He said he could tell that I wasn't going to stop running, and he knew who I was because he had been assigned to search for me when I went missing." A soft kind of fondness gleamed in his eyes as he spoke of the detective. I hadn't realized their connection was more than normal protocol, but it all made sense now—they definitely had a special bond.

"I didn't know how long I was gone for, but I didn't expect it to be almost a year. My mother was a wreck when I finally came home. Dane never really understood what happened until he was in high school. I think that was their choice to protect him. They tried putting me in therapy, but I wouldn't talk about it to anyone. I shut out the world. I didn't need friends or family."

Running his fingers through my hair, he smiled softly. "No one has ever made me laugh as much as you. I don't think I've ever voluntarily smiled until the night we met at the banquet dinner. You were so different from anyone I've ever spent time with it made me want to get to know you better."

"What do you think of me now?" I asked, unable to bite my tongue.

"I think…no, I *know* you are more amazing than I gave you credit for then."

Incapable of controlling my actions, I brought my lips to his kissing him softly.

"Thank you."

Shaking his head he replied, "No, thank you."

Pulling me tighter against him, our kiss deepened, subtly changing. The light trails of his fingers gliding up my back and neck until he was holding my face in place made me shudder involuntarily.

"Becki…" he whispered against my lips causing me to open my eyes. "Touch me," he commanded softly.

"Where?" I asked with a small grin.

Practically growling, he responded, "Everywhere."

And I did.

Chapter 26
Tuesday, September 25th

Smiling into my coffee, I took a deep sip letting the warmth coat my insides. The nuzzling against the crook of my neck sent tingles down my back.

"What are you doing up so early?" I asked, watching Eric steal my cup of coffee and downing most of it.

"No idea," he replied sitting down next to me. "This is really good. What are you having?" His grin was contagious. I headed back to the coffee pot and poured another mug full before refilling the cup in his hands. I didn't seem to be the only one in a good mood this morning.

Settling back down next to him, we enjoyed our caffeine-based breakfast in a comfortable silence. The only sound besides our breathing was the lapping of water from Barney. After his confession last night and mine the night before, I felt that we were in such a better place than I imagined could be possible in such a short amount of time. The shining of his eyes angled at me urged me to touch him again, to run my fingers through his hair. I needed some sort of self-control, though, or I was never going to make it to work. Drinking the last drop in my mug, I reached out for his and took both our cups to the sink to wash.

Placing the mugs in the drying rack, I turned around to be engulfed by arms. Sighing contently, my head tilted up, and I watched as he brought his lips down to brush mine. I heard a low growl in the back of his throat as his hands slowly made their way from my upper back down to my hips. As much as I would enjoy a morning excursion with him, I needed to be getting to work. I pulled back slightly and felt the sigh from his lips more than hearing it.

"Stay," he pleaded with his eyes still smoldering at me.

"I wish I could, but I have a job where people depend on me to be there…on time," I said, playfully pushing him away and taking a half step back.

Slinging my purse across my body, I could still feel the heat from his warm embrace, but I was almost sure it was because he hadn't taken his eyes off of me since he came down to the kitchen.

"Do you like meatloaf?" I asked, indicating for him to come closer.

"I used to have it when I was a child, but I don't really remember."

"I'm going to make it for dinner tonight; my special sauce will make you drool. Just make sure to take the beef out of the freezer by three o'clock."

"Sure. See you tonight," he said, but looked hesitant to touch me again.

Reaching out, I placed my hands on his waist pulling him close. "I hope you have a good writing day."

Seeing him visibly relax after I made the first step to touch him this time, he responded, "Thanks. I hope you have a quiet day." I smiled at him one final time before heading out to my place of work.

*****

The morning dragged on slowly as my thoughts were mostly consumed by last night's actions. I had never expected him to open up to me about his past; I never brought it up because I wasn't exactly sure I wanted to hear it. I was lucky enough that he didn't go into detail because I think I might have gone all the way with him just to erase the horrible memories in his mind. As it was, I was slightly disappointed in myself for letting the physical happen at all, but I guess over-the-clothes touching wasn't too bad.

"Knock knock!" Lily exclaimed while coming into my office with more adoption papers. "I have a favor to ask if you don't mind," she said while slowly putting the paperwork on my desk.

"What's that?"

"I have a case coming up on Thursday, and I really need to finish getting it together, but I have a few background checks that need to be done and there is no way I can get it all done today. Would you mind helping me out?" she asked, begging with her eyes.

Nodding, I started to look through the papers. "Lunch with me, too?" she asked before shutting the door.

"Will do," I responded, picking up the phone to start calling around.

*****

Grabbing a slice of pizza from our favorite pizza parlor, Lily and I settled in the corner by the window.

"So, spill," Lily demanded while sipping her Coke.

"What is there to say?" I replied, evading the subject I could already see coming a mile away.

"Tell me what is going on with you and Eric! It's obvious that you two are officially together. Have you guys done it yet?" Lily badgered. Unable to hide my smile, she started exclaiming, "You did him!"

I quickly swatted at her. "Not so loud, please, and no, I haven't 'done him.' We are just friends,' I stated matter-of-factly while biting into my pizza.

Lily, looking skeptical, said, "That's bull if I ever heard it."

"His word, not mine. I'm his only friend. It's fine because I think I'd freak out if he was doing what we did last night with someone else," I said, feeling my cheeks blush mentioning it at all but unable to avoid it.

"So you didn't have sex with him?" she questioned again, clearly confused. Shaking my head, I explained that we only let our hands explore each other.

"Becki, I'm telling you this as a friend, so don't get mad at me, all right?" Lily started, and I already didn't want to hear it. "I know how you are when it comes to guys. I caught the tail end of your relationship of Tim, but I saw everything with Gary, and I just want to help you with Eric. You are great with the relationship part, God knows I have no idea what I'm doing, but I think you should take a fun class with me. Something like belly dancing or a tantra class? It's not about the dancing part, but it's about the confidence of owning your sexuality."

"Shut up!" I commanded, staring at her with wide eyes.

"No, I'm serious. You are such a prude that you can't even have a conversation with me about it without turning ten different shades of red. I'm not saying that you aren't confident, but it would help give you a different outlook on things. Plus, if we both do it and are terrible at it, we can enjoy a good laugh. What's the worst that can happen?" Lily finished before biting into her pizza slice again.

I wanted to throw my slice in her face, but I guess I was a little uptight when it came to sexual things. "I'll consider it," I replied unenthusiastically.

"How about this weekend? Becki!" she shouted at me.

"What?" I asked, shocked by her exclamation.

"Your birthday is Sunday! We should take a class to celebrate," she said, grinning from ear to ear.

"That isn't exactly my idea of a good time," I replied, sipping my water.

"How do you think you came into this world? Take a class and learn seductive ways from different cultures," she prodded with raised eyebrows and a smirk.

"I don't think—"

"No, I'm not taking no for an answer. I will call around when I get off work to set it up, and I'll text you the time and place."

Finishing our lunch, we slowly meandered back toward the office. "Are you still happy with Will?" I inquired out of curiosity.

"I'm getting itchy feet from being with him all the time. I think this class we're taking will help me get him excited about me again."

Cocking my head to the side I questioned, "Why do you think he isn't excited about you?"

Shrugging her shoulders she said, "He just doesn't look happy to see me when I come home anymore. I like him, but I think I need to do something a bit different to entice him."

Walking into my office, my cell phone started ringing almost instantaneously. I picked it up only to hear my mother's voice on the other end. "Well, hello, dear. I'm glad that I caught you."

She started and I could do nothing but let her ramble on. "I wanted you to be the first to know that we are going to be having a small Halloween Party set for October 27th and your father and I are requesting you to join us. I hope this is far enough in advance so you can fly down?"

Looking at my calendar, I marked the date as it was free. "Yes, Mother, I should be able to make it for the party."

"I would love for you to come for the whole weekend. You can easily fly here Friday night and go back Sunday evening," she stated matter-of-factly.

"I'll do what I can," I said, knowing how much it sucked to be flying after a long day at work.

"You can bring that fellow you've been dating if you feel like it, dear. I'm sure we can find somewhere for him to sleep," she said, trying to entice me with the incentive of meeting the man in my life. I was with

303

Gary for about three years and they couldn't have cared less to meet him.

"Actually, Gary and I broke up, Mother. I'm seeing someone else right now, but like I said, I'll do what I can. I must get back to work."

"Oh, I'm sorry to hear that. Talk to you soon?"

Shaking my head I replied, "Yes, I love you. Bye."

"Love you more. Bye," she said sadly, hanging up.

Chapter 27
Tuesday, September 25th

I finished the background checks for Lily before working on my newest case and managed to help get two of our elderly dogs adopted which was really hard to do. People always seemed to want puppies, so I found it very fulfilling that the older ones were taken in together by a middle-aged couple. The tinkling of my cell phone made me slide my hand into my pants pocket. The caller ID showing that it was Eric surprised me.

"Hey, what's going on?" I asked, confused. "You don't normally call me at work."

"I was calling to find out the same thing. It's almost seven o'clock."

"Oh, I'm running a bit late, sorry. I got a lot done today, though, so I have less to worry about tomorrow," I replied, putting my files away in my desk.

"I put the beef in the fridge so that it wouldn't go bad."

"Thank you. Actually, I'm glad you called. Do you have plans for October 27th?" I inquired while staring at my calendar. The background noise on his line sounded like he was heading into the office.

"No, I don't. Why?"

"I was invited to a Halloween Party and I have to be there. And I was wondering if you wouldn't mind joining me so that I can actually have a fun time?" I asked, trying to persuade him without the details.

I didn't want him to think I was bringing him home as my boyfriend or something since he only thought of me as a friend. Ugh...the word gave me indigestion.

"That sounds like fun. Count me in," he said excitedly. He wouldn't be so enthusiastic after he found out who was throwing it.

"All right, well, I'm heading out of here in a few minutes. No munching before dinner," I cautioned him.

"I'll be good. See you soon," he said before hanging up.

Sending a quick email to Lily to let her know that I finished her paperwork, I turned off my computer and shut my office door. It was pretty obvious that I was the only person still in the office area—the only workaholic staying late on a Tuesday night. Chuckling, I checked the kennel room to make sure everyone had enough water for the night.

Walking out of the building, I pulled out my car keys from my pocket. As I headed to my car a few feet away, an odd feeling of being watched sent a chill down my back. Deciding the best option was for me to quickly get in my car, I picked up my pace and unlocked the car before hopping in and slamming the door behind me, rapidly hitting the lock button. I put the key in the ignition and as the car purred to life, I quickly looked around my surroundings, but I saw no one in particular. I was such a nut. I just needed to get home.

While driving home I contemplated ordering fast food tonight. There was no reason to make a huge meal, especially since it was already so late. Meatloaf was one of my specialties and the urge to make it for Eric was extremely powerful. I should've just admitted my feelings openly to him; it might not be so scary if I just put it out there because he obviously likes me, too; and it would finally cease his use of the word 'friend.' Turning up the radio, I sang along while remembering the lovely night we had together.

I happily recalled the memory of Eric kissing me passionately and not panicking when I confidently rubbed my hands across his chest. The way his hair hung around me when he hovered to suck on my bottom lip and the caress of his fingers on my chest. I couldn't wait to get home to see the absurdly handsome author with whom I finally shared a romantic night. Almost missing my exit, I tried to keep my thoughts on the present. I just needed to get home safely so I could relive it.

The sight of the driveway was as glorious as seeing the first flakes of snow in winter. I slowed down and parked in the usual spot almost giddy with anticipation. I grabbed my laptop bag putting it over one shoulder and setting my purse on the other. Stepping out of the car, I walked steadily to the front door as my stomach started to flutter with eagerness.

The ringing of a phone inside the house caught my attention; I'd never seen Eric use a land line. Actually, when I thought about it, I'd never even seen it. I turned to take a step up the stairs, and just as I started to get that weird feeling of being watched again, I realized that I was falling to the pavement.

Chapter 28
Tuesday, September 25th

My first conscious thought was about the awful smell that was way too close to my nose for my liking. Backing away from the offending odor, I distinctively heard and felt heavy chains on my limbs. Trying to decipher my whereabouts, my left eye wasn't cooperating like it should have, and that's when the back of my head started to pound with the most intense throb I'd ever felt in my life. Above my head through the floor boards, an odd mewling noise reached my ears, but I couldn't seem to pick up any other sounds.

A nicely decorated basement surrounded my body—there were white couches arranged by a coffee table with a big screen TV. Four tiny windows were covered with drapes and the walls were wood-paneled. This was a swanky place...but why was I here? Where was here? Glancing down, I saw that I was chained more or less to myself so that I couldn't get up and walk away, but I wasn't chained down to the floor.

The putrid smell attacked my nostrils, and the urge to vomit doubled with assistance from my head injury. My eyes scanned my surroundings looking for the cause. I was startled to see Curtis's lifeless body against the bottom of the staircase. At least, he looked and smelled dead. What was going on here? My hands patted down my pockets but to no avail. My phone wasn't there. None of my belongings were here.

I brought my hands up to my face and felt that my left eye socket was pretty puffy and tender. I must have come down pretty hard, that was me...sack of potatoes. Taking a deep breath, I tried to stand, but it was no use. Crawling didn't work either as the stupid chains didn't allow either of my legs to move separately. Trying to keep my tears at bay was useless as the situation really started to settle in. My vulnerability of being attacked freely here in this grand basement was pretty high.

The mewling noises finally ceased which made me look up to the ceiling. Was it a cat? A door creaking followed by slow and heavy steps was my only warning that someone was coming down the stairs. The first detail I took in was his black construction worker boots. Another step revealed his light faded jeans; another showed his brown baggy t-shirt with strong arms and hands gripping the railing.

Finally, his broad shoulders led the way to his thick neck with a frown looking permanently etched on his face becoming clearer the closer he reached the bottom of the staircase. His dark brown eyes were set like stones as he reached the bottom step and kicked Curtis's body over to the side. His shoulder-length blond hair looked dirty and matted.

"You fuck up," the man commented before kicking the body again, stepping over it and noticing me. "Well, look who finally woke up."

Stunned silent by his actions and worse, having him acknowledge my existence, my heart started jumping in double time. Walking slowly up in my general direction, he stopped a few feet before he was within reaching distance.

"Damn, your eye looks pretty bad. I didn't even get the pleasure of doing it myself, but don't worry, I'll have my fun with the other one." As he sunk down to one knee at my eye level, I instinctively tried to scoot back from his range, but the chains hindered my movement.

"What do you want from me?" I asked, almost biting my tongue off from trembling with fear.

"What don't I want from you? You just happened to be in the wrong place at the wrong time," he admitted before smacking me across the face with his open palm. Crying out in pain from my bruised face being assaulted a second time, I couldn't stop the instant tears from pouring down my face. My captor watched with an amused grin.

"Are you going to kill me?" I asked, shakily.

His eyes gazed directly into mine. "Eventually...when I get my fill." His words crawled over my skin like moss on a boulder...slowly, but unrelenting and unwanted.

"Please..." my lips mumbled and his lips lifted even more.

"Begging already? We haven't even begun." Tucking his hair behind his ears, he fisted the chains where my legs and hands were connected tugging until there was no space between us. My hands pushed back against his advances but were not much use. "Now, will you be good? I don't have any qualms about hurting you."

Panicked, my head nodded but the instinct to fight was strong. How could I get out of this? Reaching into his back pocket, he pulled out my cell phone and hope flared instantly in my chest. "You get to make one phone call. You only get to say what I allow, understand?"

This was my chance for help; my body involuntarily started to shiver with the adrenaline pounding. Accepting that as an answer, he punched a few buttons putting it on speaker phone.

The echo of the ringing lasted only a moment before a familiar, frantic voice answered. "Becki, are you okay? Where are you?"

My eyes closed at the sound of his rugged voice, soothing even throughout this ordeal.

"I'm okay." Fingers quickly pinched my chin to raise my head, demanding I look straight at my captor.

"Where are you? I'll come to you," Eric asked again.

"I don't know."

"What? Did someone take you?" My mouth opened to reply when his grubby hand clamped over my mouth. A piece of folded paper was put into my hands and while reading it over, the reason for this call finally hit me.

"Listen to me, please. I need you to do everything that I tell you to the letter, all right? That is the only way."

"Is he there with you right now?" Eric persisted, practically growling into the line which caused my captor to smile even more.

Ignoring his question, I continued, "No more police involvement."

"Rebecca—"

"Just listen to me!" I shouted at him over the phone as my nerves jumped under my skin. "The penalty for anything that goes wrong is..."

My captor nodded for my mouth to continue, but my will to speak eluded me. How did he expect Eric to react?

Grabbing the phone from my hands, he finished, "Her demise. It won't be quick and painless, either. And she will have you to thank for that."

"Curtis, why are you doing this?" Eric demanded and my captor chuckled.

"Curtis is decomposing ten feet away from your girlfriend." The silence stretched over the phone line for a moment.

"Eric, please," I begged in hopes that he wouldn't antagonize him.

"Take your time...we can wait," he sneered before backhanding me across the face causing an involuntary yelp.

"No! Stop hurting her!" Eric shouted across the phone as my whimpers flowed out.

Before my eyes could even process what was happening, he was on top of me shouting in my face. "Shut up or I'll shut you up!" Punching me in the stomach, I could do nothing but try to catch my breath.

"I'll do it, just stop!" Eric yelled over the phone listening to my cries and grunts of anguish.

Squinting his eyes back at me, he said, "I think I'm going to have some fun after all..." His hands gripped my throat. Unable to catch my breath, I pleaded with my eyes for him to stop, but a disturbingly genuine smile crossed his face in response to my panic. This guy wasn't going to let up. I couldn't believe this was it; I was going to die right here. Eric was going to know what it sounded like when I died.

My mother was right; I should have stayed in North Carolina. Trying to slip my hands apart and out of the chains hurt so badly, but it gave me reason to fight against him. Unfortunately, he doubled his efforts against my windpipe and blackness enveloped me entirely.

Chapter 29

"Fucking cops." I heard grunting somewhere near my feet. My head kept spinning around causing my focus to lag.

The sound of a police scanner in the background sounded loudly, "We have the lead. 10-4."

My captor, crawling up my body sneering, advised, "We're taking a trip."

He quickly stood, pulling me up with him and slinging me over his shoulder. My pounding headache reappeared in triplicate, and I felt like my eyes were going to fall right out of my head.

"Thank God you're not a fat ass," he commented while stepping over Curtis's body and ascending the stairs.

I checked my hands to see that they had been re-chained to each other and my feet bound the same way. Maybe I could hop away? He hauled me through the doorway, and I recognized my surroundings as a fancy kitchen. My eyes started looking for a knife set, anything for protection from this psycho who almost choked the life out of me.

"Kyle!" I heard a woman's voice screaming from another room. I wasn't the only one here?

"Shut your face, Jenny, before I do it for you...again," Kyle called back callously while swinging us around to a door. Kyle...as in Curtis's brother? I could feel the tension in his shoulders against my stomach while his arms were darting around across a dresser. With a seemingly quick move, he dumped me onto a bed where he continued his search with frenzied fingers.

"Where are your keys?" Kyle demanded without looking in our direction. Twisting in the direction of Jenny, my stomach tightened and my teeth gritted.

Jenny's face was completely bruised black and blue with a purple line across her neck that I was sure matched mine. Her hands were bound by rope to the headboard, but I couldn't stop looking at the dried blood on her chest. Did he cut her?

Before I could assess anymore damage to the woman, Kyle chuckled, "If only I had the time. I'd love to have a ménage à trois. However, you know what they say, out with the old and in with the hot and younger." He found the keys and quickly grabbed my bound legs and dragged me down the bed before pulling me over his shoulder again with a swift slap across my behind. The mewling I had been hearing last night came to mind, and I wish it hadn't.

With keys in hand, he walked us back out to the kitchen area slamming the door behind us. From my awkward view, I tried to pick up on some generic sign to tell me where I was, but I could only see bushes and trash cans. The popping sound of a trunk alerted me to my new destination. After painfully being dropped in, I glanced up at the sky—the sun didn't look too high yet. It was still somewhat early. Attention was abruptly brought back on Kyle as he pinched my face in between his fingers.

"Don't be jealous. I'll make it worth your while." Smirking, he leaned in and smashed his lips against mine and the urge to vomit almost overcame me.

315

Taking a step back, he slammed the trunk shut on me. Well, this was terrific, how was I supposed to get out of this? My hands felt around above my head, but I didn't feel anything useful, just towels or blankets I assumed. Moving my feet back and forth together I couldn't feel anything down there at all. Rolling around due to the car turning corners, I tried to think of an escape route or at least get a clue as to where I was. The sound of the engine revving up loudly clued me in to the fact we were merging onto a highway.

Getting an idea, I rolled my body up against the back of the trunk and tried pushing with my fists. Finally feeling a little give, I rolled backwards and then used my body weight to help push forward, and I found myself rolling out into the backseat of the car. Noisily, I might add.

"What the—" Kyle started to say, hastily checking his rearview mirror and spotting me on the backseat. Pulling my legs forward, I sat up and looked out the window and saw we were crossing the George Washington Bridge. So I was still in New York, but he was taking the lower level toward New Jersey.

"You've got spunk, little lady. I'll give you that," he said, before changing lanes all the way into the slow lane, presumably to pull off and stick me back in the trunk. There were people around me here; this might be my only chance. Without thinking, I leaned back pulling my feet up and started kicking the back of his driver's seat hard.

"You bitch!" he started yelling while trying to drive with his left hand and grab at me with his right. Evading his reach, I gave one last kick toward the headrest and watched as his head instantly pushed forward bouncing on the steering wheel.

The sickening snap I heard made me stop as I watched the blood pouring all over the wheel and his clothes.

"Fuck!" Kyle shouted as he tried to grab the steering wheel, but the blood made his hands slick. The car started screeching and pulling towards the railing as he tried to re-correct it, but it was too late. The speed pushed the car head on right into the railing of the bridge causing the airbags to pop out hitting Kyle in his bloody face. I couldn't help the scream that sprouted from my mouth as I was forced off of the backseat onto the floor, bashing my head against it.

I could barely think through the pain of my head, but I didn't have a choice. This may have been my only shot. Trying to sit up, I was quickly gripped by the throat. "You stupid bitch! You broke my nose!" he shouted at me while gripping even tighter.

I tried to pry his hands off my throat with my fingers, but to no avail. Feeling that sensation of haziness again, I thrust my still-bound hands into his face. My left hand hit his nose and my pinky finger went right into his eye. His fingers instantly let go of me to clutch his face, and I reached up quickly trying to open up my back door. My finger unlocking it, I pushed it open and began to drag myself out by the elbows, wiggling like a snake.

"Oh no, you don't!" Kyle screamed, trying to grab my foot to drag me back inside, but my body was mostly out anyway. Using gravity to my advantage, I leaned forward to the best of my ability and fell onto the pavement.

Rolling away from the car, my hands grabbed onto the railing, and I hauled my body up to a standing position. My head hated the movement and the nausea hit hard. Waving my arms from side to side to get a car to help seemed impossible—they all kept flying by. With only one option at my disposal, I started to hop in the direction back towards New York, but I heard Kyle grunting after me.

The louder his footsteps sounded, the faster I hopped. The feel of his hands wrapping around my waist from behind made me scream bloody murder. Spinning me around, he smacked me across the face with his full force knocking me back against the railing.

"You must have a death wish," he said, lifting me to a sitting position on the rail.

"Hey, are you guys all right?" asked a shocked voice from behind Kyle. Glancing at the kind citizen, he looked middle-aged wearing a Yankee baseball cap and jacket with jeans.

"We're fine. Get the fuck away from us," Kyle shouted back.

"NO! Please help!" I shouted, but the sting hadn't even registered on my face. My adrenaline was pumping, and I refused to be left alone with this man.

"He's going to kill me!" I shouted again which earned me a punch in the stomach. My breath whooshed out of my lungs painfully. The stranger retreated back to his car, and all I could hope was that he was calling the police for help. The salty smell of Kyle's blood caused my stomach to rumble in protest. Or maybe it was revolting from the abuse it was taking.

Kyle, beyond enraged, grabbed my shoulders and started pushing me backwards, but I tucked my legs behind the middle bar to keep from going over the railing.

"No, don't!" My mouth shouted in his face, but it only made his eyes narrow.

"You're no longer of any use to me," Kyle spat back in my face. He must have gotten Eric to agree to meet him. That is the only explanation as to why he didn't need me. His fingers began to grip my throat again.

"Let the girl down!" shouted the stranger from farther away.

"If you don't fuck off, I'll toss you after!" Kyle screamed back at him but paused as he saw the stranger was behind two police officers pointing a gun at him. I couldn't stop the tears from pouring down my cheeks with relief that at least someone knew where I was; someone was trying to protect me.

"Set her back down on the pavement. And put your hands in the air," one of the officers demanded from behind the police cruiser. Kyle grabbed me by the hair and tugged my head back painfully and my legs almost lost their hook.

"I'll do it. She won't survive the fall."

Officially losing my mind and control of my mouth, I started spouting off like a mad woman, "I'm Rebecca Austin from Rye! Kyle Reynolds has me hostage!"

I didn't expect Kyle could be crazier than he was, but I was once again surprised when his glare turned straight into an evil grimace. His fingers once again started to strangle me, and I couldn't think of any way out of it. I tried to reach up again and claw at his face but his grip tightened so much that the haziness started to set in rapidly. My legs unhooked from the middle rail, and as I felt myself slowly leaning backwards, I heard shots ring out.

The strong fingers instantly loosened on my throat as his body weight began to slowly slide down mine weighing my legs back down toward the bridge. Unable to stop my body from going down with Kyle's, I slid right down with him into a heap. I felt so weak and exhausted, but I used my feet to help move my body away from his.

The sound of Kyle groaning sent an intense shiver down my back. My legs scooted me further from him until firm hands grasped my waist tugging me up. Glancing up into the eyes of the kind stranger, tears slipped down my cheeks in relief.

The ambulance and fire engine sirens rang out loud and clear as they approached our area on the bridge. My attention befell the scene before me—one officer frisking Kyle while the other kept a gun trained on him. Not finding any weapons, he was put in handcuffs and given the Miranda rights. The ambulance pulled right up behind the cruiser where two EMTs piled out.

"Please get these off of me," I pleaded to one while glancing down at my hands; I' was way too tired to lift them.

"Just hold on one moment," he said, eyeing the firefighters piling out of the truck.

With a wave of his hand, one comes over to my side. "Do you have bolt cutters?" the EMT asked the firefighter. I looked down at my feet and notice that I'd lost one of my flats somewhere along the way.

"Ma'am?" asked the EMT apparently assessing if I was all right.

"I'm not dead," I stated, not wanting to mention all the aches and pains.

The firefighter came walking back with huge cutters and started going to town to free my feet and then my hands. The relief of being able to move my arms freely made me stretch them out in front of me.

"You fucking bitch!" I heard being screamed out from a few feet away. I saw Kyle cuffed to a gurney and loaded into the ambulance with blood stains all over his chest.

Another ambulance and police cruiser pulled up when I was approached by one of the original officers. "I'm Officer Ramos. Ms. Austin?"

"Yeah," I groaned both in pain and relief.

The officer grimaced once he began to examine my face. Without waiting, I rehashed the whole story of how he kidnapped me in a revenge attempt on behalf of his brother. The EMTs from the new ambulance came to check out my cuts and bruises, but I pushed them away.

"I'm fine. I just want to go home," I insisted.

"It would be in your best interest if you were checked out. All of this blood isn't yours," Officer Ramos advised, and I agreed silently. Great. To add insult to injury, Kyle may have gotten his blood on my body. As my adrenaline slowly started to run out, more aches made themselves known.

"My phone...Kyle stole my phone."

The officer left my side to converse with his partner, returning a few minutes later holding it out to me. "I need this back for evidence, but call your family."

My fingers couldn't move fast enough calling the one person I needed. "Hello?"

"Eric, it's me."

"Becki, are you all right?"

More tears slipped down my cheeks. "Kyle is in police custody. I'm being taken to the hospital."

The words barely leaving my lips, he replied, "Where? I'm coming." Providing all the needed information, we hung up, and I was escorted to my own ambulance.

Chapter 30
Friday, September 28th

Seeing my reflection in any surface had caused tears to slip down my cheeks for the last couple of days. The fact that I made the effort to get out of bed and stare blatantly in the mirror was a miracle in itself. It was nice to see that the discoloration around my left eye was all that was visible after the swelling finally went down.

The swelling in my cheek had finally settled down, but my chin still had bruises from his fingers pinching me in for that kiss. The bruises on my neck on the other hand would take a while longer. Using my liquid cover up gave the illusion that I was healed and back to normal. Not that I needed it...no one around me was fooled.

Sitting down on the bed, my feet slipped into my sneakers. Grabbing my purse and slinging it across my body, I picked up Barney's leash while heading down the stairs. I poked my head into the living room to find him cuddled up on the couch while Eric was gently stroking his head, watching TV.

"Time for your walk, Barney," I said softly. Hearing his name, he jumped down from the couch and padded over while wagging his tail in excitement. As I clicked his leash to the collar, I headed to the door to unlock everything.

Eric, holding the door open for us, quietly followed outside. The only places I was allowed to go alone were my bathroom and closet now. I wouldn't mind so much except for the looks he gave to me, like he was waiting for me to fall apart. And usually after he gave me that look, I did. I knew that he felt responsible for what happened to me and was trying to make it up to me, but oddly enough, I would have rather just been left alone so I could forget. Taking the usual walk around the block, Barney spotted his favorite tree to pee on.

The tension between Eric and I was pretty thick since our argument last night. He kept trying to coddle me like a porcelain doll. Giving me his sad eyes and telling me how sorry he was, the urge to scream almost overtook my throat. I finally had to kick him out of my room and forced him to stay put in his own for the night. Of course, that didn't last long since I ended up having a vivid nightmare and screamed my head off until Eric practically broke my door off its hinges coming to the rescue. There was nothing I could do or say to make him leave. And when he wrapped his arms around me and kissed my forehead, I sobbed until I fell asleep.

Finishing our walk around the block, I was surprised to see Detective Johnson waiting at our front door.

"Afternoon, you two," he greeted before quickly bending over to rub Barney's head. "And hello to you, too."

"What brings you around?" Eric inquired, unlocking the door letting us all in.

"Well, I've got some updates for you," Detective Johnson said, looking strictly at Eric. I unleashed Barney and locked the door prior to going into the kitchen for a water bottle. Hearing the men head into the living room to chat, I decided to hang back.

The tinkling of my new phone made me pull it out of my pocket. "Hey, Lily, what's up?"

"I'm on my way. I have a surprise for you," she said seriously. I really didn't want any more company, but girl time may loosen the tension around here.

"Sure, see you in a bit," I commented before hanging up. As I started to head up the stairs, I was called back down by Eric. I really shouldn't have been so aggravated with him.

"Yes?" I asked from the doorway.

Detective Johnson gestured for me to come and sit down. Sighing roughly as I sat down in an overstuffed chair, crossing my legs and staring at my knees, I gestured for him to begin.

"Ms. Austin, I just wanted to let you know that Kyle has pled guilty so you don't have to worry about a trial. With all the evidence we were able to collect it would be highly improbable for him to get away with anything other than life without parole." Nodding, I continued studying my knees. There was no real reason for me to look at anybody.

"It would be helpful if you could come to sentencing. As a witness, this would ensure a long term sentence for him." The idea of having to retell and relive the horror I suffered because of him caused my body to involuntarily tense up.

"You don't need me for that." My fingers knotted and unknotted repeatedly. I'd already recounted the story a dozen times between the hospital and the precinct.

"Becki...anything you can provide will help. When you left for Arizona, Kyle followed you there but

325

refused to attack you as he didn't know the lay of the land," Detective Johnson persisted.

"Why?" my mouth asked without really wanting it to. The detective gave Eric a strange look that I didn't understand.

"It has to do with me," Eric stated. "Kyle wanted to meet up for some reason. He didn't explain why, and at this point...it doesn't really matter."

"It doesn't matter?" My blood started to boil and anger started to make itself known. Detective Johnson cleared his throat before interrupting.

"What he means is that it doesn't matter why he wanted to meet up now that he is secured in jail. If Kyle wants to talk about it, he will."

My anger slowed down my thought process, but I fought against it anyway. The letter was pretty clear that Kyle wanted Eric to meet him. There was no address that I read, but I also never made it to the end of the conversation. Did Eric know something that he wasn't telling me about? My eyes flicked over to him examining if he was hiding anything, but he only reflected concern and worry. Maybe this wasn't such a good idea for me to dwell on.

"Depending on how you feel about Curtis, fortunate or not, Kyle couldn't stand him and knew that he would screw up going after Eric. Curtis had the plan but never got to fulfill it as Kyle took him out. The good news is that Kyle is locked up tightly and you and his former girlfriend are safe."

I took a deep breath and looked back up to the detective. "Thank you for your help with everything, but I...I can't listen to any more of this," I stated before standing up and going to my room.

Laying my head on my pillow, I tried to relax and forget almost all the information that I just learned. Especially remembering Jenny in that room. None of it changed where I was right now. I just needed to get through today. The gentle knock on the door roused me from my thoughts and caused me to sit up.

"Come in."

"Hey, gal pal!" Lily exclaimed coming into my room and sitting down on the bed with a big bag and box.

"Becki," I heard Eric say softly at the door. Glancing up, I comprehended the wariness in his eyes. "If you both want a snack, I can make some popcorn for you," he suggested hesitantly.

My feelings towards him hadn't changed, but clearly I'd led him to believe differently. My mood had been crazy up and down, but I shouldn't have been taking it out on him. I nodded, trying to convey a small smile. Eric returned my smile with one of his own before closing the door gently.

Lily, kicking off her shoes, plopped right down next to me. "If you really didn't want to go to the belly dancing class, you could have just said so," she joked. I had totally forgotten about my birthday plans.

"Oh, my gosh, I forgot all about that. I'm down for it if you still want to." My eyes widened just as much as hers in shock. I couldn't believe I just agreed that I would go along with her crazy idea. I did need to get out of the house and just do something, though. I couldn't stay cooped up in here.

"Well, then, open this box," Lily said, handing it to me.

As I placed it down on my lap, I could hear a slight jingle and couldn't contain the grin spreading across my face. I ripped through the wrapping paper, pulled off the cardboard top and pushed the white tissue paper aside to see a black belly dancing dress with a gorgeous leaf design in gold and emerald. There was a slit all the way from the upper thigh area down to the floor where the leaf design covered it.

"You should put it on to make sure it fits," Lily encouraged from my side. I took the dress into the closet and slipped into it carefully.

The dress fit perfectly. I hadn't even seen it in the mirror yet, but the feel of it was incredible. Walking out of the closet, Lily started hollering, "That's my girl!"

I closed the closet door behind me and did a small spin to check myself out thoroughly.

"I...I can't believe it."

"Becki, you look fabulous! You know I'm the best, right?" she said, coming over and checking me out, too.

The door opened slightly as Eric popped his head in with a big bowl of popcorn. His reaction was priceless—jaw dropping silence with bugged out eyes. I could almost hear a pin drop inside of his head.

Lily, not being a person to miss a moment, asked, "Eric, doesn't this dress make her look completely edible?"

She grabbed my hand and twirled me around. The dress scarcely covered my chest and left my stomach bare before the skirt started just under my belly button. The stunned silence continuing, I stared back up at Eric and watched his eyes blaze. Nodding as his only response, he leaned back against the door frame just staring me down.

"Thank you for buying this for me, Lily."

"What kind of friend would I be to drag you to a belly dancing class for your birthday and not set you up with an outfit?" she said, hugging me tightly, and I tried not to wince as my skin was still a bit sensitive.

"What's in the bag?" I asked out of curiosity but also to make her let go of me.

"That is a gift you need to open up alone. You will thank me later, I'm positive," she said gleefully. "Well, I have to head back, but I'll see you bright and early on Sunday," Lily advised while slipping her shoes back on.

I nodded as she headed out the door with Eric following closely behind her. Using my closet to change back into my jeans and t-shirt, I hung up the dress properly so it didn't get wrinkled. Lifting up the cardboard box, a soft jingle rattled again. Curious, my fingers skimmed throughout the tissue paper until I came across the matching black hip skirt with gold coins dangling on the edges. Wow. This was really going to happen on Sunday.

I sat down on the bed and peeked into my birthday bag. Oh, no...she didn't do this. Before I could reach in to pull the items out, I heard a soft tap on the door and spotted Eric. Things were already awkwardly strained between us; Lily's gift wouldn't

329

make it any easier. I slid the bag to the floor and used my foot to shove it beneath and out of sight.

Eric's expression warned me that something was on his mind, and I hoped that it wasn't more information from Detective Johnson. The thought alone made me frown.

"Why didn't you tell me?" he asked, hovering near the foot of the bed.

"Tell you…?"

"That your birthday was coming up. Why didn't you mention it?" Shrugging my shoulders, I laid back on my pillow.

"I don't enjoy celebrating my birthday, really. It's just another day," I replied. Noticing him cross his arms over his chest, I patted his side of the bed encouraging him to sit.

"Are you sure?" he asked warily.

Sighing, I nodded my head as guilt seeped into my stomach. I didn't mean to chew him out so badly last night. I was just…aggravated.

Sitting stiffly next to me, he glanced at my birthday bag and shredded wrapping paper. "I'd like to give you something for your birthday. If that's okay?" he added.

I grabbed his hand and tugged him down until he was lying down next to me.

"Sure," I responded and very gently snuggled into his side. "Eric, I'm sorry," I admitted, incapable of staying frustrated with him. "I just don't like being smothered. You weren't trying to—trust me, I know

330

that—but I was just so tired and aggravated that I took it out on you and I shouldn't have."

He gently lifted my chin with his finger to look into my eyes. "I understand. I apologize, too."

*****

"Becki," I heard a muffled voice say.

"Hmmm?"

"Your phone is going off," Eric said, rubbing my back while it tinkled away at us both. Checking the caller ID, I saw that it was my mother.

"Hello?" I answered in a raspy voice.

"Rebecca Marie Austin, how dare you!" my mother started shouting at me.

"What? What happened?" I asked, trying to collect my thoughts from our nap. Eric pointed to himself and then back at the door, but I shook my head for him to stay with me.

"It's all over the TV! How could you go through all of that and not tell us? You are to come home right away. I will not let that rotten city put its hands on you again," she demanded.

Cringing at the memories that she brought up, I calmly replied, "Mother, this isn't a good time to talk. I'm still recovering, and I just can't go there to discuss it right now." Eric had purchased a new cell phone for me, and I stupidly gave that number to Mother right away.

"Are you deaf? You are to come home this instant!" her shrill voice drilled right through me.

The urge to yell right back was so strong that my teeth clenched down on my tongue causing it to bleed. As painful as it was, I knew deep down that I must endure it because the words about to leap from my mouth would destroy any semblance of a relationship I had left with her.

"I understand why you would feel that way, Mother," I began slowly, "but there are important things that still need to be taken care of. I have doctor appointments, court appearances...I'm sorry, but I can't." Eric squeezed my hand gently assuring me that he was by my side.

"Rebecca...please come home," she sobbed into the phone line. "Why would someone do that to you? I just want you here so I can hold you to me. I need to know that you are okay."

My chest tightened with the intense pressure of emotions crowding together. Purposefully ignoring her question as to why, she didn't need to know about Eric's past incident. The wheels started turning slowly in my mind once again. Why would Kyle continue with Curtis's plan if he hated him so much? What did Kyle have up his sleeve? Clearly, I was missing something.

"I am okay, I promise," I stated clearly into the phone while looking into Eric's eyes. I knew deep down that he was worried about how I would handle this. I was worried, too. "We all just need to move on with our lives now. I can't change the past; all I can do is work towards my future," I continued, advising my mother.

"Will you call me tomorrow? I need—"

"I know and I will. I love you." I replied, trying to comfort her the best way I knew how from so far away.

"I love you more."

Hanging up, I snuggled against Eric's chest and closed my eyes, but my body refused to settle down. I should have just hit ignore on the stupid phone. The encouraging words passed from my lips to my mother's ear lingered in a haunting way. Would I truly be able to move on?

I had been able to avoid the radio and TV since the ordeal. Eric was amazingly understanding as to why, and since he had already gone through something like this, he never once asked what was done to me or if I wanted to discuss it at all. It was bad enough that he heard some of it over the phone. I'd never been more grateful for him than now because I could already sense the incoming of calls I was going to get regarding the situation.

"Hey," he said, breaking my train of thought, and I looked up into his eyes. "Calm down, I have you."

As tears slowly started to prick my eyes, he pulled me up into a warm embrace. "You're home now. Home with me," Eric whispered in my ear, and I couldn't help the waterfall of tears cascading down my face.

"My parents want me to move back to North Carolina," I managed to squeak out. With those words finally making their way to his ears, his warm embrace turned into a rigid hold.

"Do you want to leave?" he whispered roughly. I tried to pull back to see the expression on his face, but his hold wouldn't let me move a muscle.

"Do you want to leave..." His voice trailed off and my heart picked up.

Laying my head back on his shoulder, I thought through all the pros and cons like he taught me. My pros for leaving would be getting out of New York. I would be back home where I knew almost everyone and they knew me. I wouldn't have to worry if I couldn't get a job right away because my parents would make sure that I was well taken care of. I wouldn't be so paranoid about being watched while out at night, and I certainly wouldn't need a bodyguard to sleep with.

The cons would be giving up my job that I loved so much. Not only did I make a difference in other people's lives, but they made a positive uplift in mine. I would be losing the independence that I had been trying to get since I left home in the first place. My mother would smother me with questions about every action I committed. I wouldn't see Tim on our drinking nights at the bar; I wouldn't see him at all. Nor would I be able to spend my time with Lily whom I have come to love as much as a sister. She made being here fun, entertaining and worthwhile.

And one of the biggest cons for me would have to be leaving Eric. He was the most amazing and important person in my life. This man who chose to become my friend against years of isolation. He was the reason I didn't have nightmares when he was holding me at night; he was my shelter, and his easy acceptance of my silence since the ordeal was comforting. Could I survive going back home knowing that he was here? Did I want to try to live a life without him being part of it?

I leaned in close to his ear. "Does it look like I want to leave?" Snuggling tightly against his body, I gently kissed his neck where he responded gruffly.

"That's not an answer."

I slowly kissed up his neck to his jaw line. "I didn't tell her I would, did I?" I felt his arms let go of me and pull me back again slightly.

"That isn't an answer either. Just tell me…the truth."

Taking a closer look into his eyes, I saw there was something there. I couldn't put my finger on it, though. "I have no plans to move back to North Carolina. Why? Do you want me to go?" I asked, trying to decipher the uncertain emotion in his eyes.

"I wouldn't blame you for wanting to go, Becki. I know your parents are crazy controlling over you, but you do understand it's because they love you. They are concerned about you and…maybe they were right in the first place."

What? He wanted me to leave? I hadn't really considered how much of a pain I must be in his life if he was trying to send me so far away. I must have done something wrong to make him want to kick me out. Or maybe now that there wasn't a threat coming after me, he no longer felt the need to keep me around.

"Oh," I said as the only response and pulled away from him completely. Protection duty was apparently over. The burn of rejection made my thoughts speed more quickly in my head while it slowed down the movement of my mouth. That must be it. Curtis was dead and Kyle was behind bars. He didn't feel obligated anymore.

"Hey," he started to say, but I sat up and crawled off of the bed. I guess my eviction date had come; I was so stupid to think that this would become something more. He was pretty clear about us only being friends. I just didn't want to believe it.

"I need to be alone," I said numbly.

"I wasn't saying that—"

"I need to be alone," I stated more firmly. With my back to him, I waited to hear the door shut before turning around back to the empty room. I knew what I had to do.

Chapter 31
Friday, September 28th

Settling down in my motel room, I placed a water dish down for Barney and rolled my suitcase to the side of the bed. Opening the lid, I began to place my clothes into the drawers and hang my work outfits in the closet. Glancing at my king-sized bed, I crawled up to the pillows and practically sunk down to the floor. It was so amazingly soft, I found myself rolling from side to side enjoying every inch of it. My delight quickly darkened as my phone started to tinkle.

Checking the caller ID, it read that it was Lily, so I answered it in relief. "Hey, what are you up to?"

"Shouldn't I be asking you the same thing?" she asked in a slightly irritated tone. What did I do now?

"I don't know what you mean."

"Becki…Eric called me." The relief I was holding on to slipped right out of my body.

"He thought you were with me. Where are you?" Lily asked, a bit agitated.

"I'm in a motel in New Roc. I packed my suitcase and took Barney as my bodyguard," I explained.

"Why would you do that? He was so bewildered that you were gone that he could barely get the words out. I don't know him very well, but it sounded like he was panicking. Didn't you talk to him before you left?"

I didn't want to talk to him…I still didn't. "No, I needed to be alone. There are some decisions that I need to make for myself and I couldn't…there was no way I could stay there anymore."

"I love you, and I don't want to force you to do something that you clearly don't want to, but please, please call him."

"Lily…I don't want to," I stated, clearly asserting my point.

"I know you don't, but think about this. You've just disappeared like the night you were kidnapped. Imagine the terrifying thoughts now coursing through his mind. Is that what you want to do to him?"

My stomach tightened at the thought of actually causing him pain. That was one of the reasons why I left—to avoid that exact thing. "Fine, I'll get in touch with him."

"Do you want to hang out tomorrow?" Lily asked, trying to be slightly less frustrated with me, but I declined the offer.

"I just need to be alone right now. I'll text you tomorrow," I advised before hanging up. I knew she meant well, but I wished she would have just told him to take a hike. She doesn't understand, and now I'm being guilt tripped into calling him.

Being too much of a chicken to phone, I texted him instead: Lily called. Looking for me?

Feeling the bed sink at the bottom, I looked down and saw Barney lying down for the night. Turning out the light on the end table, I laid back in my pillows enjoying the darkness around me. I looked down as the phone vibrated.

338

I wanted to make sure u got to ur destination safely. Oh…he shouldn't still be worried about me.

I made it safely. U don't have to worry anymore. Good night. I texted back and closed my eyes. I was shocked when my phone started ringing.

"Hello?"

"Why are you doing this?" Eric's voice asked heatedly.

"I'm not doing anything," I replied.

"You left. You packed up your stuff, took Barney away and left me a bullshit note. You couldn't even talk to me?" he said angrily.

"There isn't anything to say. You have your life, your job and your home. I don't—"

"This is your damn home, too, Becki! Do I have to spell it out for you?" he shouted at me. Unable to find any other response I just conceded.

"Yes."

Hearing a frustrated grunt on the other line, I braced myself for the words that I was sure I didn't want to hear. "I want you here with me," he said slowly.

"Why?"

"I care about you. You already know this. You're my friend," he stated, and I couldn't help the sob that broke out from my chest.

"No. No, no, no, no!" I sobbed out over and over, unable to stop my lips from moving.

"What do you mean, 'no'?" Eric asked, shocked, and if I wasn't mistaken, a bit hurt.

"I'm *not* your friend. I may have been in the beginning, but I'm not now," I replied, wiping my tears away and sighing. If I was going to hurt, I might as well do it all at one time. "I have to be honest with you. I...don't consider you a friend at all."

Hearing a sharp gasp from the other end of the line, I pushed myself to finish with, "You're more."

There was silence for a moment, then, "What?"

"I shouldn't have to explain. Either you feel it or you don't, and you obviously don't." I said, trying to control my feelings but my voice broke at the end.

"Becki—"

"Please don't. I get it, trust me. It would be best for me to be on my own. I can't live with you anymore," I said weakly.

"Stop cutting me off!" he shouted back out of frustration. "We need to talk. I need to see you."

"I have to collect the rest of my things," I said softly which earned me a growl.

"Sunday, come over on Sunday."

"I'm going out with Lily," I said, trying to get out of it.

"After that, come over. I just want to talk to you, and if you still feel the need to finish getting your things, I'll help. Okay?"

"Fine," I replied curtly.

Sighing, he continued, "See you then," before hanging up on me.

Saturday, September 29th

Munching on my sandwich I brought back to the motel from my favorite deli, I was disturbed by the tinkling of my phone. "Hello?" I answered in between bites.

"How are you, sugarplum?" inquired my father.

"I'm okay, how are you?" I took a sip of my water to clear my throat.

"I'm worried about you. Are you sure you don't want to come home?"

I couldn't help myself from rolling my eyes; he was starting to sound just like Mother. "I'm okay, Dad. Really. What have you been up to lately?"

"Nothing much, things are starting to slow down around here," he admitted. That must be the real issue; he was spending way too much time with Mother around the house.

"How's Mother doing?" I asked, not really wanting to know.

"I wouldn't be surprised if she hopped on a plane to go get you and bring you back here kicking and screaming," he chuckled.

"Dad...you understand why I can't. Don't you?"

"I understand your determination, sugarplum. You get that from me. However, I don't want you to back yourself up into a corner where you don't have any options. Please at least consider it, okay?" he asked.

"I have considered it. Other than the legal reasons as to why I can't move back right now, it's not something that appeals to me. I want to have a life," I confessed honestly.

"No one is stopping you from having one." My horrid childhood memories came flooding back, and I cringed into the phone. No, there was no way I was moving back there.

"I want to do this so badly for myself. I feel like Mother is trying to undermine me at every turn," I admitted.

"I don't think that she is even aware of it. She just sees it as unconditional love," he laughed abruptly.

"It's clingy," I stated sourly.

"Just have patience with her. She isn't the only one missing and loving you."

"I love you too, Dad. I'm going to finish eating, and I'll call you guys tomorrow. Will you let her know that I called?"

"Becki, I called you," he said, his voice filled with worry. "Are you sure you're all right?"

"Oh, right, so you did. Yeah, I'm okay." I forced myself to sound brighter than I really felt. He didn't need to know the details of what I was really going through. I'm just losing my mind again. Nothing unusual here. "Can you give Mom a little distraction?"

"Of course I will. The Halloween Party is a few weeks away but I'm sure I could get her working on that. Especially since you'll be there?"

"Yeah."

"All right, sugarplum. Enjoy your meal."

"Thanks, Dad. Bye."

Finishing up my sandwich, I cuddled with Barney on the bed. Was I being selfish? Was it not normal for children to move out and have a career? Maybe this was my future, starting a fresh life on my own. Renting a new apartment without past memories of dead relationships, a blank canvas to splash new vibrant colors upon. Rebecca Austin...a new life in Technicolor.

Chapter 32
Sunday, September 30th

"I hope Will didn't mind watching Barney for me," I worried to Lily.

"He loves dogs. I wouldn't be surprised if he wasn't trying to scheme a way into taking him from you," she replied, laughing aloud.

"No, he is mine," I stated sternly which made Lily laugh even harder.

"Do you want to bring Barney with you to see Eric?" Lily asked. Shaking my head, she finished with, "He cares about Barney, too, you know."

"You're supposed to be on my side," I huffed out, agitated.

"No, I'm supposed to help you get what you deserve because I care about you," Lily spat back at me. There was no use in fighting with her when she got like this.

"I'm going to need all the room I can get to pack his car up with my stuff." Trying to be logical didn't make me careless. Without a response, she continued driving back to her place anyway. I would've killed her if I didn't care for her so much.

As she pulled up to the curb outside of her apartment building, Will was standing there with Barney by his side. Lily unlocked the doors and Will led Barney into the backseat while sliding in beside him.

"Did you ladies have a fun time?" Will asked while getting Barney to lie down next to him.

"I didn't realize how much of a workout it was to belly dance," Lily responded, and I nodded along with her.

"We have a few more sessions to go to, but I like it."

When we finally hit the highway, Will started to speak up. "So how attached are you to this one?" he asked nodding in my pet's direction.

"Extremely," I said sharply, trying to bite my tongue. I'd already lost everyone in my life; he was not taking Barney away from me, too.

"Message received," Will said, chuckling with his hands up in an innocent gesture. "I was wondering, though, if you ever need a pet sitter I'm willing to help out. He is such a great dog."

Unable to stop my smirk, I nodded back. "You'll be the first person I call on."

The sight of Eric's house coming into view quickly diminished my mirth. Lily, noticing my change in mood, piped up, "Listen, if you need me for any reason to come and get you, you only have to call." I nodded, unable to speak as my teeth were grinding together. As she pulled up to the front of the house, she put the car in park and turned to me.

"Becki, look at me." Turning my head to the left she persisted, "I know you are frustrated, fed up and sick of life screwing you over every chance it gets. But please, for the love of God, give him a chance. Let him say whatever it is he needs to get off his chest before you bite his head off."

345

I nodded, unwilling to say anything else. She wasn't going to listen to a word I had to say anyway. Opening my door, I felt Lily's hand on my shoulder. She leaned in and whispered, "I'm sure he is just as scared as you are."

Shrugging my shoulders, I stepped out of the car and let Barney out of the back seat. Barney, seeing the familiar house, got excited and started tugging the leash toward the front door. Yeah, thanks a lot, Barney. I rang the bell out of respect for his house, regardless of the key still on my key ring. I had to remember to leave that here, too.

The sounds of all the locks being undone started to unwind some of the tension in my back. I hated how my body was constantly working against me. As the door slowly opened up, Barney started to whine impatiently.

"Hey there, Barney," Eric greeted while pushing open the screen door for us and petting him on the head. As he started to stand back up, my eyes of their own accord took in his faded blue jeans and a navy long sleeve button-up. Wearing his hair loose accentuated the attractiveness of his face and crystalline eyes.

"Hi," Eric said softly, welcoming me into his home.

"Hi," I replied, just as softly. I could feel the calmness of just being in his presence affect my body. Taking Lily's advice was better than not; I could try to be civil. "Thanks for inviting me over," I said, looking down at the floor.

"Do you have your ID on you?" he asked, and I nodded.

"Why?"

"I told you that I wanted to give you something for your birthday," he advised before heading into his office. Furrowing my brow, I couldn't help feeling like I was being set up in the worst way.

Eric reappeared back into the hallway but with a black backpack slung over one shoulder. "Come on, Barney," Eric said, opening the door for us.

"Where are we going?" I asked, even more confused.

"Somewhere special," he replied softly, and as I stepped outside, I noticed Lily's car still parked outside. What in the world was going on? After locking up the house, I watched Will reach for Barney's leash and whisper something in Eric's ear. With a small nod from Eric, Will waved at me and then took Barney and they drove off.

"Ready?" Eric asked while unlocking the car. Speechless, I just followed his obvious plan and got in the passenger seat. There was no point in his trying to do something 'special' for my birthday. It would just make it harder for both of us when I left.

"What's wrong?" he asked, noticing my scowl. Shaking my head, I stared out the window.

"Just thinking." Taking a deep breath, I tried to relax some of the tension between my shoulder muscles. After a half hour of driving on the highway, I was stunned to see us take the exit ramp for White Plains County Airport.

"Where are you taking me?"

347

"Relax, Becki. I just want to show you something, that's all," he said, reaching his hand out to touch my knee but remembering our tense relationship pulled back at the last moment.

Winding through the airport lanes, he finally parked the car in short term parking. Maybe we were meeting someone here? Picking up the backpack he put it back over his shoulder and escorted me to the check-in area. Handing over two tickets, he started to pull out his driver's license.

Following suit, I whipped mine out of my wallet before we were ushered into the security line. I pulled off my sneakers and placed them in the empty bin with my purse. Walking through the metal detector I was all clear and picked up my shoes and shoved them on quickly while slinging my purse across my body.

"This way," Eric directed, leading us toward the boarding area. "Are you hungry or thirsty?" he asked, but I shook my head.

I was hungry actually, but I didn't know where we were going, and I'd rather fly on an empty stomach. Following towards the right side of the airport, I was surprised to see how small this one was compared to JFK International. Sitting down in our assigned boarding area, Eric leaned in close to my ear.

"Do you trust me?"

"Yeah..." I said warily. What did he have planned that I needed to trust him so much? He picked up my hand and squeezed it gently before tugging me up and to his side to walk towards the glass.

Oh, no. Why would he put me through this again? "Don't panic, this will be fine. I would never purposefully put you in a position where you would be harmed," he said, trying to calm me, but my tension had skyrocketed, and my eyes kept searching for one of the exits.

The small, white plane with black underbelly and bronze racing stripe design was sitting right in our section, a stupid Piper plane. "Eric, I have to go to work tomorrow. I can't afford to take any trips anywhere. This isn't a good idea. Can you just take me back?" I begged, starting to panic, but he lifted my chin up until I could do nothing but stare into the whirlpool of his eyes.

"This won't take long; I'll have you back in a few hours."

The female attendant waiting to take our tickets to board got an eyeful of Eric. I wouldn't have noticed but for the fact that she was busy staring at him instead of taking my boarding pass. Her nametag said her name was 'Cindy'; it went perfectly with her bright smile, blonde curly hair and long legs. Stupid woman was going to get fired if she couldn't keep her tongue in her mouth and assist all of the passengers. Eric, being polite, smiled at her but kept flicking his eyes in my direction. Rolling mine, I handed over my ticket to Eric which made him smirk a bit while handing it to 'Cindy.'

Not waiting for it to be returned, I walked through the corridor and down the steps outside. I took a deep breath looking at the puddle jumper; I didn't think I could do this again. Glancing back towards the airport, Eric was standing right behind me. Was it that obvious that I was ready to run? 'Cindy,' not getting

349

enough attention from Eric, encouraged us to continue and assisted us getting settled in our seats. As I stepped up into the plane, I saw it only seated four passengers. The roof and walls were white but the upholstery was all tan.

Eric put his hand on my lower back and encouraged me to sit in one of the two seats in the very back of the plane so we both had window seats. As I sat down, I put my seatbelt on while placing my purse on my lap. I pulled my cell phone out and turned it off.

"Are you sure there is nothing else I can help you with?" Cindy asked Eric.

I stared out the window not wanting to even bother getting worked up over something so lame. He wasn't interested in me so why should I stop him from meeting someone else?

"No, I don't think so. Becki, do you need anything?" he asked, but I declined.

"Are you ready?" he asked.

"To ride in a death trap?" I responded with a slight smirk.

"Stop that. It's perfectly safe and extremely comfortable. We should arrive at our destination in about an hour roughly." A memory hit me upside the head right away.

"Eric...this is your first time on a plane."

He nodded with a small smile. "You remembered." Why did he pick this tiny thing as a first try? "I looked up what I wanted to give you for your birthday and this was the best way for you to receive it," he said, leaning in close to me.

I watched the pilot and copilot crawl into the cockpit giving us a quick wave. Laying my head back, I closed my eyes and tried to imagine myself on the beach. I was on my towel getting a tan for the summer. I was jolted from my daydream by the feeling of Eric's hand on my knee. Taking a deep breath, I decided to not make a big deal out of the gesture. We used to be close, and if this was the last time were going to spend time together, then I wouldn't deny him.

Looking to my right, I caught Eric staring out the window with an uncertain emotion. "Where are we going?" I asked curiously.

"You're not one for surprises are you?" he commented.

"Not really. I'm a terrible birthday girl because usually I know what is going on," I admitted with a chuckle.

"Not today."

As the plane taxied to the runway, I glanced down at Eric's hand resting on my knee still. I couldn't seem to help myself from touching him. Carefully placing my hand on top of his, I glanced out the window as we started to rush down the runway.

Chapter 33
Sunday, September 30th

The flight wasn't very long; it seemed as if we had just leveled off in the sky before we were already descending down to Rochester Airport. As much as I hated to admit it, the flight wasn't scary at all. Now that we were safely on the ground, I think his presence may have had something to do with it. I couldn't even openly deny how right he was about the comfortable seating. Although I'm not one for Piper planes, this one may be the exception. Since we didn't have any luggage other than his carry-on, we were able to walk right through the airport.

"Hey!" I heard a voice exclaiming in our general direction.

Eric's hand placed on my lower back ushered me toward a friendly face that I thought I'd never see again.

"Happy Birthday!" Dane said while pulling me into a tight hug.

"Oh...thanks." I tried to change my expression from pure shock to a small smile before he noticed. While trying to readjust to our company, I saw Dane give Eric an enthusiastic hug, as well. I thought I handled it better than he did.

"I'm going to head to the restroom," Eric stated before handing his backpack to Dane to hold. Was my surprise in it? Cocking my head to the side, I stared at his younger brother.

"Do you know where we're going?"

"Of course I do. I'm your chauffeur," he said with a huge smile. Raising my eyebrows, encouraging him to proceed with more information, his eyes widened in alarm and he shook his head vehemently. "I'm not going to spoil the surprise. You are so close, just a half hour more."

Rolling my eyes at his attempt to mollify me, I pulled my cell phone out of my purse and turned it back on. "Can I ask you something? Non-birthday related subject."

"Sure," he said while running a hand through his wild, bed head hairstyle.

"What do you think of your brother?" Watching his mouth pull tight, he gave me his best impression of deer in the headlights.

"I think he is okay. Why?"

The feeling that he was trying to be manly about his affections for his brother made me smirk. "Do you miss him?" I asked, pushing him.

"Yeah," he replied while staring down at the floor shrugging his shoulders.

There was no rhyme or reason to explain what I did next, but I pulled him in for a snug hug and whispered in his ear, "You should tell him. He needs to hear it just as much as you do."

Stepping back into my personal space, I bumped right into Eric. "What are you two doing?"

Thinking quickly on my feet, I admitted to trying to make Dane spill about our destination. Eric, laughing at my failed attempt, grabbed his backpack from his brother, and we walked out to the short term parking lot.

Approaching the navy vehicle, Dane got in the driver's seat while Eric, being the gentleman that he was, opened my door for me. Slipping into my seat in the back, I placed my purse on my lap, and to my surprise Eric got into the seat next to mine. While driving along the highway, I looked around the differences between New Rochelle and Rochester until my mind started to wander about where he could possibly be taking me. Then suddenly it hit me, he wouldn't take me home to his parents, would he? I mean, he would warn me before that, right?

I grabbed his hand and squeezed it tightly. "Tell me where we're going, please?" He pulled me tight against his side and wrapped his arm around my shoulders.

"It will only take a few more minutes. Please be patient. This means a lot to me, and I want to share it with you," he whispered into my ear.

Dane turned up the radio for background music as we hit Highway 104, and my panic set in. Hanging from the rearview mirror was one of those tree air fresheners and pink plastic flip flops. This car clearly didn't belong to Dane. The tension in my shoulders must have been a clue to my unease because Eric gently started to rub my arm up and down.

"Becki, look at me." Following his instructions, I did and instantly regretted it. His eyes enraptured me in total control. "I'm sure it is obvious to you that I'm bringing you to my hometown. There is a special place that I used to spend all of my time as a child, and I want to show you why."

I took a deep breath and nodded, but I couldn't take my eyes off of his. Without even realizing it, our faces got closer and closer until our lips were practically touching. My rapid heartbeat made me pull back and look away quickly.

Dane slowed down along the side of the street and then parked. "I'm going to go take a walk. Take as long as you need. My phone is on me," he advised before ducking out onto the street.

Eric, opening the door to his side, beckoned me to follow out his door onto the sidewalk. I scooted out but refused to take his hand and shut the door behind me...his eyes have done enough. I just had to remember that we weren't together, we weren't friends. I was just appeasing him so I could collect my belongings and go.

Following behind him, I wasn't aware of my surroundings until we were walking on grass up to a wrought iron gate. I was truly at a loss for words. This was not where I thought he was taking me.

"This way," he said as he guided me, while walking to the left side of the grave site. Walking towards the back, I watched Eric slow down before stopping in front of a grave. Peering down at the headstone it read: George Whitman, Soldier, Husband and Father 1969-1991.

"This was one of my favorite places to be growing up. I couldn't stand to be home or anywhere near other people. I wanted to be close to the one person I loved, who loved me just as much. I blamed my mother for his death; she should have made him stay with us. Even now as an adult and understanding reality, I can't help the small amount of resentment I

355

have for her. I swore to never let anyone else in, not because I disliked other people but because I...I didn't know how I would manage to go on if I lost another loved one."

Gazing at him, I finally saw what his problem was. It was me. He had told me once before that it wasn't me, but it was, and now I understood.

"Eric?" I asked, coming closer to his side, but he shook his head. The look of sadness on his face from staring at his father's grave broke my heart.

"I wanted to introduce you to the only other person who has touched me as deeply as you have," he said softly. I had no idea what it felt like to lose a parent, but I did the only logical thing in my mind. I leaned down to the headstone and rubbed my fingers across his name before placing my lips gently on the word 'Father' before standing back up.

"It's my pleasure to meet you," I whispered kindly.

Turning around to face Eric, I watched a lone tear sliding down his cheek as he watched me. I reached out and used my thumb to gently wipe it away. "What's wrong?"

"I haven't been here in so long. And to have you here with me...it means...so much." Unsure of what to say, I wrapped my arms around his waist and just held him tight to me. We stayed wrapped up in each other for what felt like an hour, a content silence between us.

When we finally broke apart, my arms felt stiff from being in one position for so long, but it was worth it to comfort him when he needed it so badly. It's the first time he had allowed me to ease his pain. He always put up this front like nothing could touch him, like the past didn't affect him. At least I could be there for him.

We began to make our way back to the car. "Hungry?" he asked quietly, clutching my hand in his, and I nodded, lightly squeezing his hand.

Opening the car door, I was surprised to see a platter sitting on the front seat with two bottles of water. I got in and scooted to my side of the backseat while Eric followed me inside, shutting the door behind him. Handing me a ham, turkey and cheese sandwich, I practically inhaled the first half in a few bites. I was starving, and if I had to choose whether to eat or breathe...eating would win out. Raising his pale eyebrow at me with a small smirk on his face, luckily he didn't comment on my eating habits.

When I opened my water bottle, I chugged it right down and the coldness made me shiver right down to my toes. "Thanks for thinking ahead. That was amazing," I praised while laying my head back against the seat trying to catch my breath.

"Now that we have filled our stomachs, it is time," he stated in all seriousness.

"Time...for what?" I asked, puzzled.

"The talk." He scooted his back toward the door angling in my direction.

"You're a little late for the birds and the bees discussion," I replied, trying to deter him from ruining our calming silence.

"Becki," he stated in an emotionless tone. Yeah, I knew where this was going already. Rolling my eyes, I gestured with my hand for him to proceed.

"You stated that you don't consider me a friend. I must admit...it hurt to hear that. It hurt worse when you said that you considered me more."

My eyes widened in utter shock. "Why?" I never meant to hurt him by confessing my feelings.

"If I meant more to you then why did you leave me that note? Why couldn't you be honest with me about how you felt?"

I opened my mouth to respond but nothing came out.

"Just tell me the truth. That's all I've ever wanted from you," he said, pressing the issue. I opened my mouth again but still nothing came out...this was beyond infuriating.

Picking my words out carefully, I tried again. "The note contained what I couldn't say to you."

"That's bullshit and you know it, Rebecca. It only said that you were moving out because you didn't feel living with me was a good idea anymore. You were moving in with your friend until you figured out a new place to live. And that wasn't even true," he stated, frustrated with me. Well, I was right there in the land of frustration myself.

"The friend I was referring to was Barney for one, and for two, I *didn't* feel living with you was a good idea anymore," I spat right back.

"Why? Did I do or say something to make you want to leave?"

I looked down at my hands trying to keep calm. I really didn't want to rehash the whole thing. Why couldn't he just accept that I didn't want to live with him?

"You told me that I should go back to North Carolina. That moving here was a mistake. I don't know how else to interpret that other than 'you are no longer wanted here.'" The most mortified expression covered his face before he reached out and grabbed my hands.

"I wasn't trying to kick you out. I just didn't want to force you to stay if you didn't want to stay in New York anymore after...you know." Deftly trying to avoid that subject, I confessed something that I'd been dying to say for weeks now.

"Eric...you are not my friend. I don't sleep with my friends on a normal basis. I don't make out and...do what we did with my friends. And every time you called me your friend..." I looked out the window, shaking my head, unable to control my frustration and hurt.

"I wasn't trying to upset you, please believe that," he said, scooting over to my side of the car. "I didn't want to force you into something that you may not have wanted. You and Gary have only just broken up. I didn't want to be your rebound. I'm not an idiot. You and I are much more than friends but I...I've never done this before." The feel of his fingers stroking my cheek made me glance in his direction against my better judgment.

"I've never wanted anyone to be in my life. I never needed...until you." My heart rate picked up at the timbre of his voice before swelling with heartfelt joy.

"You want me?" The intensity of his stare bored right into me, and I recognized the naked fear in his eyes. I repeated myself just so that I was crystal clear. "You want me. And I want you." A tear slowly slid down my cheek as the words rang true. I'd finally admitted whole-heartedly what I'd been trying to show to him since I got home from Arizona.

Unexpectedly, he pulled me in for a deep kiss. "Yes."

He growled against my lips but didn't stop. I could feel his fingers running through my hair and clutching my face tighter to his while his mouth sensuously assaulted mine. I wrapped my arms around his neck and let my hands run up into his hair. His natural scent overwhelmed me from his breath, but also the taste of his lips made me want him more.

I sucked his bottom lip into my mouth which earned me a groan from deep in the back of his throat. As our lips broke apart, I gasped to feel his lips on my neck, and I was unable to stop myself from speaking the truth. "I want you…so much."

That little admission earned me another groan as his lips skimmed up my neck until our lips touched again. This must be what rapture and elation felt like wrapped up in one. Eric wanted me. Eric wanted to be with *me*.

His phone ringing softly from his jeans pocket slowed down our intensified make out session. I laid my head back against the window and took a deep breath. I couldn't believe so much had happened since this morning. Eric having to raise his hips up to reach down into his pocket made me laugh. I guess there were some disadvantages to being so tall.

"Where are you?" I heard him ask into the phone before he started laughing and finished with, "Yeah. Come on over."

Tilting my head to the side with a questioning look on my face, he just laughed and shook his head. A moment later, the driver's door opened and Dane slipped inside. Oh, no…was that him on the phone? Was he watching us? My face heated up with embarrassment refusing to look in his general direction.

Without a word, he pulled off into the Sunday afternoon traffic back up the 104 towards the airport. I noticed Eric reaching into his backpack from the corner of my eye and smiled when he pulled out a small box wrapped up. Opening his arms up in invitation, I slid over to his side of the backseat and snuggled into him.

"Happy Birthday," he said kindly while handing the gift over to me.

Against my usual nature, I didn't shred it to pieces but took my time unwrapping it to find a small, white box. Removing the lid, I gaped down at the most delicate looking piece of jewelry I'd ever seen. A gorgeous set of diamond tear drop earrings with my birthstone set in the middle gazed right back at me.

"Oh…oh," I said as my fingers lightly grazed them. "They're so…" I couldn't seem to finish anything that came out of my mouth today.

"You deserve them," Eric said, placing a gentle kiss on my forehead.

The half hour ride back to the airport was much more relaxing than arriving had been. The warm embrace of Eric's arms around me while I laid my head against his chest was so peaceful that I almost fell asleep. I was so certain on the way here that it would be the last time I would see him by my choice. And now my mind carried on fantasies of movie nights, romantic dinners, and possible vacations to enjoy together.

Arriving at the departure area, Dane dropped us off on the sidewalk with a hug good bye.

When he leaned in for mine, I whispered, "You should come visit us. Maybe for a weekend?" Dane gave me a small smile before nodding.

"Are you ready to go home?" Eric asked, clasping my hand while walking to the check-in.

Smiling up at him I replied, "More than ready."

Chapter 34

On the way home from the airport, Eric insisted that we stop by the motel to pick up my things to bring back. At least I had only packed my suitcase and a few of Barney's things when I left originally, because he was not to be messed with on this issue. By the time we pulled up into his driveway it was half past eight. I was surprised to see Lily and Will parked in front waiting for us when we returned. My suspicions kept rising at the brighter her smile became the closer we approached. What was she up to?

"Shall we go get something to eat?" Will asked to no one in particular.

"I could eat. What about you?" Eric asked me, and I nodded.

Packing up my clothes had taken longer than unpacking them had been. Eric, unlocking the front door, encouraged all of us in, but Lily took point by grabbing my hand and hauled me up the stairs to the bathroom.

"Shower, but don't wash your hair. We don't have time for that," Lily ordered before firmly shutting the door on me.

My suspicions grew into concern about this situation, but I followed my orders. I took a hot shower, scrubbing and shaving everything that needed attention before toweling off. I knocked on my bedroom door and Lily slowly opened it for me.

"I took the liberty of shopping for you today, and you are going to love me, I promise!" she said excitedly while leading me to the closet.

Handing me a brand new pair of black lacy panties and a black pasty-type push up bra, she shoved me in and slid the door shut behind me. Without question, I slipped on the undergarments wondering what plan she had up her sleeve.

"Lily, where are we going?" I pleaded, getting nervous again. I really did hate surprises.

"Are you decent?" she asked, and I responded by opening the closet door. I stopped dead in my tracks when I noticed my prized navy dress lying on the bed.

"You're joking, right?" I asked, stunned, but Lily taking post again pulled me into the room shaking her head. With her assistance, I was able to step right into the dress where she easily zipped me in and examined her work. Putting her hand in a plastic bag, she pulled out a shoe box.

"These are perfect for tonight." I slipped into my new pair of black pumps with diamonds on the heels. They looked magnificent with the dress, but I had absolutely no idea where I was going or why I was being treated like a Barbie doll.

"Do you have your earrings?" Lily asked, and I suddenly realized their purpose.

Eric had planned this all along so I would have an opportunity to wear my favorite dress. Like I really needed another reason to appreciate him. I went into my purse and pulled out the small, white box and put the earrings in my ears.

"Okay, sit on the bed very gently and don't squirm," Lily commanded while pulling out my hair brush and hair spray from my dresser.

After she fixed my hair up into an elegant bun and perfected my face flawlessly with makeup, I couldn't even look at myself in the mirror without my eyes welling up.

"None of that. I've worked my best magic on you, so no crying!" Lily scolded while swiping a few stray streaks and fixed my face. "All right, Cinderella, it's time for you to go to your ball," Lily said laughing, and I couldn't help but join in.

"I feel like her, kind of. My fairy godmother just came in here and beautified me." I smiled appreciatively at my best friend.

I walked slowly out the door behind Lily and descended the stairs to find Eric patiently waiting at the bottom. Dressed in a black tailored suit that accentuated his attractively fit body, black dress shoes and his hair left down and tucked behind his ears, it was hard to believe that he wanted me. As I came into full view, I watched him smile at me knowingly.

From behind his back he pulled out another box, but this one was bigger and wasn't wrapped.

"One more thing," he whispered softly as he circled around behind me. I felt him place a necklace on me and after he snapped the clasp shut, I looked down to see the matching piece to my earrings.

"Thank you...so much," I said, turning around to face him. "Words can't express how much I love my birthday gifts." With a gleam in his eye, he wrapped his arm around my waist and planted a chaste kiss upon my lips.

Eric, with his hand on my lower back, guided us to the back door. The soft sounds of music came drifting to my ears the second we stepped out onto the patio. I couldn't stop the gasp escaping from my lips as I looked around the backyard and spotted a huge tent with candles and a small dance floor set up. Eric, walking me inside to the table that was laid out with candles and the soft music, put me at complete ease.

We uncovered our meals and began to eat our delicious grilled chicken and vegetables. Lily was an amazing cook, and I couldn't believe she helped him set this up. I was dead set against being with this man nine hours ago—how did she know that I'd end up here?

I sipped my water with lemon before asking, "When did you decide to put this together?"

Eric, chewing his chicken, swallowed before replying. "After you left. I called Lily to find you...I had the ideas, and she planned it out." Taking a bite of my baby carrot, he surprised me. "I wanted to make your birthday unique."

I smiled thinking back over my day from start until now. I had never had such an eventful birthday. "Well, you've succeeded with flying colors."

Gently wiping my mouth clean, I placed my napkin down on top of my plate. "May I have this dance?" Eric asked bowing, and I smiled at the gesture.

I stood from my seat and curtsied. "I'd be honored, sir." Taking my hand into his, he led me to the dance floor holding me tight to his body. My body of its own volition melted right into him, and I sighed softly enjoying every moment of it.

"So..." Eric began, causing me to glance up to see him smirking at me. "You want me," he said suggestively with raised eyebrows. I couldn't help wanting to whack him just like the night we first met. And without another thought about it, I smacked his arm.

"What was that for?"

"You keep making inappropriate remarks to people and one day someone...namely me...will be inappropriate right back."

A dark look crossed his face before he said, "I'll show you inappropriate."

Sweeping me up until our lips touched, he slid his tongue right into my vacant mouth. My returning moan was all the response that was required. When he released my lips, he slid me slowly down the length of his body until my heels touched the floor again. The powerful connection that flowed throughout my body when we kissed was getting stronger and stronger.

Leaning down to my ear he whispered breathlessly, "Shall I tell you how beautiful you look tonight?" Unable to wipe the smile from my face, I nodded. "I've never seen anyone look as gorgeous as you do right now." His words caused a flutter in my stomach and my smile widened. Yeah...compliments are a definite weakness. Especially from him.

367

I gently ran my fingers up and down his chest playing with his suit jacket lapels. "You look very handsome in this. I may force you to go to more social events just so I can see you in it."

Smirking at me again, he said, "I could just wear it around the house. It could be my new pajama set." He winked fiendishly.

Thinking on my feet, I came back with, "Well I wouldn't be able to see it in bed, especially with your room being across the hall and all." A small scowl crossed his face before it was replaced with a serious expression. Uh oh, what have I said?

"I want you to stay with me. No more running." Eric gazed into my eyes exuding the full force he empowered.

Wasn't this what I'd wanted for weeks now? The hope I'd been holding onto that Eric would feel the same way for me as I did for him? I pulled back from his arms a half step and kicked my heels off before smiling up at him.

"What are you doing?" he asked, cocking his head in the gesture that I'd grown to love.

I wrapped my arms around his neck while gazing deeply into his eyes and softly replied, "Trying."

The End...For Now.

Here's an excerpt from

Hope Has a Glare,

the tantalizing sequel to *Glimmer of Hope*

Excerpt

If I had thought of where I was going, I'd have drawn a blank. If I had been stopped in traffic, maybe I would have changed my route. If the phone had rang once, maybe just maybe, I wouldn't be sitting where I was. But I hadn't been thinking, the roads were strangely clear, and no one had called. Sometimes there were signs that couldn't be ignored and unfortunately left me in the last place I ever expected.

I wouldn't be sat at a tiny cubicle looking at an empty chair. The only protection a thick glass with a phone hung up beside it. How did I even get here? Just as the thought passed, the guard opened the door leading in the one person who had starred in my nightmares. The only person that had given me reasons enough to be the wreck I had become.

A bright orange jumpsuit decorated with handcuffs at the ankles sat down before me. His blond hair was cut short and close to his scalp, allowing his dark brown eyes to pierce right through mine. He appeared to be only slightly shocked to see me on the other side of the glass but it didn't last long. He grabbed up the phone with purpose while my fingers trembled around the handle of my own.

"Couldn't stay away, could you?" Kyle sneered.

My voice had abandoned me. My thoughts drew a blank. Why had I come? What did I expect to get out of this? The lack of response didn't appear to bother Kyle as he chuckled and raised his eye brow. The gesture seemed too normal, too calm. Was he expecting me to show up?

"I...What...Why?" I stumbled out, my insides trembling with fear even with a guard as protection.

"If you came here thinking I was going to spill my guts to *you*, you've got another thing coming." Kyle stated before a smirk broke out upon his lips. "Unless you wanted something else?"

What could he possibly offer from a jail cell? If he wasn't going to give out information about why he did what he did, he had nothing left to offer. It was a wasted trip. A wasted conversation. A wasted experience.

Kyle licked his lips, "We both know what you came here for."

My heart started to pick up in pace as realization came. What a pig. I'd rather die than allow him to ever touch me again. It wasn't possible to scrub my mouth hard or long enough to take away the memory of his lips pressed against mine. But I tried. It was just another part of the horrific memories that I needed to forget.

"Why did you take *me*?" I asked, "You didn't want me."

"I didn't?" he asked darkly.

"You said I was in the wrong place at the wrong time."

"So?" He replied, "Maybe you were…"

"This was about Curtis getting his revenge on Eric. Why-"

"You don't know anything. And I'm not going to tell you so stop with the questions." Kyle snarled, irritated.

Frustrated, I clenched my teeth together. I could badger him with questions to which he wouldn't answer and waste more of my time or go home. Anywhere would be better than here, even with the drama awaiting back home. I sighed realizing that this was a lost battle.

I stood ready to hang up the phone when one more question pummeled my mind. I had to ask. I just had to. Kyle started to hang up his phone when I gestured for him to give me one more minute. He wasn't surprised but stood before the glass. He was probably already deciding not to listen but I was glad that he hadn't hung up.

"I know you won't answer my questions but please just answer me this-"

"Begging again?" Kyle quipped with a snide smirk.

"Why were you taking me to New Jersey? Why was Eric to meet us there?" I asked in a rush.

The question only made his smirk widen to a full ear-to-ear smile as he shook his head.

"Who said we were going to New Jersey?" he asked.

That was the direction we were headed in. Where else would he have taken me? As a kidnapper he could have technically gone anywhere but we were going south on Interstate 95. What else was I to think?

"I told you. *You* don't know anything." He stated sharply before throwing in, "Next time, I expect a conjugal visit."

With those repulsive words ringing in the phone, he hung up and retreated out of the visitation room. Leaving nothing but more questions and worse. A nauseating but tempting invitation to come back.

Don't miss the next installment of the exciting Hope Trilogy!

About The Author

M. L. Newman is an independent writer who lives in rural Connecticut with her wonderful husband. She is a member of the RWA. She has a bachelor's degree in Social Sciences from Marist College. She is active in community theatre and has played characters ranging from Brigitta Von Trapp in The Sound of Music to Ms. Hannigan in Annie which has inspired the many fun aspects and personalities for the characters in her romance novels.

M. L. Newman is currently hard at work on the upcoming novel, *Hope Has a Glare*, the sequel to *Glimmer of Hope*, but she'd love connecting with you on her Facebook page https://www.facebook.com/pages/M-L-Newman/508027985916037 and on Twitter https://twitter.com/MLNewman1

Looking for exclusive content and more?
Visit www.mlnewmanauthor.com

www.ingramcontent.com/pod-product-compliance
Lightning Source LLC
Chambersburg PA
CBHW070759180626
46818CB00001B/28